Dragon
Fury

Also by Lisa McMann

» » « «

THE UNWANTEDS SERIES
The Unwanteds

Island of Silence

Island of Fire

Island of Legends

Island of Shipwrecks

Island of Graves

Island of Dragons

» » « «

THE UNWANTEDS QUESTS SERIES
Dragon Captives

Dragon Bones

Dragon Ghosts

Dragon Curse

Dragon Fire

Dragon Slayers

Dragon Fury

» » « «

FOR OLDER READERS:
Don't Close Your Eyes

Visions

Cryer's Cross

Dead to You

LISA McMANN

THE UNWANTEDS QUESTS

Dragon Fury

Aladdin

NEW YORK   LONDON   TORONTO   SYDNEY   NEW DELHI

This book is a work of fiction. Any references to historical events, real people, or real places are used fictitiously. Other names, characters, places, and events are products of the author's imagination, and any resemblance to actual events or places or persons, living or dead, is entirely coincidental.

ALADDIN

An imprint of Simon & Schuster Children's Publishing Division

1230 Avenue of the Americas, New York, New York 10020

First Aladdin paperback edition September 2021

Text copyright © 2021 by Lisa McMann

Jacket illustration copyright © 2021 by Owen Richardson

Also available in an Aladdin hardcover edition.

All rights reserved, including the right of reproduction in whole or in part in any form.

ALADDIN and related logo are registered trademarks of Simon & Schuster, Inc.

For information about special discounts for bulk purchases, please contact Simon & Schuster Special Sales at 1-866-506-1949 or business@simonandschuster.com.

The Simon & Schuster Speakers Bureau can bring authors to your live event. For more information or to book an event contact the Simon & Schuster Speakers Bureau at 1-866-248-3049 or visit our website at www.simonspeakers.com.

Book designed by Karin Paprocki

The text of this book was set in Truesdell.

Manufactured in the United States of America 0721 OFF

2 4 6 8 10 9 7 5 3 1

Library of Congress Control Number 2021940672

ISBN 9781534416109 (hc)

ISBN 9781534416116 (pbk)

ISBN 9781534416123 (eBook)

Contents

O Liesa! My Liesa! Our fearful trip is done! (Apologies to Walt Whitman.) To you, dear editor, for every magical moment of this very special journey, and for the gift of your creative heart. You made this series infinitely better, and I am forever grateful to have written these fourteen books with the one and only you.

The Chase

Thisbe Stowe had failed to obliterate the Revinir.

Her spell had struck the ground and exploded behind the dragon-woman, knocking her down, but only for a moment. In seconds the Revinir was back up—and furious. While Aaron and Ishibashi exchanged fire with the Revinir, Thisbe and Rohan escaped into the forest of Grimere. But the evil ruler was soon on their tail again, roaring and spraying fire in all directions.

The two dodged the flames from the Revinir's blasts and kept running. They knew she couldn't see them, and she couldn't squeeze her body between the trees to go after them,

LISA McMANN

but her random bursts of fire could still reach the fugitives—and all the timber surrounding them.

"You betrayed me!" the Revinir shouted down. Her voice hitched. To Thisbe, she sounded . . . devastated. And . . . possibly in pain?

Between roars and flames, the dragon-woman reached her claws into her mouth and scraped around, trying to dislodge the throwing star that Ishibashi had implanted there moments ago. The first two weapons that had hit her in the forehead had barely nicked her thick skin and bounced off, one of them leaving a trickle of blood. But the metal star in the back of her throat was stuck fast, and the tissue surrounding it was swelling up.

Below, Thisbe's expression flickered as thoughts about all that had just happened pounded her. What a terrible mess she'd made! She was devastated by her failure to use the obliterate spell properly. Now everything was in chaos. She'd put Aaron and Ishibashi in danger and left them to fend for themselves. And she and Rohan were about to get burned to a crisp.

The two didn't respond to the Revinir's shouts. They ran as quietly as they could for a while, then spied a large fallen tree and slid under its branches for cover. Too late, they realized the remaining dead leaves of the tree were brittle—the leaves would catch fast if the Revinir figured out where to aim her blasts. But their smartest option was to stay still and quiet.

"How do we get out of here?" Rohan whispered.

Thisbe looked back the way they'd come. "The desert is back there," she said, "so that means the road and the crater lake are this way." She pointed to the south, then frowned. "I think." Neither of them knew their way through this end of the forest. They were far from the castle and the city of Grimere. The thick expanse of trees spread through the entire center of the land of the dragons: One end was near the castle; the other was close to the cavelands where the ghost dragons dwelled. Dragonsmarche and the crater lake were somewhere between those two points on the other side of the road.

No matter where they were at the moment, Thisbe knew that they had to stay hidden in the thicker parts of the forest in order to keep the Revinir from diving down and snatching them up in her claws or blasting them with her furnace breath. They could hear her circling above the treetops.

"Rohan," the Revinir called, slurring her words a bit

because of the metal star in her throat, "I command you to stop Thisbe! Bring her to the dragon path where I can see her!" Then she muttered, "I should never have ordered him to obey that traitor."

Thisbe and Rohan's eyes widened. The Revinir still believed Rohan was under her mind control. She hadn't yet figured out that they'd been tricking her all this time.

"What should I do?" Thisbe whispered, her chin in the dirt. "The version of Thisbe I've been pretending to be would try to take control of the situation. Not apologize for almost killing her, but accuse her of hurting Fifer and telling her she deserved to be attacked. That would startle her, I think, in the right way. Should I tell her that's what I was reacting to, and declare that I'm sorry I didn't manage to kill her?" She paused and cringed. What would that lead to? "Or should I try to explain some other way?"

Rohan looked at her, concerned. "I . . . think it's over, *pria*."

"What? What do you mean?"

"This whole act you've been doing." He shifted in the detritus under the tree as ants crawled on them. "It's done. There's no coming back from what happened."

Thisbe stayed silent, the blood draining from her face as she tried to comprehend what he was saying. Rohan continued gently. "Do you really think you can go back to her and try to salvage this fake relationship? I just can't see it ever being repaired. It took you so long to get her to trust you, and after what took place back there—after what you just did to her—the farce is over. You tried to kill her, Thiz. And she's well aware it wasn't a mistake."

Thisbe's thoughts continued whirring as she attempted to come up with a way to reconcile with the Revinir and keep this going. She'd worked so hard to get here. Poured her heart and soul into this! But the damage had been done. Thisbe dropped her head into her hands. There was no explaining away her attempt to kill the dragon-woman—it had changed their strengthening relationship in an instant, and the Revinir would never forgive her, no matter what story she concocted to try to explain it. Thisbe had messed it up. The fragile trust had been broken. The Revinir was way too hardened, and this betrayal would only harden her more. There was no way to fix it. "It *is* over, isn't it," Thisbe said, resigned. She lifted her head to look at Rohan as the weight of it all came down on her. "Everything I've worked toward and all we sacrificed for this . . . I just messed it up in a single move."

"You still have one obliterate component," Rohan reminded her. "Do you want to try again?"

Thisbe peered up around the fallen tree, trying to locate the Revinir above the treetops. "Too many branches. I can't even see her. I'll miss again." She sighed and gathered her thoughts. "We need to focus on getting out of here, I think."

Rohan nodded. "Yes. Find the others and see about Fifer's injuries. I hope she's all right."

"The Revinir is going to round up her people and dragons," Thisbe said, thinking about what would happen next. "We need to be ready when she comes after us. Oh," she moaned, "what have I done? I've put everyone in so much danger!" She thought of the interaction with Aaron and Ishibashi. They hadn't fled with her and Rohan, which meant they probably believed Thisbe had turned on them for real. "They're going to hate me. And all of this damage . . . for nothing."

Rohan reached for Thisbe's hand and laced his fingers with hers. "We're going to figure this out," he said, but he didn't sound sure.

"And Fifer," Thisbe whispered, her voice catching. "I wonder what happened to her. We're going to need her help. And Dev's."

Almost as if on cue, an echo of a whisper filled Thisbe's ear. *Water.*

Thisbe turned to Rohan. "Did you hear something?"

He shook his head and put a finger to his lips. The random fire strikes were getting closer, and they could smell smoke.

Thisbe was certain she'd heard the word. It had to be from Fifer. Could their telepathic communication system reach this far? And why *water*? Perhaps, in her injured state, she was in need of a drink. *Somebody please give Fifer some water!*

In that quiet moment, the crackles of the forest around them grew louder and more consistent. Rohan shifted to look behind them, and he gasped. "The trees are burning," he said. "Lots of them."

Thisbe forgot the whisper in her ear and turned sharply to look at the areas of flames growing around them. The Revinir had set the forest of Grimere on fire. And Thisbe and Rohan were trapped in the midst of it.

LISA McMANN

Taking Care

Aaron, holding Ishibashi's dead body in his arms, could barely get out his instructions to Quince. "Fly as quickly as possible to Ashguard's palace." He choked, then added, "Please hurry." The rest of the team members would be there already. He looked down at the silent, small body of the man who'd taught him what goodness was. The man who'd loved him when he'd felt unlovable. Ishibashi had given him a second chance to make something good with his life. He'd died pushing Aaron out of the way of the Revinir's flames, even though he was immortal. Or so Aaron had thought.

He closed his eyes. "I'm so sorry," he whispered. "I hope you didn't suffer." After a long moment, Aaron lifted his head. He reached into his vest and found a send component. He opened it, took out the tiny pencil attached, and wrote:

Dear Kaylee,

Gather Ito and Sato. Brace yourselves for shocking, terrible news, and hold each other close, for I must tell you that our beloved Ishibashi has died. He was killed by the Revinir as he saved my life. It was a swift, unexpected attack, and I have minor burns but am otherwise all right. Shock is still muddling my thoughts, but I wanted to let you know right away.

Love,

Aaron

Aaron let out a ragged sob, then took a breath and blew it out slowly. He concentrated on his wife and released the send spell. It left a trail of smoke to the east and disappeared. Then he pulled out another component to tell a similar story.

Dear Florence,

Brace yourself for shocking, terrible news. Ishibashi and I ran into the Revinir, Thisbe, and Rohan. Thisbe confirmed our worst fears, but then she changed suddenly and tried to kill the Revinir with an obliterate spell. She missed, which is so unlikely, and the Revinir retaliated and killed Ishibashi. Thisbe and Rohan ran off into the forest. I'm unsure about where my sister stands, but I fear she's gone rogue against us all, and we've lost her forever. I'm on my way to Ashguard's palace with Ishibashi and Quince. If you have time . . . prepare a burial spot.

Your friend,

Aaron

He sat back, his skin on fire, burns weeping, body aching, and he closed his eyes again. Ishibashi had died, and that was not only shocking and sad, but confusing as well. To what extent had ingesting the glowing seaweed affected them? Aaron and the scientists had all thought it made them immortal. Ito and Sato were both over 115 years old by now and still functioning quite well. Ishibashi had only taken one dose in his lifetime, when he was already a middle-aged man. Aaron had been a teenager when they'd administered the dose to him to save his life. But it was apparent now that the seaweed didn't save them from everything. Perhaps the small amount had been ingested so long ago that it had made Ishibashi vulnerable. In that case, what did it mean for Aaron? And for the other two scientists?

It was something he'd have to discuss with Ito and Sato when he returned. *If* he returned. It was still too soon to know what was going to shape their lives in the coming days, but one thing was now painfully clear—there was no promise that Aaron would survive it.

Added to that, while he was worried about Fifer, he was extremely confused by what had happened with Thisbe. Her actions were inexplicable. She'd said horrible things to him, then suddenly turned and attempted to kill the Revinir, but . . . missed? Was she going for an even bigger power grab than anyone had imagined, taking on the Revinir *and* all of Artimé?

Or . . . had she missed the Revinir on purpose? It wasn't like Thisbe to mess up a spell. He didn't know if she'd ever done it before. As one of Artimé's best mages, Thisbe didn't make mistakes when it came to launching a spell she'd handled before. So what had happened there? And why had Rohan gone along with all of it? Did she have some sort of power over him? Had she figured out how to control people in the same way the Revinir had done?

Something felt terribly off. Thisbe had become someone they all might need to be afraid of. Did the people of Artimé have two enemies now, including the identical twin of their head mage? Was history repeating itself before Aaron's very eyes, but he'd been too stubborn to see it for what it was until this moment?

With Ishibashi gone in an instant, Aaron was deeply worried about the Revinir's vast firepower. She could've taken Aaron out just as swiftly. Would any of his other friends fail to survive whatever lay before them? Aaron had never felt so much darkness in all of his life. Things had gone too far—and the Revinir and Thisbe seemed unstoppable. What if there was no way out of the disaster that seemed to be steamrolling toward them?

On the Run

Thick smoke billowed through the forest and hung over Thisbe and Rohan. Sprays of fire scorched and ignited the trees around them. When flames crept to the fallen tree they were hiding under, setting the dead leaves around them ablaze, the two knew they had to run for it.

"This way," Thisbe whispered, trying to stay calm as smoke burned her throat. They held hands and kept low. Thisbe felt sick. This reminded her of when they were in the castle dungeon searching through the maze of passageways for Maiven Taveer while the drawbridge and building burned. If

LISA McMANN

only the results of this venture turned out as well or better, maybe things would be okay. But that was a big if. Just thinking about her flub forced a groan from deep inside her. She'd been so close to ending the Revinir's reign, freeing the people and dragons of Grimere, setting the ghost dragons free to go to their next lives, and restoring the rulership to Maiven and the dragons. And she'd completely biffed it. It made her want to give up.

The two caught sight of the river but didn't take the time to get near enough for a drink. Instead they continued moving forward through the thick mass of trees and hoped the forest canopy would give them the best protection from the Revinir's keen senses. With any luck the smoke would shield their scent from the dragon-woman. They skirted around spot fires and ducked when another blast came through the foliage. When Rohan's shirttail caught fire, Thisbe shoved him to the ground to put it out.

She helped him to his feet, and they continued painstakingly, trying not to let the leaves and twigs crunch under their shoes. Hoping whatever sounds they did make were masked by the crackle of fire. Praying they were going the right way. How far would they have to travel before they spotted the road? Before the Revinir realized she was destroying her own land? Before the smoke completely disoriented them and they were lost for good?

As the forest became thick with smoke and the fiery sections more plentiful, Thisbe started to panic. Would they ever make it out? Were they even going in the right direction? Soon they could barely see ten feet in front of them because of the haze, and they struggled not to cough and give away their location. They came upon an entire section of the forest ablaze and had to detour around it.

When the trees began to thin and smoky sunlight filtered in between them, Thisbe realized the edge of the forest couldn't be too far off. She looked up, catching a glimpse of the Revinir's wings overhead. The dragon-woman snarled something about the forest fire, and then she belted out a mighty roar.

Thisbe and Rohan cringed and ran as the roar triggered images to flash in their minds. "This is bad," whispered Rohan as the new, real scales on his arms and legs stood on end. "She's calling in more dragons. We'll never get out of here without being seen."

LISA McMANN

Many of the dragons were already close by since the Revinir had roared in anger at Thisbe for trying to kill her. As the first ones circled around her, the Revinir shouted an order. "Get water from the river and the crater lake! And put this fire out before my entire land is destroyed." She was quiet a moment as the air swarmed with more arriving dragons. Then she added, in a menacing growl that was more to herself than to the dragons, "If you see Thisbe Stowe, don't bother bringing her to me. Just kill her."

Slipping Away

Thisbe glanced fearfully at the river. Would it be too dangerous to use it to escape? With flames closing in, she and Rohan might not have a choice. The smoke was making their eyes run and their lungs seize up. They struggled to breathe. They had to get away from the Revinir, no matter the risk. "Into the river," Thisbe whispered.

"But the dragons will be downstream fetching water," Rohan argued in a harsh whisper. "She's ordered them to kill you!"

"It's our only way out of here," Thisbe replied. Tears from the smoke streaked her face. She thought about how Dev had

LISA McMANN

hidden from the Revinir and the red dragons in the river. "The dragons are heading for the largest clearings along the dragon path, where it's easier for them to land and move around. We'll sneak in over here, away from them," she said, pointing in the direction she believed was the right way out. "We'll stay low in the water and hope nobody sees us. Then we'll float in the current until we're out of this forest, under the bridge, and on the other side of the road." She coughed violently into her sleeve, and they both froze, waiting to see if the Revinir had heard her. When nothing happened, Thisbe continued. "Have you learned to swim yet?"

Rohan gave her a look. "You mean in my spare time?"

Thisbe stifled a grin. "I thought Ms. Octavia was going to teach all of the people from Grimere."

"She did start lessons," Rohan admitted, "but Maiven and I had to leave after the first one because of . . . well, because of you becoming a traitor. But I'll be fine."

"Just hold on to me."

"I intend to."

Thisbe raised an eyebrow, and despite the urgency, she gave him a soft kiss on his ash-smudged cheek. "Come on," she said. "Let's go." She led the way with Rohan close behind her, and they crept across the forest floor, breathing through the fabric of their shirts to try to keep from inhaling too much smoke and inducing another coughing fit. Finally they made it to the riverbank. Enormous dragons were descending into a clearing in the depths of the forest, far away along the river.

"That must be the dragon path, down there," Rohan whispered.

Thisbe nodded. Seeing her chance, she slipped into the river.

Rohan hesitated, eyeing the distant dragons. When he was assured they hadn't noticed Thisbe, he followed her in, still scared—the river was wide enough that the dragons could travel the length of it without having to knock down too many trees to get to them. "Stay low," he whispered to Thisbe as he reached for her hand again. "We can't be seen, or you're dead. And if you're dead, I'll be lost forever." It was too devastating to think about. Especially since he'd thought he'd lost her once already.

Thisbe threaded her fingers in Rohan's and waded toward the middle of the river, where the water was chest deep. They

LISA McMANN

both took a long, much-needed drink as they crept forward.

"Everything is bumpy," Rohan whispered. "How do you know what you're stepping on?"

"You don't."

Rohan cringed and stayed close to her. "Do the fish, like, *do* anything to you?"

"They might slip up your trouser leg and wiggle around," said Thisbe. "Be careful."

"You're . . . joking."

Thisbe gave him an eerie look. "You never know with fish."

Rohan's face turned gray. He decided not to ask any more questions. They half floated with the current in the brisk water. The air was clearer directly above the water, which made it easier to breathe if you weren't busy worrying about fish flopping around inside your pants.

They could hear a group of dragons ahead of them, presumably along the bridge. The creatures were jostling for a spot near the river to suck in a mouthful of water as instructed. "I think we have a problem," Thisbe whispered. "How are we going to get past them?"

"Wait it out?" suggested Rohan. "Maybe there will be a

break in the flow once this batch collects their water and heads out." They continued forward, water lapping their chins as they remained hunched. "Can you see anything yet?"

"Not much." The tree branches, covered with leaves, obstructed their view, but smoke-filtered light shone stronger now. They were getting close.

Finally the edge of the forest was in clear view, and the two could see an expanse of grass with the road beyond it. The river flowed several feet below a bridge. Dragons moved about alongside it, gathering water.

The smoke wafted over Thisbe and Rohan, but it was less thick here, and the crackle of fire became softer behind them. The two watched the majestic mind-controlled dragons do their jobs. Thisbe peered down the road, trying to figure out where they were. Nothing looked familiar. When she looked to the east, in the direction of the castle, she couldn't see it at all. But she could see hills peeping up and soon recognized them as the ones between Dragonsmarche and the crater lake. She'd climbed over them a few times, and that was also where she and Rohan had first met Quince and Gorgrun. The ghost dragons had arrived just in time to bring them to the castle to save Maiven Taveer. The distance to those hills told Thisbe that they were a long way from anywhere civilized, which meant she and Rohan might not be all that far from Ashguard's palace in the other direction, to the west, where Fifer and Dev were. Could they possibly find it? The road would lead them in the right direction. But first, could they get past these dragons?

Thisbe wasn't sure how long they could wait to make their move. The water wasn't freezing, but it was brisk. Her teeth wanted to chatter, but she held her mouth closed.

The reminder from Fifer's whisper returned to Thisbe. *Water.* They were definitely in water now. Thisbe tried to send a message back to Fifer. *Are you okay? Rohan and I are in the river.*

There was no response. She tried again. *We're trying to escape dragons so we can get to you. Is water the secret to us getting out of here?* Still nothing. Thisbe looked at Rohan, who was studying the sky. "I don't think this is going to work," she whispered.

"The dragons just keep coming," Rohan said. They were like flocks of giant birds circling and swooping down, waiting for their turn to gather water as the Revinir had bidden them to do.

"We'll have to wait it out." Thisbe shivered, and she and Rohan huddled together to share their warmth. She thought again about Dev and how he'd made it through his ordeal, and she told Rohan about it to give him strength too.

They stayed quiet in the forest shadows, twenty yards or so from the road, waiting for all the dragons to have their turn. But there was no end. Thisbe spotted Ivis the green, doing as the Revinir had commanded, and a pang of longing pierced through her. Why couldn't things be back to normal? Why had Thisbe missed with the obliterate component? This nightmare would all be over if she'd done her job right.

Pan came down after a while. It was a sad sight to see the ruler of the sea doing the Revinir's bidding. Waves of emotion caught Thisbe unprepared once more, and tears sprang to her eyes. Was there any chance they could fix this after she'd messed it all up? What had she been thinking? How could she have bungled such an important spell?

Thisbe closed her eyes and gave in to the truth. She knew how. She'd felt sorry for the Revinir. It was deeply painful to admit, but it was true. The dragon-woman's story of childhood loneliness had touched Thisbe; there was no denying

LISA McMANN

it. And in that instant of sending off the deadly spell, Thisbe had wavered. Now all her work over the past months had been for nothing. They were further from overthrowing the Revinir than ever, and the blame for that rested squarely on Thisbe's shoulders. "Ugh," she muttered, shaking her head.

"Are you all right?" whispered Rohan.

Thisbe opened her eyes. "Yeah," she said, resigned. "Just . . . thinking."

Rohan gazed at her, concerned. He released his embrace and saw that her lips held a bluish tinge. He felt the cold water rush in between them and returned to her side, wrapping his arms around her to preserve their waning warmth, and perhaps offer comfort for whatever she'd been ruminating over. They were stuck here for the foreseeable future, unless something amazing happened.

Just before they could take the cold no longer, something amazing *did* happen.

Drock the dark purple dragon appeared, flying low along the edge of the forest, trying not to act like he was searching for anyone. Trying to appeared glazed and obedient, like the rest of the dragons.

"Look," Rohan whispered, releasing Thisbe.

Thisbe looked. "It's Drock!" she whispered. The two surged forward in the water, hoping his keen eye would connect with them in the shadows of the forest's edge. Hoping he was looking for them after the Revinir had made it clear that Thisbe was out here.

Drock flew over the river, then circled around, waiting his turn. When a space opened up along the road nearest them, he landed with his back to them. He drew water into his mouth and trained his eyes on the river, turning his head slowly to look behind him. Somehow sensing the two, Drock spotted them, and he gave them a meaningful look. Then, in one motion, he lifted his snout and flung his long, ropelike tail into the water toward them.

Thisbe looked at Rohan. "This is risky."

"We don't have a choice."

They waded forward and grabbed ahold of the dragon's tail. Drock curled it around them and brought them onto his back, trying to do so quickly yet stealthily so they wouldn't be seen. The two flattened, but they knew they were still visible. Drock was no ghost dragon when it came to anyone being able to hide on his back. But they'd have to take their chances.

Drock loosened his grip but kept his tail coiled around the two humans to give them some cover. If anybody looked closely, they'd think the sight strange. The dragon lifted off, trying to get higher than all the other dragons before anyone noticed he was carrying two stowaways. He dropped his mouthful of water onto the burning forest, then headed out toward the crater lake, pretending to go after another load of water.

The Revinir, hovering above the forest, narrowed her eyes and watched him go.

Barely Hanging On

A send spell reply from Kaylee made its way to Aaron as he neared the palace.

Aaron,

Your news of our dear Ishibashi's death has rocked us all. Ito and Sato are devastated, and Sato has taken ill. We've heard from Carina, who is on her way here with the fleet of ghost dragons to pick us up and join you in the fight. I'll tell her what happened in person.

I'm hesitant to leave Daniel with Ito under these circumstances since he has Sato to look after. So much going

LISA McMANN

on. Take extra care, please—we all love you so much.

Kaylee

Aaron blew out a breath and wiped his eyes, then dropped his hands in his lap. He could only imagine how Ito and Sato were taking the news—could they even believe it? It worried Aaron that Sato had taken ill over it. He wished he could be there with them to tell them everything. He hoped that, on the other side of the pain, the men would find a bit of peace in Ishibashi's death. Like Aaron, alongside their grief they must have immediately thought that there was hope for them to someday be able to pass on as well. Aaron knew that would comfort them eventually, if not right away. For so many years they'd wondered if the seaweed had made them immortal—and they'd assumed it had caused their unprecedented long lives. That stress of long life had taken its toll, especially on their bodies that continued to age.

"Is everything all right back there?" Quince asked. He looked over his shoulder at Aaron holding Ishibashi's lifeless body. The dragon's eyes flickered as if he just remembered what had happened. In a more sympathetic voice, he asked, "Are you holding up?"

"I'm all right," said Aaron. "Anxious to get to Ashguard's palace, which is where we are going, right?" Even in his stunned grief he knew to keep reminding the forgetful ghost dragon of their destination.

"Ahhh," said Quince, turning to look ahead again, and then to the left and right. "Yes. Yes, that is where we appear to be headed. Is Ashguard expecting us?"

Aaron closed his eyes. He didn't have it in him to remind Quince that the old black-eyed Suresh family leader hadn't been seen in years and was presumed dead. "They're expecting us," he said, and left it at that.

After a while they spotted the crater lake to their left. Quince angled slightly away from it, turning west, and soon Aaron could make out a small hill with a large, broken-down palace situated on it. To the right was a mountain range that separated the palace from the cavelands. On the other side was an orchard, and a village rose up beyond that. As they drew closer, Aaron could see four red, motionless masses around the palace. With a sickening start he realized they were slain dragons—which meant Fifer had been truthful about being surrounded by them. Somehow, someone had gotten them all.

Aaron's mind returned to Fifer, and his worries spiked anew. Was she all right? With death in his arms, he was reminded of the fragility of life. And with four dead dragons on the grounds, Aaron knew that whoever had slayed them could have life-threatening injuries. He scanned the overgrowth, spotting Astrid and Gorgrun resting outside near Florence, who was standing with Seth, pointing to the dead dragons. The Magical Warrior trainer seemed fully repaired and back to her old self.

Relieved, Aaron sat up higher and tried to push away the darkness. "Quince, let's land in that open spot near the other ghost dragons," he directed.

Quince did as requested, and once they were on the ground, Florence and Seth came swiftly toward them. Simber emerged from the courtyard, which had been turned into a temporary hospital ward for the two injured teenagers. With solemn faces they greeted one another. Then Florence took Ishibashi's body and carried it to the grass. Seth laid a blanket over it. Aaron slid down the ghost dragon's wing, and Florence greeted him with a gentle embrace. Simber and Aaron exchanged a strange look. The cheetah was one of the few who knew the truth about the magic seaweed, so news of Ishibashi's death had been especially shocking to him. There wasn't a chance to discuss it in private at the moment, though.

"Are you all right?" Florence looked Aaron over, then checked his wounds. She started pulling medicine out of her waist pouch.

"I'll manage," Aaron said. "How is Fifer?"

"She's woken up a couple of times," Seth said. "I think she's going to be okay. Dev, on the other hand . . ."

"Dev? He's here too?"

Seth nodded. "He's badly hurt. There are a lot of strange things happening that we don't understand."

Florence agreed and began treating Aaron's wounds. "I'm hoping we'll be able to find out what's going on when Fifer awakens for good."

"You have enough medicine to spare?" Aaron didn't want them to use any on him if they were running low.

"Yes, we have everything. We just need more time." Florence smiled grimly, then took a long look at Ishibashi's body. "I can't imagine . . . That must have been so hard for you. We're all a mess over it." She looked like she wanted to know more but didn't want to press him.

Aaron's face went numb. He nodded. "I've informed the others back home. Kaylee is going to tell Carina when she arrives—she should be there in a day or two, right? I can't seem to keep track of the time."

"It depends on how fast she can get the ghost drrragons to fly," said Simber. "They'rrre not the speediest mode of trrrans-porrrt, but we'll take what we can get. I expect it'll be severrral days beforrre they arrrive back herrre."

"We'll come up with instructions for them on the route to take so they're not detected," said Aaron. He winced as his burns began to throb. "I could go for some herb capsules for pain if you've truly got enough to spare, Florence. And I'd like to see Fifer and everybody else."

"We brought half of Henry's supply of herbs with us," Florence said. "And he'll bring more. In fact, I'll write to him to make sure. We need every protection we can get." She turned to Seth. "Will you stay with the body? We'll be back soon to dig the grave."

"Oh," said Seth, alarmed. But he wanted to do whatever he could to help. "Yes, of course." He settled into the idea, then added, "Make sure you try to give Fife some water. She keeps asking for it, but then pushing it away."

Florence flashed a grateful look. "Thanks. We will."

Deep Thoughts

Seth had never watched over a dead body before. And the fact that it was Ishibashi, someone he'd known and thought of as a grandfather almost all his life, made it even weirder and sadder. The man's clothes had been scorched and his body burned. It had been shocking to see, and Seth was grateful for the blanket covering Ishibashi now. But Seth was sure he'd never forget it, which made him even more distressed. He tried to replace the image with a different one— Ishibashi smiling in the greenhouse. That helped a little.

He wondered things as he sat with the sun on his back. Had Ishibashi languished, feeling all the pain from the Revinir's fiery breath? Or had he died instantly, like Alex had? Seth had thought a lot about death ever since that incident with Alex. What happened when life was over? Was it just . . . nothingness? When a person's body failed to stay alive, what happened to their personality? Their spirit? Their emotions and everything that was invisible inside their bodies—weren't those things that couldn't be killed? Did they just . . . disappear? Or were they, like, hovering in the air all around? Or off on some afterlife adventure with all the other dead spirits?

Seth shifted in the grass and slowly turned his head, looking for souls in the air. Perhaps there was some other place they all gathered, like ghost dragons flocking to the cavelands to wait for whatever came next. Seth hoped that was the case—it was easier to think of the ones they'd lost that way. Together. Having an adventure. Maybe it was silly and childish, but it eased Seth's pain.

He would miss the lost ones in the meantime. Tears came to Seth's eyes when he thought about what life in Artimé would be like without Ishibashi. Obviously the grandfathers were very old, and everyone had expected them to die by now, but it still seemed so wrong and strange to picture life without them.

LISA McMANN

Seth cried for a few minutes as some of the numbness wore off. Ishibashi had invited him and Thisbe and Fifer into his greenhouse when they were small to learn how to grow delicious applecorn and other hybrid produce, as well as the herbs that were infused with magic and used for healing. He'd let them tinker with the instruments they'd salvaged from shipwrecks and play hide-and-seek in the maze of stone hallways in the scientists' living quarters.

Every time someone died, Seth was struck by pain stronger than he could remember from the previous time. He hadn't known his real father, who'd died in Artimé's first battle, so that death didn't affect him like the others. Sometimes Seth felt bad about that when he saw the pain in his mother's eyes. Even though she was happy in her relationship with Sean Ranger, Seth knew she wouldn't forget his father. He wished everyone could all just go home and have nothing bad happen ever again.

Seth let out a heavy breath and wiped his eyes. He looked around the property and noticed Simber and Aaron in a quiet conversation by the river. Seth had explored the grounds a little in the short time they'd been here and wondered if perhaps burying Ishibashi by the orchard would be nice. It felt right. With a pang he thought about Kaylee and the other grandfathers. They would miss saying good-bye.

Maybe it was better for them not to see the body and the burial. To remember Ishibashi with his clever smile and kind words. Alive. Not like . . . this. Seth didn't think he'd ever forget the way Ishibashi had looked before he'd put the blanket over him. He didn't want Ito and Sato to see that.

Florence returned with a shovel she'd fashioned out of a sapling and a piece of metal she'd found in the open-air kitchen. "Come, Seth. Let's say our good-byes." She reached down and carefully picked up the body.

"I was thinking near the orchard would be nice," said Seth.

"I agree. Here come Aaron and Simber."

Soon after, Sky and Maiven emerged from the center tower to meet up with the rest. "Maiven showed me a comfortable library in the bulb at the top of the big center tower," Sky told them, as the others hadn't had a chance to venture inside yet. Maiven had of course been a frequent visitor to the palace many years ago before the coup, but she'd also been by recently, after her prison escape, to see if the library still existed and to borrow some of Ashguard's books.

"We plan to transport Fifer and Dev up there," Sky continued. "They'll be more comfortable. I think we'll be stationed here for a while."

"The staircase is made of iron and stone," Maiven informed Simber and Florence. "It seems wide enough and strong enough for you, although the opening to the library might need some construction work done to enlarge it for Simber to get through. He'd be able to hear everything from the top of the stairs, though, for now."

"Thank you," said Florence. "That's good news. We'll all have a look after we pay our respects." Florence weaved around the dead dragons, and Maiven and Seth and the rest of them followed. None of them remarked about the enormous eyesores, or the fact that the dead beasts were already attracting flies and other insects. There was no way to move them. It was depressing.

Everyone gathered around at the edge of the orchard. Soon Florence's shovel gave a sickening zing as it hit the dirt. Sky caught Seth's eye from across the gravesite, and they both flinched at the second zing. How many more graves would there be before this was over?

Speculation

After Ishibashi's body had been placed in the grave, Florence, Aaron, and Seth said a few words about how Ishibashi had affected them. Aaron spoke through tears and sobs. "I wouldn't be here if it weren't for him," he said when he could get the words out. "He changed my life. I'm just . . . sick about this."

Florence spoke about Ishibashi's unselfishness and his willingness to help in all situations. Seth mentioned how much he'd learned from the man about healing and plants, navigation and science . . . and kindness.

They said their final good-byes, then all helped push the

LISA McMANN

dirt back in. Seth, who'd found one of Ishibashi's throwing stars tangled inside the fabric of the man's tattered pocket, used it to fashion a marker for the spot. Then they turned back to the palace to check out their new living quarters.

As they walked, Sky wrinkled her nose and squinted. "Something's on fire," she said. She pointed to the clouds of dark smoke polluting the sky. "That's the direction of the forest." Everyone stopped in their tracks to look.

Aaron's expression became alarmed as he added up what he knew. "Thisbe and Rohan ran into the forest with the Revinir chasing after them," he said. "I hope she hasn't set the whole thing ablaze!"

"I rrreckon that's exactly what happened," said Simber. He looked at Florence, then Aaron, unsure who to address when his head mage was unconscious. "What do we do about Thisbe? We can't . . . We can't just abandon herrr forrr good, can we? Even afterrr everrrything she's done?"

Aaron tore his eyes away from the smoke. "I . . . I'm at my wit's end with her," he said. "I don't know what to think. I don't understand what she's doing. And with her betrayal—I guess I feel like we have other . . . priorities." He blew out

LISA McMANN

a breath. "That sounds harsh, but I don't think we have a choice." He was terribly torn up inside. He knew he shouldn't blame Thisbe for Ishibashi's death, but the irrational part of him couldn't help but tie this tragedy to her. After all she'd done to betray them, his sister was the last person he wanted to help right now, as bad as that sounded.

Sky shook her head in disagreement. "I spent so much time with her and Rohan. She confided in me about all their hopes and dreams to restore this land to its rightful rulers. I just cannot imagine this is a permanent path she's taking. She despises the Revinir."

"I still wonder . . . ," Seth began, but then he grew quiet. His feeling that Thisbe and Fifer had been plotting something secretly against the Revinir wouldn't go away, but no one else had taken him seriously. "Did Thisbe plan all of this just to try to get the Revinir alone so she could kill her?" Could that be it? But why not tell everyone that's what she was doing?

"It's been on my mind," Florence said. She told them about what she'd found in Fifer's robe pocket—the empty container that had held an obliterate spell and the instructional note from Thisbe.

LISA McMANN

"After what I witnessed today, I do think that could be a possibility," Aaron admitted. "But she gave me nothing—not a hint of that! And if it's true, what happens now that she bungled it? She just ran off. Her actions were extremely confusing. She's like a puzzle, and I can't understand how any of the pieces fit together right now. Thisbe, Fifer, Dev, Rohan—none of them are able or willing to explain what they've been doing, and it's very upsetting. Not to mention Ishibashi's death has rattled me in a rather . . . unexpected way." He glanced at Simber. It had rattled the cheetah as well, and the two had had a moment of privacy by the river to start unpacking this new development. But nothing made sense anymore.

After a deep sigh, Aaron continued. "All I know is that Thisbe said horrible things to my face when the Revinir was too far away to hear her, so she's not doing a great job of convincing me that she's still on our side."

"My main issue," said Florence, "is that I have a hard time imagining how Thisbe would miss with that obliterate spell. That's completely out of character for her."

"I agrrree," said Simber. "Therrre arrre many layerrrs to this storrry. Maybe she rrreally did intend to miss."

Seth frowned. "It's not adding up. I wish Fifer would wake up so we could ask her what's going on. I have a feeling she knows everything."

They were all quiet for a long moment as they watched the smoke billow in the distance. Then Maiven asked, "For those who think Thisbe missed purposely, do you believe it's because she had some prior agreement with the Revinir to act that out?"

Sky blew out a breath. "I hope that's not it."

"How could she have?" asked Aaron. "She didn't know Ishibashi and I would be happening along that way at that time."

"They could have hatched the plan when they saw you coming," said Maiven. But then she shook her head. "Why, though? It's all so mysterious. And Rohan just went along with it?" The lines in Maiven's face seemed to deepen. She'd had big plans for Thisbe and Rohan, but now . . . she might have to look to someone else to carry on her legacy once she joined her friend Ishibashi in the dirt.

After a while, Simber snarled and walked away from the others. "I'm going forrr a fly-arrround. I want to see wherrre everrrything and everrryone is. And have a look at that firrre. Maybe . . . maybe I'll find . . ."

Maybe he'd find Thisbe, they were all thinking. The others knew to let him go, despite the risk of fire being able to destroy the winged-cheetah statue. They filed back to the courtyard, where Dev and Fifer still lay, covered in blankets. Nobody quite knew what to do next for them, other than take them up to the library and continue to nurse them back to life.

Simber made a beeline in the direction of the forest. He barely made it halfway before he sensed Drock approaching. Confused, Simber squinted, but he couldn't see the dark purple dragon. Was Drock carrying riders? And if so, who? Someone from the castle? Simber sampled the air, picking up Thisbe's scent. Drock and Thisbe were together? Intentionally? Or had Drock secretly gone after her? Did Thisbe have some sort of hold over him, too? Wearing a frown, Simber sped toward them, prepared to fight.

A Dark Meeting

Drock had flown to the crater lake and stayed above the other dragons to hide his riders from view. Then, instead of swooping down for a mouthful of water, he turned off to the west, hoping few noticed. The Revinir was far behind them, tending to the burning forest, but Drock couldn't trust any of the dragons not to tell her he'd disobeyed a command and had gone off course. The other dragons appeared set on their tasks, and no one came after them, which left Drock cautiously relieved.

They approached the rolling hills of Ashguard's domain, with the mountains in the distance, and Drock was finally free

LISA McMANN

to talk normally. "Tell me what's going on," he demanded, glancing over his shoulder at Thisbe. "You've caused a great deal of harm."

Thisbe and Rohan exchanged a nervous glance. They looked around and found it safe to sit up. "Well," Thisbe said hesitantly, "it all started when Fifer and I got dropped through the roof of Ashguard's palace, and Fifer had this impossible-sounding idea." Thisbe went on to explain everything that had happened from that moment on—how Thisbe had balked at first, and how Dev had come into the picture, and how they'd all decided this was the one way they thought they could beat the Revinir. They added that they felt it was best to tell no one else of the true plan because, if captured, they could be compromised by being forced to take the dragon-bone broth.

Except for the occasional fiery snort, Drock remained quiet as he listened to Thisbe and Rohan. It wasn't for him to judge, but Thisbe, despite her levels of evil, appeared to be telling the truth.

Every now and then, as the story unfolded, Thisbe peered anxiously around Drock's neck trying to see the palace. But it was growing dark. Rohan kept an eye on their tail, making sure they weren't being followed. Behind them, the clouds of black smoke over the forest grew.

"Simber is approaching," Drock announced. "He's still a good distance off. He's coming from Ashguard's palace."

Thisbe and Rohan exchanged an uneasy glance. "Is anyone with him?" Thisbe asked.

"Not that I can tell." Drock sniffed the air. "But he brings the smell of death with him."

Thisbe's eyes widened in fear. "Whose death?"

"I can't tell."

"This is sickening," Thisbe whispered. *The smell of death?* Anxious sweat beaded on her forehead. Was it Fifer? Who else could it be?

"Can you tell if Simber is searching for us?" Rohan asked. "Perhaps Aaron sent him."

"I'm not a mind reader," said Drock. "But that seems within the realm of reason."

Thisbe bit her bottom lip, feeling apprehensive. If Aaron had gone straight to Ashguard's palace after the incident, it seemed likely he would have made it there hours ago to tell everyone what had happened. And now Simber was out on the prowl alone. "Get ready for some angry roars." Thisbe's stomach hurt. There would be so many questions.

"He's spotted us," Drock said. "If you want my opinion, I think you should just explain everything like you've been doing for me. This is complicated, and they're going to be mad for a while. They might not believe you at first. But it's best to just get it out and start fresh with a new plan going forward."

It was a relief to get the calming advice—and from Drock, of all dragons. He'd really stepped up, Thisbe realized. She trusted him. After feeling like she was on her own against the world for so long, having a dragon on her side felt like a comfort. "Thank you, Drock. I hope Simber listens to me." Then she ventured, "Do *you* believe me?"

Drock was quiet for a moment, and Thisbe wondered if he was testing her levels of good and evil. The thought made her cringe, for if that were true, and he used that as a measure, he'd definitely say no.

"Yes, Thisbe," Drock said after a moment. "I believe you have the best of intentions for the land of the dragons and for Artimé."

Thisbe grew tearful. "Thank you. Maybe Fifer and Dev

have already spilled the secret plan to the others by now, and Simber's not going to be mad at all." She frowned through her tears. Fifer was the one who'd been so insistent about keeping this secret from absolutely everyone. Was she aware that the whole plan had been trashed because of Thisbe's mistake? If Fifer thought the plan was still in play, she wouldn't lay out the truth. So what was Fifer telling them? Was she too injured to explain anything? Or worse—dead? Thisbe was a ball of nerves as Simber grew close enough to be seen in the darkness. "I guess we'll find out soon enough," she said.

Drock slowed, and Simber circled around and came up alongside the dragon as they continued flying. Simber greeted Drock, then peered at Thisbe and Rohan. The stone cheetah looked angry. That wasn't a good sign.

"Hi, Simber," Thisbe said, trying to be brave. "I'm sure you've heard from Aaron and Ishibashi by now. And you've probably been very confused about my actions over the past weeks, but I assure you my intentions have been solely for the good of Artimé and the land of the dragons. I'm ready to tell you the truth."

LISA McMANN

Simber narrowed his eyes.

Thisbe faltered. "Honestly, Simber. I can explain every-thing. But first, Drock said . . . he said he could smell . . ." She couldn't get the words out. She gripped Rohan's hand, digging her nails in.

"Was there a death?" asked Drock. "We're all concerned."

Simber turned away and blew out a breath. After a moment, he said, "Ishibashi is dead."

A Confrontation

hat?" Thisbe was sure she hadn't heard Simber correctly. "It's Ishibashi? How?" A small wave of relief that it wasn't Fifer was steamrolled by shock and grief at the news.

"I thought you knew," said Simber. Suspicion crept into his voice. "Aarrron said you werrre therrre. You missed the Rrrevinirrr with the obliterrrate spell. Then she firrred back and hit Aarrron and Ishibashi. And yourrr grrrand-father . . . died."

Thisbe felt like she was going to pass out. She started sweating, and her stomach cramped. This couldn't be true.

LISA McMANN

Ishibashi? Dearest grandfather to them all? How? "Is Aaron okay?" she whispered.

"He'll be all rrright," said Simber, softening a bit once he saw Thisbe's reaction.

Rohan gripped Thisbe's shoulders to keep her from flopping off the side of the dragon. "After Thisbe's component missed," he told Simber, "we took off running. We didn't realize the Revinir had retaliated." He felt the jolt as well. "I'm . . . extremely sorry. We ran for our lives to the forest and didn't look back. We had no idea."

"Well," said Simber gruffly. "Obviously Thisbe still has a lot of explaining to do. You both do, and I'm not forrrgiving you—you've hurrrt a lot of people and caused irrreparrrable harrrm. But I apologize forrr my bluntness. I can see that you'rrre trrruly moved." He paused. "I wasn't surrre what to expect frrrom you afterrr everrrything you've done to upend the worrrlds."

Thisbe put her hands over her eyes. Had she caused this? Was Ishibashi's death her fault too? Had she made this terrible situation worse instead of better? "Oh, Simber," she said. "I'm sick about it."

Despite his softening heart, Simber remained curt. "Ishibashi saved Aarrron's life. It could be yourrr brrrotherrr that you'rrre mourrrning."

"Simber," Drock said sharply. "Really? She's already lost one brother. Have a heart."

Rohan strained forward to address the winged statue. "You must believe me. We had absolutely no intention of hurting anyone but the Revinir."

"You have a strrrange way of showing it," Simber said. "You should know that no one at this time believes that to be the case."

Drock gave Simber a hard look. The cheetah was blunt and could be insensitive at times. And he also had made numerous assumptions about Thisbe that obviously needed explanations, so it made sense that he wasn't feeling very soft toward the girl at the moment. But everyone knew Simber had a tender heart as well. The cheetah noticed Drock's gaze and did a double take as Thisbe bent low, her face in her hands.

"Of course I know that, Simber," Thisbe moaned.

If there was one thing about the four Stowe siblings that Simber knew to be true, it was that they took their mistakes to heart and dwelled on them for a very long time. In some cases, it seemed like they'd never get over them. Simber monitored Thisbe's reaction. And he imagined the years of grief the girl would now place upon herself. The cheetah's heart stirred even though Thisbe still had a lot to answer for.

Simber mulled over what Rohan had said. Eventually he agreed that Thisbe could not have predicted Ishibashi's death based on the confrontation that had occurred. It had been wrong of him to imply that Aaron could've died because of what Thisbe had done—she wasn't in control of the Revinir's actions. But she *had* played a part in setting those actions in motion.

He sighed heavily as the two flying creatures advanced toward Ashguard's palace. "Thisbe," Simber said gruffly, "the Rrrevinirrr is a monsterrr that nobody can contrrrol. Why don't you tell me what's going on. Let's starrrt therrre. And then we'll see how farrr we have to go beforrre everrrything is back on trrrack."

Thisbe didn't move. She was sick over Ishibashi's death, but also hurt and angry that Simber had put the Revinir's actions on her. Thisbe had tried to kill the Revinir, and she was the only one at the moment who could do it. Yes, she'd faltered and missed. That happened to the best mages sometimes. But she was not the reason Ishibashi died. Thisbe hadn't intended to give the Revinir a chance to retaliate. It had just happened.

She lifted her head. "Simber, I'm not a child anymore. I am in line for the throne of the castle in this very land we're flying over. So . . ." She took a breath and plowed forward. "So I would appreciate it if you would stop scolding me as if I were still young in Artimé." She cringed and looked away. Perhaps now wasn't the right moment to say that. But she *had* said it, and now it was out there. "You never saw me grow up. But I did. I was forced to."

Simber appeared struck by the words. He remained silent, absorbing them.

"That said," Thisbe went on, "I admit I have done some things that I'm sure are very shocking and troublesome to you and the rest. And I'd like to tell you everything." She glanced at Rohan. He squeezed her hand in support.

"I have not betrayed Artimé," Thisbe said. "Fifer and Dev will confirm that if they haven't already."

"They arrre both unconscious afterrr fighting the rrred

drrragons," Simber said icily. "So, no. They haven't been able to speak at all."

Thisbe recoiled again. "Why didn't you say so?" she exclaimed. She knew very little about this, but it seemed worse than she'd imagined. She was dying to know what had happened. "Are they going to be okay?"

"Florrrence believes so. Fiferrr should be, at least. Dev's injurrries appearrr morrre serrrious."

Thisbe blew out a breath. "Oh no," she whispered. They *had* to be okay. How many more things could go wrong? She took a few moments to get a grip on the situation as they drew near their destination. Fifer must have been hurt badly, and Thisbe had barely had time to think about it. And Dev seriously injured? What had happened that they'd had to go after the red dragons? A thousand questions pounded her. She knew she had to clear her name and regain everyone's trust, but Fifer and Dev's situation was pounding her from another direction. It was almost too much. She glanced at Rohan.

"We'll get through it, *pria*," he said softly.

Thisbe nodded, but everything was bleak.

The palace was in sight. Glowing highlighters lit the windows of the center bulb—Dev's glorious library. Thisbe felt a pang of homesickness. She'd spent weeks there with Fifer and Dev, plotting all of this. They'd agreed this was the right plan to end the Revinir. And now Thisbe was left alone to defend that plan. Her two cohorts were unaware, unable to speak. Would anyone believe Thisbe after what she'd done?

Facing the Others

S ave yourrr explanation forrr now," Simber said to Thisbe. "You'll only have to tell it again." He was still disgruntled with Thisbe and wanted to know why she'd done the things she'd done, but he was also feeling remorse over how harsh he'd been in updating the two about the injuries and death. "We'rrre apprrroaching Ashguarrrd's palace, and the rrrest of the team will want to hearrr."

"All right," said Thisbe, a bit stiffly. She was reeling in shock and feeling defensive at the moment. If Simber was being this harsh with her, how would the others be? She gripped Rohan's hand tighter.

Rohan didn't know how to comfort her. "It's going to be rough for a while," he whispered. "I'll be here with you."

Thisbe nodded and tried to steel herself for it. Soon Simber and Drock landed. The dark purple dragon seemed horrified by the dragon bodies strewn about the lawn. "This is unacceptable," he muttered. "I'm going to take care of this before I go back." Thisbe and Rohan slid to the ground.

"Thank you, Drock," Thisbe said. "For everything. You've been a good friend, and you saved us."

"I believe your story," Drock said pointedly, making sure Simber heard.

The cat grunted, and the two teenagers walked with him across the lawn to the pavers.

While Drock called Quince, Gorgrun, and Astrid together to begin removing the red dragon carcasses, Simber stopped short at the entrance to the tower. "They've moved Fiferrr and Dev inside. Therrre's some sorrrt of librrrarrry up herrre."

"I know," said Thisbe icily. "I lived here for weeks."

Simber grunted again. He stepped through the doorway, wings grazing the sides, and peered up the spiral stone-and-iron staircase to see if he could fit. Thisbe and Rohan hesitated

LISA McMANN

behind him, stuck. "This is the sturdiest tower by far," Thisbe said in a less icy voice, "so I'm sure it will hold you if you can fit around the curves of the staircase. Can you navigate it all the way up?"

"Just barrrely, I think," Simber said. "But in case I can't, go ahead of me. I'll follow you."

"And Florence?" Thisbe asked, beginning to be concerned about all the weight the two statues combined could add to the library bulb. There hadn't been any water damage to the ceiling and floor there, but Simber and Florence were really heavy—though they managed all right in the mansion back home without falling through. Maybe this undamaged part would hold them all right. "Is she already up there?"

"I assume so. Maiven and Sky told me I might not be able to get thrrrough the opening to the top floorrr."

"They're right," said Thisbe. "But you can get close. Just don't venture onto the floors themselves—the parts beneath the flat roof." She kept her eyes not quite on his for fear of detecting even more disapproval. "Those floors are rotten. We fell through a few of them when the Revinir dropped us through the roof."

Simber glanced at the girl, and some of his irritability faded. "Drrropped you thrrrough the rrroof?"

Thisbe nodded primly and continued ascending. "Yes. We were both injured."

"Fifer told us you took a fall," Rohan said. "She didn't explain how."

"What she told you was true enough," said Thisbe sharply, making sure neither of them tried to imply Fifer had said anything inaccurate. Not when her sister wasn't conscious and able to defend herself.

Neither Rohan nor Simber was about to challenge her on that. Clearly Thisbe had been through a lot, and Rohan and Simber said no more. Simber backed out of the space so the two humans could go first. Thisbe sprinted up with Rohan right behind. At the top floor, they emerged into the library. "They're here," Sky murmured. "Simber found them." The winged cheetah remained at the top of the stairwell and poked his head through.

Being back here brought on a wave of emotion. Thisbe's lip began to quiver when she saw Aaron, looking haggard and grim. He gave her a hard look but didn't come to greet her.

"Aaron," Thisbe whispered. "I'm sorry about Ishibashi."

LISA McMANN

Aaron frowned. He shook his head slightly and looked away. The irrational feelings took over him again. When he looked at her, all he could picture was what had happened right after she'd run off to the forest. He knew it wasn't technically her fault, but he was having trouble working through it.

Thisbe blew out a breath. This was going to be horrible.

Sky and Seth were on the other side of the room, near Florence, who was spread out on the floor to keep from putting too much weight in one spot. Fifer and Dev rested on sofas that had been pulled near the fireplace. Thisbe forgot her brother's reaction for the moment and rushed over to her sister's side. She knelt, then took her twin's hand. It was warm but limp. "How is she?" she asked, turning to Florence, then dropping her gaze. Florence looked livid.

"She's improving," the warrior said, her voice measured.

"Hey, Thiz," Seth said. He came up to Thisbe and stood awkwardly nearby as if awaiting a hug that didn't come. "She's been awake a few times. The medicine is working."

"Hi." Thisbe held Seth's gaze, trying to judge if he was angry with her too. Trying to sense the temperature of the room. "It's good to see you. What about Dev?"

"We're . . . not so sure about him."

Thisbe's heart wrenched, and she looked at him, gray and lifeless on the sofa. The sight made her ill. "What happened? I can't believe the red dragons would attack without provocation. They let us live here peacefully for so long."

"Did they?" asked Seth, his gaze flickering to Aaron.

"Yes, as long as we didn't try to leave the grounds," said Thisbe, trying to act normal and fight off tears, even though everyone was really tense and clearly not sure about her. "The only way they wouldn't attack if we tried to leave the property was if we asked to go to the Revinir. That's how I got out safely."

Florence looked over the railing and exchanged a dubious glance with Simber. Aaron narrowed his eyes, and Sky seemed troubled. Maiven waited patiently to hear more, but even she shifted uncomfortably. The tension ramped up instead of deflating, and Thisbe knew she'd have to start explaining everything. But there was Aaron, still sitting in the corner, most certainly blaming Thisbe for Ishibashi's death, and that felt awful. Thisbe wasn't sure how to start telling them what had happened. She wished Drock would just poke his snout

LISA McMANN

into the tower window and do it for her, now that he said he believed her. Or maybe Rohan, since he knew the whole story . . . but that wasn't fair. He'd only been a witness to part of what was happening. Tears welled up in her eyes, and she turned to face the fireplace as she bit the insides of her cheeks, trying to stop falling apart.

Maiven got up and approached. She put her hands on Thisbe's and Rohan's shoulders, making Thisbe jump. "I'm glad to see you both," the queen said quietly. "We all are. And despite our mourning for Ishibashi, we want to hear from you. Are you prepared to tell us what's going on? You must give us everything exactly and truly, or you will risk losing us. This is very serious. I hope you understand that."

"Of course I do," Thisbe said, her voice cracking. She turned to her grandmother, searching her face. Knowing there was so much to explain, but also feeling annoyed that her grandmother was speaking to her like a child. Thisbe knew full well the consequences she would face—she'd agreed to them weeks ago when she'd bought into Fifer's scheme.

Maiven's face changed when she looked Thisbe up and down. "You're wearing my uniform," she said.

Thisbe started. It seemed like months ago when she'd chosen to wear it, but it was only this morning. "I . . . yes. I found it in the closet in my room in the palace. Rohan believes I resemble you. Don't you agree?"

"I do," said Maiven. "You look very smart in it." Then the warmth faded from her voice, and she repeated, "Are you ready to tell us what happened?" The queen's stern face held, which gave Thisbe a fresh wave of insecurity. Surely her grandmother would believe her story, wouldn't she? What if they refused to hear her out? Clearly they believed Thisbe had been a traitor to the black-eyed rulers and to Artimé. Maiven had also given Rohan a similar look. He was in no way cleared from guilt.

"It's a very long story," Thisbe said hesitantly, turning to face the others. She slipped her hand into Rohan's and searched the room. Her gaze landed on Sky. The woman gave her an encouraging smile—the first person to do so. Sky might actually believe Thisbe—they'd been through so much together. Shoring up her confidence, Thisbe kept her eyes on Sky and falteringly began to speak.

Telling the Truth

First," Thisbe began, trying to keep her voice from faltering, "regarding what happened today, I didn't know that the Revinir had . . . killed . . . Ishibashi, or that she even attacked you at all. Rohan and I learned of it a short time ago, when Simber found us and told us. And I'm absolutely sick about it. I didn't mean for that to happen, nor did I expect it. Not at all. I can explain everything—I promise. But I'm having . . ." Her voice trembled, and she started to cry but went on through the tears. "I'm having a hard time knowing how to start this story. Especially because it begins in Fifer's brain."

Thisbe glanced at Fifer and Dev, still unconscious, and tried to send Fifer a mental message. *Wake up. I need you. Please, Fifer. Help me.*

Fifer's eyelids flickered but didn't open. Thisbe would have to tell this story alone.

Rohan stood by, his shoulder touching hers as if to remind her he was there. But he stayed quiet, knowing that even though he supported her and understood everything, his words wouldn't hold the weight of hers. Besides, he was being treated nearly as suspect as Thisbe at this point.

"Rohan," said Maiven, "are you of sound mind?"

"I—" said Rohan, taken aback, but remembering the last time he had seen her, on the back of the ghost dragon. "Do you mean free from the Revinir's control? Yes."

"No, I mean free from Thisbe's control."

Rohan's lips parted. What were they all thinking here? "Yes. Thisbe has never controlled my mind, nor would she."

"That seems like something a mind-controlled person might say," said Aaron.

Rohan looked at Aaron sharply. He respected the man greatly, but he wasn't about to let him get away with this

LISA McMANN

madness. He walked over to him and looked him squarely in the eye. "Aaron, I'm under no one's control but my own. Would you prefer I stand here next to you? I'm quite sure it would be allowed."

Aaron harrumphed.

"I don't mean to be sharp with you," said Rohan, sounding more apologetic now, "especially under the circumstances and with the pain you must be feeling. But I am very saddened that you think Thisbe would ever partake in such a thing, despite your current perspective. I hope you will soon understand what Thisbe has gone through in trying to protect you all."

Aaron crossed his arms over his chest. "We'll see."

Rohan glanced at Maiven. "Are you satisfied that I'm under no one's mind control but my own, Grandmum?"

"Yes, Rohan," she said. "Thank you." She looked at Thisbe. "I'm sorry for the accusation, but you must understand how your actions look to us."

"Of course," Thisbe said, feeling numb and taking a moment to collect her thoughts. She wanted to look at Aaron, but she couldn't get herself to do it, for fear of what she'd see in his eyes. Earlier, in the desert, he'd blamed himself for influencing her actions, to Thisbe's surprise. But that was before Ishibashi died. Had Aaron's opinion changed since then? He was so upset and angry at her—she'd never seen him like this before. He'd always been so even, so rational, so tender with the girls compared to Alex. But he was very upset now. Everything was such a mess, and it was clear that most of her friends and family in this library blamed her for all of it—which she thought she was prepared for. But now they thought she'd done something unconscionable to Rohan, too. She hadn't anticipated that. What other accusations would she have to face alone? "When Fifer, Dev, and I hatched this plan," Thisbe said, "I thought that at least I'd have them to lean on when it came time to explain it. But it seems like everything has backfired."

She looked up at Sky again and steadied the worries that bombarded her. There was nothing Thisbe could do but tell them what had happened from the moment the Revinir had swept up her and Fifer from the shore of Artimé.

After a deep breath, she began. "The last time I communicated with any of you," she said, "was right after the Revinir abducted Fifer and me from Artimé. I sent a message asking

LISA McMANN

you to help. Fifer also sent a message, which, at the time, I assumed was a call for help as well. Unbeknownst to me for the next couple of days, she had actually told Florence to stand down and wait for further instructions." She glanced at Florence. "During that time I thought you must have been following us and had run into trouble. Fifer finally broke down and told me what she'd done."

Florence frowned. "That seems . . . out of character for Fifer."

"Oh gods," Thisbe moaned as it dawned on her what she was up against. Thisbe closed her eyes and took in a slow breath. Already Florence was doubting her. "I know it seems that way. I know you all think Fifer is pure and perfect and would never lie." She wanted to say more, like pointing out that Fifer had actually killed an Unwanted recently when she put an end to Frieda Stubbs, but she held her tongue for fear of sounding too defensive.

"There were some other factors," Thisbe said instead, "like our injuries after the Revinir dropped us through the roof. But Fifer will corroborate my story—I guarantee it. Dev will too. He arrived here not long after Fifer hatched this whole . . .

plan." She hesitated, then looked around the room. "It sounds like I'm blaming Fifer—I'm not. I signed on, and I still feel like it was the right choice."

Florence shifted. She wore a grim look. "Continue."

Thisbe talked late into the night. She shared how Dev had shown up. And she explained Fifer's idea about actually being able to beat the Revinir if Thisbe could get close enough. She talked about finding the Revinir's weaknesses, and how they'd realized that one of those weaknesses was that the dragon-woman so badly wanted Thisbe to join her.

Thisbe admitted that she and Dev had thought Fifer's scheme was an impossible one at first, and that they'd actually fought her on it for a while because it seemed so preposterous. But then they slowly realized it just might work. "And after months and months of us all trying to find the solution to taking out the Revinir," Thisbe said, turning to Florence, "we finally agreed that this plan was viable. So . . . I created a new version of Thisbe. Just like I'd create a character that I would play onstage back home in the theater."

Florence's face flickered, and she turned to look at the fire.

Thisbe went on to share about her painstaking time in the castle and the plans that she and Fifer and Dev had made to deceive everyone. "Believe it or not," she said wearily, "we chose not to tell you the plan in order to protect you in case the Revinir captured any of you and forced you to drink dragon-bone broth. She'd get the truth from you that way." She paused. "We needed you to think the worst of me so that if you were ever tortured or taken prisoner, you wouldn't be able to give away the truth about the plan."

"I knew it," Seth muttered, and everyone, who'd been silent all this time, turned to look at him. "I told you all there had to be a reason!" He turned to Thisbe. "I told them. I believe you, Thisbe."

Thisbe blew out a breath. Her knees felt wobbly with relief. "Thanks, Seth."

Rohan nodded at the boy. "I remember you saying it. You were right."

Simber sighed deeply from the staircase. Aaron put his face in his hands.

Thisbe, even though she was exhausted, felt a small lift knowing one dear friend believed her. But the silence from the

LISA McMANN

rest of them was heavy, and Thisbe couldn't tell if they were rejecting her explanation or if they were buying it. Her two key witnesses remained unaware and unhelpful. She dropped to rest on the arm of Fifer's sofa.

Rohan took that as his cue. "The Revinir and Thisbe discovered Maiven and me on our covert mission with Quince outside the castle ballroom, as I'm sure Maiven relayed to you all. The Revinir took me inside, and she immediately, and quite sneakily, put two vials of dragon-bone broth in my tea." He pulled up his sleeves and showed his scaly arms as proof. "Real ones this time," he said, looking at the former queen. "The Revinir tried to hide what she was doing, and even Thisbe didn't know she'd done it. But, because I know that monster as well as Thisbe does, I was expecting it. Luckily, I had ingested enough of the ancestor broth in the catacombs to counteract the effects, or I could have wrecked Thisbe's plan."

"Well . . . ," said Thisbe. "I managed to do that myself today. But yes."

She and Rohan told the rest of the story, including that morning when they'd paraded to Dragonsmarche with the Revinir to declare their joint rulership, and how that had failed.

LISA McMANN

Thisbe concluded the tale. "And all of that led us to the desert. We were on our way to see if the ghost dragons had vanished when we met face-to-face with Aaron. I know it was confusing, Aaron. But you must believe that I was still playing my role until that last second, when Rohan whispered to me that the Revinir was alone—I'd been trying to get her on her own the entire time so I could use my obliterate spell. And she was finally in a place where no one else would be hurt. I could safely take her out. So . . . that's what I tried to do." Thisbe looked miserable. "And obviously, under such great pressure, I failed." She paused. "So there you have it. Believe me or don't. That's the whole story."

Thisbe took a break to drink some water as the others talked quietly among themselves, piecing Thisbe's story together. It seemed to help the others to know that the Revinir had immediately tried to control Rohan's mind upon his arrival at the castle. It made them realize that Thisbe's reasoning for not telling them the truth from the beginning might have been valid. A few others were starting to believe her and understand how everything had happened.

But Thisbe had done so much harm in missing the Revinir

with the obliterate spell. That's where the biggest doubts remained in the minds of Aaron, Simber, and Florence.

"I don't mean to take a stab at you," Florence said to Thisbe, "but how in the world did you miss with that spell? You executed it perfectly when we practiced."

Thisbe knew how. But if she admitted it, would that only make them doubt her entire story . . . and her? She turned her gaze to the window and caught the reflection of Aaron looking at her. She dropped her eyes. "I don't know," she said. "I just . . . messed up. First time for everything, I guess. There was a lot of pressure."

Aaron frowned. He'd cautiously begun to believe her . . . up until this moment. What was she hiding? He knew that shifty-eyed look. He'd done it himself countless times. There was still something big Thisbe was keeping from them. Something sinister. How much of her story was true? And how much was a trick? Was she still supporting the Revinir, even as she stood here, pouring out her heart and getting people to support her, just like that? No one, not even Rohan, knew if she was telling the truth about her motives. The feeling in the pit of Aaron's stomach made him look away too. Was he too hard on her

LISA McMANN

based on his own past? Maybe she wasn't like him after all. But oh, how she seemed like she was. Perhaps even worse. The thought made his stomach churn. This whole thing—Ishibashi's shocking death, his sister's deception, his own past life of betrayal coming back to haunt him—felt very out of control to Aaron. And he felt himself spiraling with it.

The uneasiness in the library didn't go away. Thisbe and Rohan were exhausted, and everyone else needed to think about what Thisbe had told them. Florence and Simber exchanged a glance and a nod. Florence moved to the stairwell, and the two statues went outside for a while, while the humans looked after Fifer and Dev and prepared for bed.

When everyone else had settled, Thisbe lay down on the floor next to Fifer's sofa so she could help her if she woke up. With no definitive decisions made about Thisbe's actions, everyone else went to sleep . . . some with one eye open.

Irrepressible Anger

The Revinir retreated in fury to her castle, leaving the other dragons to put out the forest fire she'd started. She landed on the drawbridge and stomped through the immense, vacant entrance. Turning left, she swept up the staircase and, on the ballroom level, turned and went into her private quarters to brood. She was angry, but she also felt devastated and betrayed. She tried to get some sleep, but when sleep wouldn't come, she left her room and wandered the halls, knocking things off the walls as usual.

She ordered her servants to go away and leave her alone. But then, in a fit of paranoia, she demanded they return to

LISA McMANN

protect her and forced them to peer out all the windows, looking for dragons, fog clouds, or anything else suspicious. As they conducted their search, the Revinir wandered into the ballroom with the remaining glazed-eyed simpletons who were appointed to wait on her. Once the coast was clear, she retired to the balcony until the smell of smoke drove her inside. She sat by the table where she and Thisbe had eaten and bantered together, and closed her eyes.

Thisbe had tried to kill her.

The Revinir's mind whirled, trying to come up with reasons for how and why all of this had happened. How had she not seen it? She knew definitively that Thisbe had tricked her. Again. This time, though, was mortifying. With a whimper, the Revinir opened her eyes and listlessly tried to eat from the previously untouched food on the table, which had been left there by mindless slaves who had delivered it at the usual time despite the Revinir not having been anywhere near the castle. But the dragon-woman's throat was raw and sensitive. The metal star was still stuck back there. She could feel it but couldn't get a good grip on it with her claws. Soon the emptiness inside her pulled her attention away.

LISA McMANN

This gaping new hole inside her was so similar to the one from her childhood, and the memories came flooding back. Especially those of the day when Marcus and Justine had packed up a boat and left Warbler Island with Gondoleery Rattrapp and Eva Fathom, coldly saying good-bye to young Emma.

Emma had pleaded with them to come back. Shouted for them to return. Begged them, against her own good judgment, to take her in the boat with them. Though she couldn't imagine setting a single foot into that tipsy little skiff and setting sail, away from the safety of dry land.

"You're afraid of the water!" Justine had shouted back, as if Emma could have ever forgotten. "When you grow up, build a ship and come find us!" Justine had grinned and elbowed Marcus at that, the Revinir remembered. Not nicely. Like she'd won something.

"I'm not afraid anymore!" Emma had screamed, and the tears had come too. She'd run into the water—a few steps. Four or five, until the panic took over and forced her back to shore. It was a lie, and Justine knew it. Emma had been afraid of the water ever since she was a baby.

No one knew what had caused it. No one could recall a

moment when Emma had fallen into a river or the sea, or had been surprised or shocked by a sudden experience with it. Least of all her. But fear of things isn't always learned, the Revinir knew. She'd just been that way.

As she'd grown up, she'd built a ship. But she was too afraid to test it out. What if she'd made a mistake and it wasn't seaworthy? What if it sank? So she built another ship. And another. All of them seemingly sound—some still sat in the harbor of Warbler Island today. But Emma wouldn't test them. She couldn't. Her feet wouldn't let her on board. So she just kept building more.

When she took over the island as leader after her mother passed away, people began to ask her about all the ships— what was the purpose if no one was using them? They offered to test the ships out for her, but that frightened Emma even more. What if people left and didn't come back? What if they went to find Justine and Marcus and told them what a coward Emma was? And told them how she'd built all these ships, like Justine had teasingly told her to do? Would Justine win again if she found out that Emma had been smart enough to make them but too scared to use them?

LISA McMANN

Emma had grown tired of people talking about her. She wanted them to keep their mouths shut and help her build ships until she was absolutely sure they were perfect. She wanted the people to stay in Warbler and do the things she told them to do. And to just stop mentioning Emma's weird obsession with ships and fear of water.

When pirates came to inquire about the ships, Emma saw a mercenary opportunity. She could sell ships to the pirates and make a name for herself that way—then she could use the excuse that she'd become too busy and important to go after her siblings. She wasn't afraid of water, she'd say to everyone. Not afraid at all, just very busy becoming rich with pirate gold. She changed her name to Queen Eagala, because it sounded brave and bold and powerful, like an eagle. A creature who could fly over the sea and never have to touch it.

Some of the people of Warbler balked at building ships for pirates. They pestered their leader to let them test the waters. But the pirates were bringing her trunks of gold and placing orders for fleets, and Queen Eagala needed her people now more than ever.

The complaints grew, and the leader of Warbler began to

LISA McMANN

investigate methods of silencing them. She managed a bit of magic she'd learned from her siblings and their friends and put a silence spell on the island. And while it worked on the noises from wildlife and nature, it didn't silence the people. They rose up to oppose her. To ridicule her even more than before.

Dewy-eyed, the Revinir looked up from the table in the ballroom and surveyed her castle. She'd found a way to silence her people back then, all right. Using the very gold the pirates provided. Melting it into thorns and creating the thornament necklaces.

When the Warblerans had tried to escape after being silenced, Queen Eagala branded her people with orange eyes so that everyone would know where they belonged, and she kept most of them working in the underground sections of the island. Almost everyone turned away from her, but her fear tactics had worked, and they stayed.

The worst thing about the way she'd ruled Warbler, the Revinir realized now, was that she hadn't had anyone to confide in. And now, once again, she was in the same situation. She'd had a confidant for a moment, and it had felt good. But then everything had exploded.

If only she hadn't been so deathly afraid of water all her life, maybe things would have been different. Maybe she would have gone to Quill with Marcus and Justine. And maybe she'd have found herself in Artimé and been accepted as one of them.

Eventually, despite her fears, she'd gone out on a ship to Artimé, back when she thought she had a chance at taking it over—proving something to her siblings, perhaps, even though they were both dead by then. True, Captain Baldhead had insisted on her going, and Queen Eagala had known that her reign on Warbler depended on defeating Quill and Artimé. She'd gotten aboard the ship—trying to hide her shaking— and had stayed glued to the deck in terror throughout the journey. Once in Artimé, she'd been attacked by a flying dead body and forced to escape in a tender to stay alive and keep hidden. She'd floated over to Artimé's own pirate ship and found it deserted. But more importantly, it seemed safer than a little tender tipping on the waves. During the course of the battle, she'd fled up its nets and climbed aboard to stay alive. Hiding there, she'd waited for the fight to come to her.

She'd ruined Alex, or so she'd thought. But in the end, the ship had had a mind of its own, and when someone died aboard it during the fight with Alex, the ship, of its own accord, carried Eagala to its original home, the Island of Fire. She was too afraid to abandon it. When the volcano island plunged underwater, Eagala and the ship went with it. She'd been thrown violently from the ship and forced through the volcano network, then found herself in this world, being spewed from the crater lake. She'd nearly drowned. She didn't remember how she'd made it to shore alive.

That was the last time the Revinir had been fully submerged in water. After that harrowing experience, she had vowed never to touch the sea again if she could help it. The memories still haunted her nightmares.

But she had wings now, like an eagle, but better. And wings made the sea irrelevant.

By morning, the fire in the ballroom was out, and the Revinir had dealt with her tiny battered heart. Thisbe was dead to her. Or, quite literally, she soon would be. The dragon-woman hadn't lifted the kill order, and didn't intend to. She didn't care who followed through with it, as long as someone did. Didn't care if she ever set eyes on that traitorous girl again. In fact, maybe it would be best if she never did.

But Drock the dark purple was another matter the Revinir would have to look into. Had he helped the two escape? They were heading toward that abandoned palace. Perhaps the dragon had gotten confused and thought he was doing right by rescuing Rohan. Or . . . perhaps he wasn't under the mind control spell at all, which at this point was only a small problem amid the greater mess the Revinir faced. She might have to have Drock killed just to put that one behind her.

The red dragons would probably do that for her, she realized with a small smile. And if they didn't, maybe she could use Drock against the people of Artimé and beat them at their own game.

Whatever the case, it was time to fight, and the sooner the better—before the few Artiméans here brought in the rest of their troops. Today the Revinir would attempt to let go of the relationship she thought she'd had with Thisbe. And she'd round up the dragons and the people of Grimere and the surrounding villages and prepare to hunt down anyone who harbored her. The girl had dashed all of the Revinir's hopes in an instant and stopped the Revinir's dream of being a true, official dragon leader of the land of the dragons.

Thisbe would pay. All of Artimé would pay. Not just for the wrongs they'd done to her in the past few days, but for as far back as she could remember, standing on the shore of Warbler and watching her brother and sister sail away without her.

Suffering the
Consequences

All night in her dreams Thisbe tried to communicate telepathically with Fifer, and in the morning
the words were a whisper on her lips. "Wake up,
Fifer. Please. I need you." She sat up and peered
at her twin. The girl's cheeks were ruddy, which was a good
sign, but her eyes remained stubbornly closed. She'd rolled to
her side in the night, though—or someone had moved her. But
Dev's face was drawn and gaunt. The two had to wake up soon,
or they'd lose a lot of their strength. At least they were taking in
scant amounts of water via a sponge spell component Aaron had
managed to create out of some moss from the riverbank.

LISA McMANN

Florence was nearby, stoking the fire as Aaron and Seth carried several fish up the stairs to be cooked for breakfast. Everyone else was awake. Rohan appeared, coming up the stairs a moment later with an armload of apples from the orchard. He handed them out.

"We weren't able to collect many before," Thisbe remarked before biting into one. She stretched and got to her feet, still chewing.

"Many what?" asked Florence, in an attempt to be civil, though it was clear the warrior trainer still had her doubts about Thisbe's story.

Thisbe swallowed and attempted the same—they'd have to all get along in order to beat the Revinir. "Apples. Only a few fell inside the red dragons' invisible boundaries, and we couldn't cross them."

"Except when *you* wanted to leave," Florence pointed out, and the way she said it made Thisbe glance sharply at her. It seemed like Florence was challenging her story.

"Right," Thisbe said tersely, but her heart sank. She scrambled to explain. "When we three decided it was time for me to leave, I . . . I spoke to the front corner dragon. In a roar, because

I'm part dragon, obviously. And because the Revinir had given the dragons instructions . . ." Thisbe trailed off, realizing she was repeating herself from last night. And by emphasizing this part of the tale, she only sounded defensive and desperate to be believed. Which she was, it was true, but that somehow made her story seem less credible. She sighed and took another bite of the apple. "You don't believe me."

Florence kept her gaze pointed at the fireplace. "I didn't say that."

"You don't have to. It's clear." Thisbe moved to the stairs. "I'm going to the river to clean up. I'm a mess from escaping that forest fire."

Rohan bit his lip as he watched her go, wavering between following her and letting her have some time alone, and eventually choosing the latter. Then he looked at Florence. "She's hurt you don't believe her."

"I have to protect our people," Florence said, more sharply than she usually spoke. "It's my duty. Fifer is unconscious, Aaron is too stuck inside his own head, and Simber is swayed by his devotion to the twins. Somebody has to ask the tough questions, and it falls to me."

LISA McMANN

Rohan gave her a measured look. He trusted her and looked up to her leadership. And he understood at least a little why she was still skeptical despite Thisbe's explanation. "I can only tell you," he said, "that at the castle, Thisbe told me the truth about everything once I figured out what she was doing. She was very worried about me taking in the dragon-bone broth, and her fears were warranted. It's the first thing the Revinir did to me. If I hadn't had a buildup of the ancestor broth already in my system, things might have gone badly much earlier than they did. And I might not be here."

Florence nodded slowly. "Right. But now Ishibashi isn't here."

Rohan closed his eyes, pained. "Right."

Florence let out a frustrated noise. "Look. Just because I was carved out of rock doesn't mean my heart is made of stone. It's . . . hard to put this all together. Hard to use my mind efficiently when I hurt so much." She hesitated. "I still can't believe that Thisbe would miss with that obliterate spell. Aaron told me she verbally stumbled and said the wrong word. That is just . . . It's so improbable for her—for someone at her level of expertise. I believe much of her story, but I think she might still be lying about something big."

Rohan looked up, alarmed. "What?"

"About her feelings."

Rohan's lungs contracted. "Feelings for . . . whom?" he whispered.

Florence glanced at him and saw the look of dread on his face. She softened. "Not for you. I think those are true. I mean her feelings and desire for power. And her relationship with the Revinir."

Rohan looked away, troubled. He recollected that moment when Thisbe had bobbled the spell. He thought about how she had so smoothly fooled the Revinir for many days, working her way into the dragon-woman's tiny heart. She'd been so convincing, as one would expect from such a naturally skilled actor. But what if it wasn't all an act?

The thought left Rohan cold.

Thisbe returned, and everyone trickled back up to the library to eat the cooked fish together. They tended to the still unconscious ones. Florence administered another dose of medicine to them, and Thisbe held the wet sponge to their lips, trying to get a bit of water to seep into their mouths.

"Water," Fifer whispered. She choked and coughed on the dribble, and her eyes fluttered.

"Fifer," Thisbe said, holding her sister's head. When Fifer stopped coughing, Thisbe pressed the sponge against her sister's lips again. She heard the word "water" ring in her ears, as if it were an echo. Then she realized Fifer had sent the word to her telepathically like she'd done before. Thisbe frowned, puzzled. Fifer turned her head away from the sponge.

"She's been doing that for days," Seth said in a low voice. "She asks for water, but then doesn't want it."

Thisbe pinched her eyelids shut, thinking it through. Whatever Fifer was trying to communicate, Thisbe didn't understand. She sent a message back. *What do you mean? Please wake up! I need your help. Florence . . . doesn't believe me.* Tears welled in Thisbe's eyes, and she kept her head bent over her sister so her hair would hide her face. If she started crying now, she might never stop. Because maybe Florence was right to question Thisbe's intentions.

The thing Thisbe wanted to know was *why* did she feel a twinge in her heart when it came to the Revinir, after all the horrible things the dragon-woman had done? Did it make Thisbe a bad person to have sympathy for someone like that? Is that the trait Aaron was so afraid she had?

A few minutes later, when Thisbe's overwhelming wave of emotion had passed and she was helping everyone else clean up, Fifer's eyes fluttered again. But this time they stayed open. She blinked a few times, trying to clear her head. Trying to remember where she was and what had happened to her. And it all came rushing back: The fight with the red dragons. Florence in pieces and Fifer putting her back together again. Dev valiant with his homemade spears against the fierce attack of the Revinir's dragon guards. "Dev?" she called out, her voice raspy. "Florence?"

Everyone turned. As Fifer struggled to lift her head, Thisbe and Florence rushed to Fifer's side.

"You're awake!" Thisbe cried. "Oh, Fifer. Thank goodness." Thisbe bent down to support Fifer's shoulders. Tears slipped down Thisbe's cheeks, and she buried her face in Fifer's robe and tried to stop crying—she didn't want to frighten Fifer.

LISA McMANN

But the sobs exploded from Thisbe's chest, and all the sadness leaked out.

Fifer stared at her sister for a moment, her eyes clouded, her expression confused. "What's wrong? Why are you back?" she said weakly. "Does this mean . . . it's over? The Revinir is dead?"

A Heartfelt Plea

T hisbe felt her face grow hot, and she struggled to regain her composure—she didn't need anybody seeing her bawling her eyes out right now when they were skeptical of her every word and action. She lifted her head and sniffed hard. "I—no, the Revinir is still alive. I tried to obliterate her. And I missed." She felt her throat tighten again despite her efforts. "I messed up everything, Fife. Like, absolutely everything." The tears began again, and she covered her mouth as if that would stifle her sobs. "But I'm so glad . . . to see . . . you . . ." She couldn't continue. The uninvited jags burst forth again, and they broke the tottering dam that Thisbe had been trying to hold together for weeks. Fifer was awake. She seemed like she was going to be okay. Soon Thisbe would have to let her down again with more terrible news.

"There, there, Thiz," Fifer said as Simber peered up into the room from the stairs to see what was going on with the girls. With a look of relief at the sight of his head mage awake and looking all right, he settled back down again. "I'm so glad you're back," Fifer crooned weakly, patting Thisbe's back. "Whatever has gone on, we'll . . . figure it out—" Fifer noticed Dev and uttered a slight gasp. "What happened to him?" She struggled out of Thisbe's grasp and rolled to her side toward Dev, then tried to sit up but faltered. Thisbe sobbed a bit more, then sniffed and moved away when Aaron came over to give Fifer a hearty hug and help her sit up.

"Dev's alive but unconscious," said Rohan. "Florence can explain about him."

"It's good to see you awake, Fifer," Aaron said quietly. He didn't acknowledge Thisbe or her tears.

"Thanks, but I don't understand anything. How did you get here? What's going on?" Fifer looked at Florence. "Are you okay now? What happened after I brought you back to life?"

Florence, Maiven, and Sky moved over to the fireplace area, and Sky began toasting some bread for Fifer to nibble on. Seth came and sat next to Fifer, leaving Thisbe free to back away from the group, which felt more comfortable at the moment. Aaron returned to brooding in the corner by the staircase, near Simber, close enough to listen in.

"I'm fine, thanks to you," Florence replied. "We're so glad you woke up. After I shot a couple of arrows, the red dragon grabbed you with its tail and tossed you across the yard. Dev became furious and charged at it with his spear. He and I killed it together, but its head fell on him."

As Fifer took it in, the blood drained from her face. "Is he going to be okay?"

"We don't know. He seems to be healing well with our magical medicine, but he hasn't woken up. Henry sent me a note this morning with a new option to try, so we're working on it."

Fifer lifted her hand to cover her eyes as a wave of emotion washed through her. Then she rolled back on her sofa, exhausted already. "Oh, dear Dev," she moaned. "You don't

LISA McMANN

97 « Dragon Fury

deserve any of this." She took a moment to gather her thoughts, then turned back to Thisbe. "So . . . if you're here, that means everyone knows?"

"I . . . yes," said Thisbe, glancing furtively at Florence. "I mean, I told them everything. I had to. I'm not sure if they believe me, though."

"We—I do believe . . . most of it," Florence said, somewhat unconvincingly. "I just have questions. And concerns."

"As do I," said Maiven.

Aaron mumbled something from where he sat.

Thisbe pressed her lips together and looked at Fifer. "It's been a bit tough," she managed to say before her voice broke once more. With Fifer awake, and others in the room still questioning, Thisbe got to her feet. "I'm going to get some air while you all talk to Fifer—to make it fully clear that she and I haven't spoken or tried to get our stories straight. You'll see soon enough that I've told the truth."

Thisbe continued toward the bannister and rounded it, passing Aaron. He glanced up and caught Thisbe's furtive look. He didn't indicate whether he believed her or not, but his expression wasn't quite as cold as before.

LISA McMANN

Thisbe blew out a breath. As Simber slowly backed down the staircase to the fifth-floor landing, making room for Thisbe to get past him, Thisbe's mind returned to her big flub with the obliterate spell. She still felt tremendous guilt for messing it up, and that worried her. Aaron seemed unable to forgive her or believe her—did he truly know more about her nature than she did, like he'd implied in the desert? Was there still something to worry about? Was there a chance Thisbe would go astray again, even when surrounded by everyone she loved? She hesitated on the top step, wanting to ask him, but then again, she didn't want to know the answers.

Besides, how could Aaron ever understand Thisbe better than she understood herself? Thisbe knew without a doubt that there was no way she would turn on Artimé like that again. And it wasn't like she'd actually done it once already— it had all been part of the plan. Her joining up with the Revinir hadn't been real. None of it.

Still, Thisbe wondered what the Revinir was doing now. She'd sounded so hurt when they'd been hiding from her in the forest. But who wouldn't be, after an attempt on their life? Thisbe was sure she'd get over it soon. The Revinir was a monster.

LISA McMANN

But she'd been a girl like Thisbe, once.

"Stop thinking about Emma," Thisbe muttered under her breath. With the stairway clear, she started down.

"What's that?" asked Florence through the balusters. She and Maiven were looking down curiously at Thisbe as if waiting for an answer.

Simber gave her a sharp look from below. "Who's Emma?"

Thisbe ignored Simber and looked up. "No one," she said coolly. She caught Seth's gaze and held it. "Thank you to those of you who believe me."

Seth pressed his lips firmly together and nodded slightly.

Thisbe began descending again. "I'm going for a very long walk so you have plenty of time."

Sky and Maiven began to protest the need for her departure, but Thisbe slipped down the spiral stairs, calling back to them, "I want you to be one hundred percent sure you trust me. We can't have anyone doubting anyone during this crucial time." She continued down the stairs.

"What's going on?" Fifer asked, searching the faces before her. "Why don't you believe Thisbe? What's happened?"

The remaining group looked soberly from one to another,

and in the uncomfortable moment, Maiven poured Fifer some tea to go with the toast Sky had made. "There have been some questions about all the lying everyone's done," she said.

Rohan got up. "I don't need to hear Fifer's story to be convinced that Thisbe is telling the truth," he said, and went after Thisbe.

"I don't need to hear it to believe Thisbe," said Seth, "but I *want* to hear it. I'm staying."

With Rohan gone, Simber crept back up to the top of the stairs.

Once Thisbe could be seen through the window strolling toward the orchard, Aaron got up and moved to his sister's sofa. He sat on the floor facing her. "All right, Fifer," he said. "Is it true that *you* came up with a plan for Thisbe to infiltrate the Revinir's castle in an attempt to get close to her, with the goal of destroying her? And that it was a smart idea not to tell any of us about this plan?"

Fifer nodded defiantly. "It is true. And it *was* a smart idea."

Aaron blinked. "All right," he said. "Once you've had some refreshments, tell us everything from the beginning."

LISA McMANN

Half Apologies

As the day wore on, Thisbe and Rohan slowly wandered the orchard and the deserted village, holding hands and not saying much, but each mulling things over. They looked through various homes, finding them empty but mostly inhabitable. They spoke a little about what must have happened for everyone to have left. As they pieced together all of the black-eyed people's images that pounded their minds, along with the history that Rohan could remember from the books he'd read, it all seemed very sad. It added another level of discomfort to the day. But being together with Rohan, safe and not on the run, felt right and good. So that helped Thisbe's mood a bit.

» » « «

Inside the palace library, Fifer regained some strength through the magic of Maiven's tea and the toast Sky had made and was eager to tell her story in order to help her beloved sister.

Fifer's tale matched Thisbe's.

When Fifer was done and thoroughly ready to take a long nap, Florence spoke up. "Thank you. I'm sure you're exhausted. But . . . I have one question." She hesitated, as if unsure whether to continue, then pressed onward. "Do you think Thisbe has developed sympathy for the Revinir?" She told Fifer how Thisbe had missed the dragon-woman with the spell by fumbling on the verbal component.

Fifer rested thoughtfully, her eyes drooping. "I can't imagine her feeling that way at all," she said with a yawn.

Before Aaron and the rest could break the news of Ishibashi's death to Fifer, the head mage was asleep.

Florence addressed the others. "I'm still skeptical about that one thing," she admitted. "But I owe Thisbe an apology. I'll be back in a while." Her gaze rested on Aaron, and she gave him a quizzical glance. "Does anyone else want to join me?"

"I'll speak to her later," Maiven said quietly.

LISA McMANN

Aaron frowned and shook his head. "Not right now. I'm still . . . processing. I hope you can all understand. Something's not quite adding up, and I'm . . . I'm feeling pretty raw still. It's going to take some time for me."

Florence went after the couple, searching the village until she found a home deep in the center of the village with its front door standing wide open. She approached and ducked her head to look inside. It seemed as if this place hadn't been picked over quite as thoroughly as the others. The two were scavenging useful items.

"Thisbe?" Florence called out when she spotted them.

Thisbe turned, her expression as stony as Florence's. "What is it?"

"I came to tell you that I'm sorry," Florence said.

Thisbe waited, but there was no more to it. So she nodded stiffly. "All right." Then she turned to Rohan. "Let's bring this stuff back to the palace. We can start making weapons tonight."

"I'll . . . help carry things," said Florence.

"Suit yourself."

It was far from the most comfortable situation the two from

Artimé had been in together. Florence didn't elaborate on what she actually felt sorry about, and Thisbe was still hurt. Distrust hung between them.

But they went together back to the palace, where everyone who was able came down to greet Thisbe.

Aaron came first, stiffly. "I believe you," he said, but he avoided her gaze. Though they shared an awkward hug, Thisbe could tell something was still bothering him greatly. But at least they were on the same side against the Revinir.

Maiven, on the other hand, apologized wholeheartedly for the tone she'd taken, and Sky also affirmed she believed Thisbe. Simber seemed distant and slightly skeptical, still, but agreed with the others that her story was sound. And Seth felt quite proud to have believed her all along, which almost made up for the rest of them.

Despite the lingering uneasiness, it felt good to be together. Thisbe had spent so much time alone, in her head, trying to single-handedly destroy the Revinir. So having backup was a relief. The momentum from becoming focused on one goal raised their spirits, which was much needed after losing Ishibashi.

As everyone settled down for the evening, Dev stirred. He sipped water from the sponge, then groaned and sank back into unconsciousness. "I think he's going to pull through," Florence announced to the others. "Henry's suggestion seems to be working." She gave him another dose.

It was the lift they all needed. But things didn't feel normal, and Thisbe didn't know what would have to happen to make it that way. She feared her unsettled feelings wouldn't go away soon . . . especially once she found out that Fifer still didn't know about Ishibashi.

Back in Artimé

Carina and the team of ghost dragons finally made it to Artimé. Upon their arrival, Carina leaped from her dragon and ran to embrace her children, Ava and Lukas, and her husband, Sean Ranger. But when their joyous reunion was over, Sean pulled Carina aside to tell her the shocking news of Ishibashi's death.

Others soon gathered to help her process the loss: Henry and Thatcher Haluki, as well as Kaylee Jones and Lani and Samheed Burkesh-Haluki. By now the shock of the scientist's death had somewhat lessened for the Artiméans, but

LISA McMANN

witnessing Carina learning of it brought the sadness back in waves again, especially for Henry.

Artimé's chief healer knew a lot more about the reason for the scientists' long lives than anyone else did. He knew about the glowing blue seaweed that had first saved a dying tortoise's life, then that of Karkinos the crab. The seaweed had seemed to allow the scientists to live immortally after they'd ingested it—but few others knew this. Ishibashi had sworn Henry to secrecy back when he was just a budding teenage healer and had told him that he must have a human's consent before using it on anyone because of the unknown side effects.

Henry had carried some of the seaweed in his medical kit for a while, just in case . . . but then he stopped after Meghan Ranger had died under his care. She'd been unresponsive, so he hadn't been able to ask her if she wanted to take it before it was too late. The memory haunted him. But he'd done what Ishibashi had instructed him to do. It was better not to have the seaweed. There was less guilt, and he spent fewer sleepless nights wondering if he'd made a mistake. He'd never been sorry not to have it.

So how had Ishibashi come to die, when the seaweed not

LISA McMANN

only saved lives but also seemingly made those who ingested it immortal? Henry had talked with Ito about it after the news came in. The oldest scientist was at least 120 years old, and he'd taken in a great amount of the seaweed over time. It had been an experiment among the three men from the Island of Shipwrecks. Ito ate a small amount daily, Sato only when feeling ill, and Ishibashi only once when they first discovered it more than sixty years ago. Perhaps the fact that Ishibashi had only taken a single dose a very long time ago had something to do with his vulnerability to death when attacked, but no one knew for sure.

Ito was shocked and saddened and had abruptly taken ill over the news, but after a while he seemed grateful to know that it was possible to die, despite the seaweed, for he and Sato were growing frail, and they worried about their quality of life as the years pressed on.

Still, the Revinir ending the life of such a man as Ishibashi, no matter his age, was a horrible evil. There was nothing the two remaining scientists wanted more than to see their friends succeed against the dragon-woman. They would be biding their time in Artimé, hoping for everyone to return safely.

Henry was restless with wanting to know more about how the attack on Aaron and Ishibashi had happened, because the note they'd received didn't really explain much. But he'd find out soon enough. And now that Carina and the dragons were here, the fighters of the seven islands were ready and eager to go. Lani, Samheed, and Kaylee had been in communication with Florence all this time, discussing training, and brainstorming and plotting their attack based on a variety of scenarios. Their transportation had arrived, and the group of leaders made plans to have everyone depart in grand fashion first thing in the morning for Ashguard's palace, as instructed.

Inside her apartment, Carina wrapped herself in the comfort of her family; only Seth wasn't with them at the moment, and she missed him. She wondered how he was handling the news of Ishibashi's death, and she felt terrible that she hadn't been there with him when he'd found out. She checked in with him via a send spell, letting him know she was safely in Artimé and had heard the terrible news, and asked how things were going there.

While she awaited a response, she carefully set aside everything she'd need for the journey. Sean had packed for himself and the younger children already, and their bags sat neatly near the door.

Over the course of several messages, Seth updated her on what had happened with Fifer and Thisbe. They talked a bit about the trust that had been lost, and how hard it seemed to put it back in place again—how that might take a while. Seth told her that Florence and Aaron had seemed especially suspicious of Thisbe and remained wary even though the stories checked out. And they also talked about Ishibashi's death and how Seth had watched over the body, and how that had affected him. Then he added one last message.

Hey Mom,

Do you think death is just . . . the end? Or is Ishibashi someplace else? And Alex?

It was enough to make Carina pause. She sat down on the sofa in their apartment and read the words over again. She'd wondered the same thing many times. Imagined that there was someplace other than the ground for the soul to fly off to. It had helped her get through many losses, including Seth's

LISA McMANN

father. She had doubts but hoped it was true. And hope of this sort wouldn't hurt anyone in a time like this. She penned a reply.

> Seth,
> Life seems senseless if there isn't something more, doesn't it? It's comforting to believe there's a world beyond, where the ones we love and miss are sharing good times with others while waiting for us. I think it's all right to wrap yourself up in that thought. I will see you soon.
> Love,
> Mom

Carina touched the message to her lips and sent it off with a whisper to her firstborn. They'd been through a lot together. She knew he would be all right, but it still hurt to know he was feeling the recent deaths in a way Carina had felt the deaths a generation ago. Seth's father first, then Mr. Today. Her mother, Eva Fathom—that had been a complicated one to process. Meghan Ranger and Mr. Appleblossom, and even Liam Healy and more had touched them all in various ways.

Then Alex, a huge loss. And now, their dearest Ishibashi. Life had dealt the Artiméans so many blows. If they succeeded in their mission, would the untimely deaths finally end? How many more would they lose in the struggle to bring peace to all the lands within reach?

With a heavy sigh, Carina went outside to make sure the ghost dragons were comfortable in the lagoon for the night and remind them to stay there. Then she returned to her kin, kissed sleeping Lukas and Ava, and sank into her bed next to Sean, wondering how long it would be before she would know such comfort again.

An Impressive Lineup

In the morning, everyone from the seven islands who was able and ready to fight collected their components, weapons, and travel bags and met on the lawn. Carina sought out Lani and whispered a new idea to her that she'd come up with.

Lani nodded enthusiastically. "That sounds wise. Last night I sent the squid to find Talon and Spike—with any luck we'll see them later."

"Perfect."

The women split up and began directing traffic, guiding people to open spots on the lawn. The extended area soon filled up. People and creatures from Quill and the Island of Legends and Warbler joined the Artiméans. Only a few stayed behind as caretakers of the mansion. Even young Daniel Stowe-Jones joined them on this journey—Kaylee couldn't bear to stay at home when her skills were needed, and she couldn't leave the boy with Ito when Sato was so ill and in need of Ito's caretaking. There would always be people on this journey to protect him. And even if Kaylee had to stay back from fighting in order to keep Daniel safe, at least she was closer to the battle and could help in other ways.

The army of ghost dragons lined Artimé's extended shoreline, and they were bolstered by the sight of so many strangers ready to fight on their behalf. Carina, Sean, Samheed, Lani, Copper, Crow, Scarlet, Henry, Thatcher, and even Lhasa the snow lion took the lead positions on board the dragons. Each ghost dragon was then populated with all sorts of willing fighters.

Statues like the telepathic gargoyles Matilda and Charlie, the tiki, the ostrich, Captain Ahab, Jim the winged tortoise, and Kitten and Fox went with Lani's dragon. Magical creatures who could fight, like Rufus and his army of squirrelicorns,

115 « Dragon Fury

LISA McMANN

rested on Samheed's dragon—they could fly, but not long distances, so it was better to ride. With them was Panther from the jungle, who was finding this venture to be a bit angsty, but so far she was holding her own. The promise of seeing Simber soon seemed to calm her and keep her focused, and the urge to stalk and pounce on unsuspecting squirrelicorns lessened somewhat.

Legendary creatures from Karkinos joined Lhasa on her dragon—a small army of drop bears, Vido the golden rooster, and the hibagon, who kept himself shielded so no one would actually stare too long at him and fall in love, as had happened in the past with a pirate.

Sean's, Thatcher's, and Henry's dragons all carried humans from Artimé and Quill and many medical, food, and magical supplies that Florence had asked them to deliver.

Carina's ghost dragon would transport Asha, Prindi, Reza, and the other black-eyed future rulers of the land of the dragons, as well as Henry and Thatcher's children, including Ibrahim and Clementi. And Copper, ruler of Warbler, led with her assistant, Phoenix, and dozens of other Warblerans anxious to help Artimé and the land of the dragons in their

LISA McMANN

time of need. They would do anything to keep Queen Eagala from returning to take over their island again, and many of them had learned the basic freeze spell from Lani over the past weeks, which would definitely come in handy if all of their plans came to fruition.

In the moments before departure, Carina noted that the last ghost dragon in the lineup still had plenty of room on her back. Carina went to speak to her privately, and the ghost dragon nodded her head and backed into the water, creating space around her. Then Carina went inside the mansion and up to the no-longer-a-secret hallway.

There was still one door up there that no one knew how to open, but Carina wasn't thinking about that now. Instead she went into the Museum of Large and weaved her way between the large things, ending up at Ol' Tater's feet. The enormous mastodon statue stood frozen with a blissful look on his face. It reminded Carina that the last time they'd frozen him, he'd been enjoying quite a nice time playing in the water's edge after Frieda Stubbs had been taken out of power.

Carina placed her hand on the statue's side and closed her eyes. She concentrated on the place she wanted him to move to—the back of the ghost dragon to whom she'd just spoken. When she was ready, she whispered, "Transport." The statue disappeared, and Carina ran swiftly outside to make sure it had appeared in the right place.

Everything was as it should be. Ol' Tater was all set for an adventure. Whether they'd wake him up remained to be seen, but he was good to have around just in case. They could always stash him somewhere else until they needed him.

And so they set off, an army larger than the world of the seven islands had ever seen before, stretching across the sky on the backs of majestic ghost dragons. As they went, a message arrived and weaved through the masses into the proper hands.

Carina,

When you have the gorge between the worlds in sight, veer sharply to the northwest. Make a semicircle around the villages and the forest, keeping a great distance from sight of anyone on the ground and from any dragons patrolling the areas. Then turn south at the cavelands. When you cross the mountain range, you'll see an old palace and beyond it an

abandoned village. Settle everyone there, and hide yourselves
from any dragons flying about. Home base is inside the center
tower of the palace.

Florence

Carina passed along the instructions to her team leaders aboard the various ghost dragons, though she altered them slightly, for she hadn't yet told Florence about the new plan she and Lani had come up with that morning. One of them would have to make a small detour, though Carina wasn't quite sure how to do it without being seen by anyone at the castle. She knew of the ghost dragon's fog ability by now, but she'd also just learned from Seth that the Revinir had figured out how to detect them. So there would have to be another way.

As they flew, the mood was grim and purposeful. This was no lark. They were heading toward the battle of a lifetime. Some of them looked back at their dear land of Artimé, wondering if they'd ever see it again.

An Upward Turn

Once they were past Warbler Island, Carina urged her ghost dragon to push ahead of the others so she had an unobstructed view of the sea below. The woman enlisted help from Asha, Prindi, and the rest of her team to scan the waters, looking for movement—a spray of water or a flash of bronze. They were in search of Spike Furious, Alex's magically created whale with a long spike on her head, and Talon, the flying bronze giant. The two had been searching far and wide with Issie, the sea monster, for Issie's baby, who had been missing for over seven hundred years.

Several Artiméans had seen Issie's baby, Isobel, not too long ago, and she'd even rescued a few of them. But she'd elusively slipped away from the seven islands before her mother could find her. Carina glanced at Lani on a different dragon and saw she was searching too.

No one caught sight of anything, and they had to give up when it became too dark to see. "Perhaps they'll see us," said Prindi, lighting a blinding highlighter at half brightness.

"Good idea," Carina said, and she instructed others to do so as well. But still, Talon and Spike didn't appear.

"We may have to abandon that part of the plan," Carina called out to Lani.

But when they approached the place where the Island of Fire should be, the volcano broke through the surface in glorious fashion, spitting out fire, then water. And then passengers. The burning lava illuminated the travelers: Talon, Issie the sea monster, the giant squid, Spike Furious—and in the midst of them was the seven-hundred-year-old baby Isobel herself.

"Oh, look!" said Lani.

"You've found her!" Carina shouted to Talon. "They've been reunited!"

"And I see I'm not too late to join you," called the bronze giant, flapping his wings to stay in the air. As the four sea creatures splashed into the water and disappeared under the surface, safe and together at last in their world, the Artiméans cheered.

Talon circled around the army in flight, searching through the darkness for the dragon next to Carina's that held most of the legendary creatures from Karkinos. He landed with a spring in his step. "It was a beautiful reunion," he said to Carina as Lhasa bounded across the ghost dragon's back to greet him. Talon gave her a hug, then turned back to Carina. "The squid found us shortly after and urged us to return to our world, and now I understand why. It looks like we have another job to do."

Lani grinned at him from the ghost dragon on the other side of him. "You're right," she called out. "Welcome back. Your success with Isobel has just lifted my spirits tremendously. You've given me hope that we can accomplish what we are about to do."

Carina smiled faintly and nodded in agreement. She wasn't so sure. But as she'd said earlier in her written conversation with Seth, hope definitely wouldn't hurt.

"I'm eager to learn what's going on," said Talon.

From the sea, Spike Furious rose above the surface and followed along at the speed of the dragons. "You must avenge the Alex's death!" she warbled. "I am with you in spirit!"

The people of Artimé tapped their fists to their chests in solidarity and called encouragingly to Spike. They would do everything in their power to return with news for the whale. Poor Spike had never gotten over the loss of the one who had created her. No doubt she felt terribly helpless now.

With Talon here, Carina's previous idea that she'd shared with Lani was now possible to carry out. "We'll fill you in on all the details," Carina told Talon. "But first, are you okay with making a detour to deliver some important goods to the castle? You'll have to do it without being seen." She peered through the darkness, trying to find Matilda and Charlie, the telepathic stone gargoyles. Then she patted her shirt pocket, confirming that Kitten was still there. "Come on over," she called to Talon. "I'd love a moment to confer."

"By all means," Talon said, and flew to her.

Carina beckoned him to land on the ghost dragon she was riding on. "Have you ever wanted to be invisible?" she asked.

"Who wouldn't?" asked the bronze giant. "Simber says it's a lovely feeling."

"Great. Sometime tomorrow we'll be approaching the gorge. And I have a very important job for you. It's one that's going to help us out . . . a lot."

Gaining Strength

By morning Fifer was up and carefully moving around. Her body ached. Her head did too, but that was probably because of feeling terrible about all the confrontations she'd missed. Poor Thisbe had endured it all alone, and then there was the grilling from Florence and Aaron . . . eesh. Fifer hadn't planned on that and felt bad for her twin. But then they'd told her about Ishibashi's death, which had set her back on the sofa for a while, trying to comprehend it. It was sickening to learn about. It made her feel numb that he was gone. Buried. Never to be seen again. It felt so abrupt. No wonder everyone's emotions were high.

LISA McMANN

Once all the information had been shared by her and with her, and after she'd had a moment to breathe, she asked Thisbe to go outside with her. Ishibashi's death felt like a warning, and she needed to think. "Things have ramped up," she muttered to herself. Then, turning to Seth, "Keep an eye on Dev for me, will you?" Fifer asked. "If he wakes up, give him water and some more herbs."

"I know how to take care of people," Seth said, feeling a bit cross to have her dictating orders like that. "Who do you think has been nursing *you* back to health all this time?" His very close friend Fifer had doted on Dev from the moment she'd woken up. She'd hardly given Seth a glance or a word of thanks. It was annoying. And Seth was feeling completely out of sorts with nothing much to do except hang around and somehow plan for an attack nobody quite knew how or when to carry out.

"Sorry," Fifer said weakly. "I know you do. That was a rude thing for me to say. And . . . I'm grateful."

Seth shrugged. "It's all right." At least she'd apologized. But he'd been the one sticking up for the girls all this time, saying they had to have had a bigger goal in mind against the Revinir, and casting doubt on Florence's and Aaron's wild theories that Thisbe had actually gone against them. He wanted to blatantly announce that he'd stood up for them so that he could get some credit for once. But that wasn't Seth's style. He wasn't bold or brash like that. He just wanted them to appreciate him without him having to remind them to do it.

There was more to Seth's feelings now, though. Since the arrival of Rohan and Dev, it seemed like he had taken a distant back seat, and he was the only one who'd realized it. It's not that he didn't like the other boys. He thought Dev was all right, and he'd gotten to know Rohan a little. It was just . . . he didn't feel like he was as close to the girls anymore now that they had their life-altering goals to achieve, and their new friends to help them.

He watched Fifer get up, and didn't offer to help her. There was some small, momentary satisfaction in that, but it didn't linger, and after a moment of watching her struggle, he felt bad and jumped to his feet. "Do you need help?" he asked.

"I'm going to try on my own," Fifer said, glancing at him and flashing a grateful smile. "But thanks for the offer." He reluctantly smiled back and sat down again. The girls moved to the stairs and eased down them at a snail's pace for Fifer's sake. Every movement hurt, but she badly wanted some space from the others. And her mind was occupied with a lot of things. Fifer was terribly worried about Dev. Florence had said he'd actually helped slay a dragon—she could hardly believe it, but after a while it sank in and didn't seem so unlikely. Dev was . . . well, he was incredible in an under-the-radar way. And the two of them had grown awfully close after all they'd gone through.

Her heart ached, thinking of him lying there so helplessly as his body mended with the magical medicine. If only he'd wake up! He needed to drink more water and eat real food or he'd die. The medicinal herbs and some mashed apple they'd slid inside his cheek weren't going to cut it for much longer.

Thisbe had a lot on her mind too. And even though the group had come together and had tried to mend the hurt feelings, things hadn't magically felt fine again. In fact, she still felt like she was getting negative vibes from Florence and Aaron, and even Simber. It was annoying, and it made her want to shout in frustration, but she couldn't actually put her feelings into words. Florence and Aaron were talking to her. But everything felt . . . cold. What more did they want from her?

At least she had Fifer and Seth and Rohan backing her up. And Sky and Maiven seemed normal now too, so that was better than before. She held out her hand at the bottom of the steps to help Fifer. "Did the foxes ever come back?" Fifer asked, peering underneath the staircase.

"No, but I've seen them since I returned," said Thisbe. "They've been running around. I think they're glad the dragons are gone."

"Where have the bodies gone to?" asked Fifer. She started the seemingly endless walk toward the river, anxious for a bath. "How on earth did you get rid of them?"

"Drock and the ghost dragons took care of them. Quite a relief, actually. I'm not sure anyone else knew what to do."

"Could have done the transport spell once they were dead," Fifer said. "It worked on the whale bones, didn't it?"

Thisbe blinked, realizing Fifer was talking about the whale skeleton—which would become Spike Furious—that Alex had transported before they were born. "I guess." She shrugged. "It's done now."

Fifer stopped to catch her breath halfway to the river. She squinted into the orchard, seeing the fresh mound of dirt and

LISA McMANN

the grave marker. "Oh," she said, and went toward it. "Oh no. Is this . . . ?"

"Yeah." Thisbe cringed and went with her. She hadn't felt right about paying her respects. It was partially her fault that Ishibashi had been killed, and she was having trouble dealing with it. Had Ishibashi died thinking Thisbe had caused his death? The twins stood together looking at the dirt and feeling awful for a variety of reasons.

"Why do you think your spell missed her?" Fifer asked quietly.

"It was just a mistake," Thisbe said too quickly. Too defensively.

Fifer didn't say anything for a moment. Then, "You don't make mistakes like that."

Thisbe closed her eyes. She felt gutted, like all the air inside her had been pushed out and there was nothing left outside to breathe. A small swift breeze seemed to rise up from the grave, and it gave her a chill.

"Is it because you felt sorry for the Emma inside the monster?"

Thisbe's eyes flew open. How on earth did Fifer guess it so quickly? But of course Thisbe knew why. Sometimes these things happen with twins, and the older they got, the more the two noticed their connection. Not to mention, Fifer knew as much about the Revinir's past as Thisbe did, now. They'd both ruminated, silently and out loud together, about what had made Emma move so sharply toward evil. Thisbe turned her head slightly and found Fifer studying her.

"That's it, isn't it?" asked Fifer.

Thisbe was struck by how sickly her sister still looked. She sighed in defeat and turned away, but her eyes landed on the grave again. "I'm sorry, Ishibashi," she whispered. A sob escaped her.

After a moment, Thisbe couldn't stand it any longer, and she stepped back, eyes swimming and voice cracking. "I can't do this. Not right now."

"I know. It's okay." Fifer took Thisbe's arm, signaling it was time to move on. As the two continued toward the river, Fifer was deep inside her thoughts. When they reached the bank, she unfastened her head mage robe and took it off in preparation for her bath, then turned to Thisbe. "I think Ishibashi is somehow finding comfort in the fact that your compassion affected you. He would understand."

"You don't know that." Thisbe's ribs ached. She wanted it to be true, yet she hated this conversation for ripping her insides to shreds when she wasn't ready for it. She didn't think Ishibashi would be comforted at all—he'd still died, hadn't he? There was no finding comfort in anything after that. How was she supposed to live with this guilt? Would it ever go away?

Fifer handed Thisbe her clothes and slipped into the river. She let the water soothe her sore body. The two didn't talk. Both were trying to figure out life and how to live it properly, and discovering there was no way to do that. Every time they turned around, some new wrench was being thrown at them. They both just needed a moment to catch their breath, and they both kept not getting one. While Thisbe stood waiting, thinking, mourning, and trying to figure out the jumbled mess of emotions inside her, a shout rang out from the tower-library window.

"Dev is awake!" Seth called. He hesitated, making sure the girls could hear him. Then he added, less enthusiastically, "Fifer, he's asking for you!"

Brought Back to
Life

The simple words that Seth shouted had a profound effect on the ailing girl in the river. *Fifer, he's asking for you!* Fifer sucked in a sharp breath and started scrambling for the shore, forgetting how weak she still was. She stumbled and fell into the water, then emerged and tried again as Thisbe watched, agog.

"You could help me, you know," Fifer said, panting. Her limbs felt like noodles.

Thisbe threw Fifer's clothes to the grass and reached out. "Sorry," she said. "I was just flabbergasted by your reaction. You almost jumped out of your skin."

Fifer's face grew hot. "Aren't you excited to hear that Dev's awake?" she said crossly.

"Well, sure," said Thisbe carefully. She eyed her sister. "Did you two actually become friends while I was gone? You were always sort of indifferent about him."

"I'm indifferent about everyone," Fifer scoffed, and wrung out her hair, then gently shook herself to remove as much water as possible before putting her clothes back on. "Seems only natural that closeness would happen under the circumstances," she said primly. "We went through a lot together, to be honest. Not just here, but after Alex died, before the Revinir controlled his mind. We're . . . I'd call us strong friends."

Thisbe squelched a grin. "Ah. Strong friends. A very normal thing to say."

"Shut it," Fifer warned.

"It's just that you seem to have gotten your strength back and then some," Thisbe teased. "Shall we jog on over? Do you need to fix your hair first?"

"I don't fix my hair for anyone but me," Fifer retorted. She started toward the palace but slowed, her breath labored. "Wow, I'm spent," she admitted.

Thisbe took her arm to help support her. "I can imagine," she said, sounding suspiciously too concerned.

Fifer eyed her. "Do not."

"A boy like Dev can really wear out a girl."

"I *said*—" Fifer barked. "Honestly, Thiz! I've never teased you one single time about Rohan."

"That's because you're one hundred percent pure goodness. But I'm super evil."

"Besides," Fifer continued, ignoring her. "I don't *like* him." She stopped abruptly as Seth emerged from the base of the center tower. "I thought you might need help up the stairs," he said, looking at Fifer. "I can carry you on my back. Or . . . whatever." His pale skin flushed crimson.

"Thank you," said Fifer. "I'd appreciate that. I'm feeling a little light-headed, actually."

Thisbe snorted. Fifer shot her a dagger look. Seth frowned, confused, but not sure if he wanted to know what was going on.

"Climb on." He turned and bent down while Thisbe helped hoist Fifer onto his back. Thisbe and Seth, with Fifer hanging on, moved to the stairs and started up them.

LISA McMANN

"I didn't expect you to be soaking wet," Seth remarked halfway up. "You might have mentioned that."

"Sorry." Fifer kept her eye on Thisbe, but her sister seemed to have dropped the line of teasing for now, which was a relief, since none of it was true. Fifer didn't have feelings like that for anyone. Ever. She thought of herself as a person who didn't need *that* kind of love. It seemed unnecessary. Just a few good friends—not too gushy or huggy, but people she could have deep conversations with and really count on—would do perfectly fine, as far as Fifer was concerned. Thisbe and Seth were at the top of her list, of course. But now Dev was one of them too.

As she hung on to Seth's neck with her hair dripping steadily onto the top of his head, she realized she'd gone through a lot of tough stuff with him, too. Her feelings for Seth were brotherly, as they'd always been. But Dev. . . She let out a sigh. Something was different about him. Anything more than friendly relationships seemed too complicated to be bothered with. Especially when she had to get well so she'd be in top form to go after the Revinir again. If there was anything Fifer was longing for right now, it was to get out of Ashguard's palace, where she'd been holed up for months. And at this point, she didn't care if any boys came with her. It might be easier without them.

Once upstairs, Fifer forgot Thisbe's teasing, and she remembered to thank Seth profusely this time. When Seth seemed sufficiently appreciated, she went over to Dev. His eyes were closed. "How is he?"

"He's sleeping again," said Florence, "but he managed to eat some toast and take in some water." She hesitated. "We moved him around a bit—bent his legs and arms and rolled him to his side, and he seemed to handle it without too much pain. I think he's knitting back together properly."

"I'm so glad for Henry's medicine. Without it, we'd be much worse off." Fifer sank to her sofa and lay her head nearest the fireplace to help dry her hair and warm her up. As she lay there, shivering, facing Dev at arm's reach, she noticed some of the gray in his cheeks had been replaced by a dash of ruddiness. Something inside her stirred. A tiny pod of sadness—or something—threatening to crack open, but she didn't know what was causing it. She reached out toward Dev's hand and

LISA McMANN

placed hers on his sofa near it. She wanted to take his hand to let him know she was there, but she also knew how much she'd hate it if someone did that to her without her permission. So she left hers a few inches away, then closed her eyes and fell asleep, dreaming of the pain she'd felt and the struggle to communicate when she'd been unconscious. One word returned to her and pounded in her head like waves against the sand. *Water. Water. Water.*

Hours later, Fifer's eyes flew open. She sat up, sore and disoriented in the dusk, and looked around. Florence, Maiven, Aaron, Rohan, Sky, and Thisbe were discussing attack plans, saying things like "What about the statues?" and "Two main fighting areas" and "The cave could work." Her sister was about as far away from Aaron as she could get, but at least they were both in the same conversation. Hopefully, soon they'd patch things up after their misunderstanding. But she needed them both now. "Thisbe. Aaron. Can you come here please?"

"What is it?" asked Thisbe. She and Aaron hurried over.

Fifer scrunched up her face as she tried to remember what had been real in her injured state and what had been a dream.

"Thiz, did you ever get a mind message from me after I was injured?"

"No, I don't think— Wait." Thisbe frowned. "I thought I heard you say the word 'water' a few times. But that's all I can remember. I assumed you were just trying to communicate with Florence to give you a drink but you couldn't speak it, so it went to me instead."

"No," said Fifer, eyes widening. "I meant it for you! When I was unconscious, I figured out the key to everything."

"Everything . . . what?" asked Aaron.

"Everything we need in order to take down the Revinir. I've only just remembered it now."

Thisbe and Aaron looked on, confused. "And . . . what's the key again?" Thisbe asked.

"It's water," said Fifer. "Don't you see? That's her biggest, darkest fear. And I'm not sure how we're going to do it yet, but I can feel it—it's the secret to beating her. So everyone needs to be thinking along those lines. Water is the key to overthrowing the Revinir."

Water

re you feeling all right?" Aaron asked Fifer, leaning down to check her forehead for fever. Florence, Sky, and Maiven had overheard what Fifer had just said and joined them. In the low light, nobody noticed Dev's eyes flutter open. His gaze darted from one person to the next as if trying to figure out where he was and how all these people had gotten here.

Fifer moved Aaron's hand away. "I'm fine. Hear me out." She struggled to sit up. Her body was still plenty sore, but she had a lot of explaining to do.

"Water?" said Thisbe. "I don't get it." She searched her

mind to connect water to the Revinir in a way that could cause the monster's demise. But nothing made sense.

"Water was a significant factor in all of Emma's major life events," Fifer explained.

From the stairs, Simber grunted. "Emma," he said, but the rest ignored him and urged Fifer to continue.

"Water was so major that she wrote about it in her journals," Fifer said, "and we witnessed some of those moments too. When she was a little girl, she didn't want to go into the stream with Justine and Mr. Today to learn magic. She stayed onshore. But when they did magic alongside the stream, all was fine." Fifer paused for a breath before continuing. "When Marcus and Justine left Warbler, Emma was devastated, but she didn't try to follow their boat. She built ships but never used them, and she refused to allow the people of Warbler to learn how to swim or to take the ships out on the water."

"True," said Sky. "We were deathly afraid to go near the water because of her."

"Which made your escape with Crow on a raft all the more admirable," Aaron said.

"Exactly." Fifer's eyes shone. "When Eagala sent Warbler's

children to fight against Artimé, she didn't lead the ship—she stayed home and made her people do the dirty work for her. Do you see?"

"And," Aaron said thoughtfully, "when she did finally show up at the final battle, she didn't cross the water to come ashore. She hid in the ships, only moving when she absolutely had no other choice. After our ghost ship set off on its own accord with her on board, heading to the Island of Fire, she didn't even try to jump off to save herself. She rode the ship right down."

Thisbe's eyes narrowed. "Oh my. Fifer. You really do have something here. She's afraid of water."

"Yes," said Fifer. "Deathly afraid."

"That explains why she won't even catch her own fish," Dev croaked, to everyone's surprise.

They all turned, thrilled to see him awake, yet focused on the breakthrough. "Exactly!" Fifer exclaimed. Then she whispered, "You're awake!" She gazed at Dev, her heart full of joy at the sight of his face looking a little more of a healthy brown than sickly gray. "That definitely explains why she hung back from the river where you were hiding and made the red dragon catch fish for her. The Revinir hates being near the stuff," she continued, barely skipping a beat, and turned back to Thisbe. "That's what I was trying to tell you in my feverish unconsciousness."

The head mage paused for thought, then lifted her forefinger in the air. "And," she said importantly, "I almost forgot: After she grabbed Thisbe and me near the jungle, Thisbe wriggled loose and fell into the sea. The Revinir had to fly down to the sea to pull Thisbe out, and she made a strange noise, as if she were absolutely terrified. I remember thinking it was so odd—she barely got a claw wet, but she still freaked out."

"This is really making sense to me," Sky murmured.

"You kept saying the word 'water' when you were unconscious," Florence said, "but you didn't want to drink any. Is this what was going through your mind?"

"The thoughts never stopped—they just churned in my head. I kept trying to wake up to tell you, but I couldn't." Fifer tapped her chin thoughtfully. "Team, we are onto something big here. But we're running out of time, and we need to prepare for when the others get here. Let's request a status update from everyone, then figure out our plan once and for all. We

LISA McMANN

have to get it right this time. If we don't, I believe we'll be out of chances."

"What can I do to help?" asked Dev, though he was the last person anyone expected to lift a finger around there.

Fifer turned to him. "Honestly, it's just so good you're awake," she said, and everyone else chimed in with their sentiments over it. Having Dev back with them only made them all stronger, and they needed some good news for a change. "Just get better," Fifer said. "You and I both need to do some serious healing. Fast. Because this thing isn't going down without us."

The Drop-Off

When Carina's army of magical and traditional fighters approached the great, misty gorge that marked the border between the world of the seven islands and the land of the dragons, they bade Spike Furious good-bye. The whale stopped following and circled around in the waves below. She had agreed to stay there, at the west end of the sea, in case anyone needed to be flown across the gorge to escape or be taken home. It would be a lonely time for Spike, but she would do anything to help in the fight against the one who'd killed her creator, even if it wouldn't bring the Alex back—because it might save someone

LISA McMANN

else from that fate. Now that Issie and her baby were reunited, perhaps they and the squid would come to check on her and help pass the time.

Carina's ghost dragon dropped to the back of the group and hovered over the gorge, hidden from view of the castle by the mist that rose up from the pounding waterfall. Talon, beside Carina, stood on the dragon's back with limbs outstretched, and Matilda and Kitten stood next to him. Carina and a few others hurriedly painted the three of them with invisibility paintbrushes. It only took one dab to cover Kitten completely.

"This spell will give you enough time to get to the top of the castle," Carina told Talon as they hurriedly finished painting him. She gave him a sack of paintbrush components. "Once you get there, you're going to have to hide in a turret, paint yourself again, and have Matilda paint the parts you can't reach. Then I want you to fly at top speed to meet up with us." She pointed out the direction they were going to travel, which would allow them to avoid being seen by anybody. Going this route would take them a little longer to reach Florence and Fifer and Thisbe and the rest, but it could contribute to a surprise element if the Revinir didn't know this group had arrived.

Fox gave Kitten a special air-kiss good-bye—special because he couldn't really see where she was, so he sort of kissed all around in a circle and hoped one landed on her. Then Talon flew off with Matilda and Kitten through the mist, all of them invisible.

As Carina and her ghost dragon went to catch up to the rest of their party, Talon and his cohorts soared quickly over the gorge and made straight for the castle, arriving at the top of a turret before anyone could see them reappearing. There they crouched to hide and be repainted. Once they were invisible again, Talon flew the two down to a spot where they could gain access to the interior of the castle.

Kitten had been inside the castle multiple times before, so Talon put her in charge. "Stay close to Matilda until she finds her bearings," Talon instructed her. He turned to Matilda. "Please give us a status update whenever you feel safe to do so."

"You can count on me," Matilda signed.

"Mewmewmew," said Kitten, with authority. She signed something to Matilda with her teeny-weenie paws, and the gargoyle nodded.

LISA McMANN

Talon was taken aback. "When did you learn to sign?" he asked the kitten.

"Mewmewmew," she said proudly.

Talon smiled politely and nodded, though her mews told him nothing.

Matilda took one more paintbrush and applied an extra layer on Talon so he would have the maximum length of invisibility.

"Thank you. Good luck to you both, and take care." Talon left a few of the paintbrushes with Matilda in case they'd need them and darted away, leaving the two to do their job. As he flew, he calculated where he thought the army might be by now and zipped toward them as fast as he could go. His invisibility would only last about fifteen minutes, so he had to get as far as he could away from the civilized areas of the land of the dragons. He flew upward as well, so that he'd only be a dot in the sky once the spell wore off. With dragons circling all around Grimere, he wanted to be far above them so they wouldn't notice.

By the time Talon reached the rest of the party from the seven islands, Matilda had already contacted Charlie via their telepathy, letting him know that they were safely inside the castle. Charlie signed to Carina, and when he finished, Carina communicated the rest of the report to the others.

"All is well," she reported. "Matilda and Kitten are making their way down to the floor of the castle where most of the hustle and bustle seems to be happening."

"How are they not being seen?" asked Fox anxiously.

Charlie signed for a moment, then Carina interpreted.

"Whenever they get close to soldiers or servants along the way," Carina said, "Matilda poses as a statue until the coast is clear again. So it's slow going, but it helps that most of the people in the castle are under mind control. They're not looking sharply at things that might be considered unusual."

"And is Kitten okay?"

"Yes," Carina assured him. "When Kitten isn't scouting out their path ahead, she can easily hide behind Matilda's feet or hop inside her fist."

Fox seemed comforted by the news, and soon they were once again focusing on the path in front of them.

Skirting outside the edge of the inhabited parts of the land of the dragons, the entourage spotted a small village. They might not have realized it, but it was the place where Thisbe and Fifer had first seen Dev and Princess Shanti at the marketplace. They'd been thirsty and starving, and the twins had been captured and held in the prison cave while Seth stayed behind with Hux on the mountain.

The black-eyed people looked down at the land with the same awe as the residents of Artimé. Most of them had never been to this part of their world, and none had ever seen it from above. Asha pointed out various landmarks that she remembered studying about before she'd been auctioned to the Revinir. She spoke about how things must have changed in the years since Maiven had been the ruler—and not for the better.

"We have a lot of work ahead of us to take our land back," Asha said to the others. "And then we'll have even more work returning it to its former glory." She looked at the small group of former slaves and their friends who stood with them. "Are you ready to face it all? Are you ready to fight for what is ours?"

"I'm ready," said Prindi.

"Yes, we're all ready," added the others.

"We're ready to assist you," said Clementi, and Ibrahim nodded.

The black-eyed children wore the expressions of older, wiser fighters. After all they'd been through, it was no surprise. They had nothing to lose and everything to gain. They'd fight to the death for their land and their freedom. There was nothing else to do.

Preparing for Battle

The Revinir stepped outside the castle entryway and bellowed out a series of roars—angry, mournful, spite-filled roars. Her new battle cry. With the forest still smoldering in spots, the dragon-woman continued walking and came to a stop on the center of the drawbridge, watching with a dark expression as dragons came from far and wide—including the ones still trying to put the fire out—to assemble at her beck and call. It all felt a bit hollow this time.

One small gargoyle and one very tiny kitten slipped over to the corner of the entryway and peered around to see what was happening. Hundreds of mind-controlled soldiers gathered outside with the dragons, making the statues feel smaller than ever. The soldiers stood in formation, waiting for instructions as always. Unable to make any decisions on their own. When everyone had arrived, the Revinir addressed them.

"We have a battle close at hand," she said in greeting. "We'll be implementing some new measures to assess the movements of our enemies. And when the time is right, we will strike. The next few days are crucial as I prepare my plan."

There was no indication that anyone, soldier or dragon, had an opinion on this.

The Revinir faltered, feeling a gnawing emptiness inside. But she pressed on. "Ten soldiers will line the edge of our land, facing east, watching for the people from the seven islands to advance across the gorge. Half of the remaining soldiers will go out to the remote villages surrounding Grimere to enlist all of the people of this land to join in the fight against Thisbe Stowe and her people. The rest must go into Grimere to do the same. This is not optional! Everyone must fight or die!"

The way the dragons and soldiers looked at the Revinir with their empty eyes left her disturbed. Without Thisbe at her side, the Revinir had lost confidence. But she knew she had to make up for it, so she pressed on and ordered her captains to split up the group in the way she'd just laid out.

"Dragons!" she said next, trying to sound authoritative and enthusiastic. But all she could think about was that it didn't have to be this way. If only Thisbe hadn't turned on her, they could be celebrating together right now. Was it possible that she'd missed . . . on purpose?

Before the Revinir could proceed, a new dragon coming from afar landed and approached the drawbridge. It reported something quietly to the Revinir, but it was hard for her to hear over the movement and activity of the soldiers.

"What's that?" she demanded. "What did you say?"

"The four red dragons at the palace have been slain," the dragon said again in a monotone, louder this time. The Revinir paused in her instructions as the words slammed into her.

"Are you sure?" she asked. "All *four*?" It felt like her breath had been stolen from her.

The dragon nodded and stood at attention, awaiting its next assignment.

The Revinir reeled. How had this happened? Had Fifer

done it? Alone? How could that be? There was no way Thisbe could have made it to the palace and killed four dragons in this amount of time. But the fact that anyone could kill a dragon at all caused a chill to pass through her. She narrowed her eyes suspiciously. "How many of Thisbe's people are there? Surely it must have taken an army. Surely . . ." She faltered. "Surely it wasn't Fifer alone."

"I saw no humans at all," said the dragon. "Nor did I witness the attack. I only saw several ghost dragons and Drock the dark purple moving the red dragons' bodies to the foothills for a proper burial."

In the castle entryway, Matilda and Kitten exchanged a glance as the Revinir seethed. Then the dragon-woman sent the messenger dragon away. Her bruised feelings for Thisbe and the nostalgia for the way things could have been swiftly changed to fury. Thisbe had caused all of this . . . or her people from the seven islands had. Which was why the Revinir had secretly still been plotting to go after them once she had gained full control of the land of the dragons.

Even if Thisbe hadn't turned on her, the Revinir would have gone after the girl's people, though she'd told Thisbe

LISA McMANN

otherwise to convince her to join this mission. The truth was that the attack on Artimé and the seven islands would only have been delayed until after the Revinir had taken control of this kingdom. The plan had always been to go back on her word and throw Thisbe in the dungeon so she couldn't interfere . . . though it had been getting harder and harder to picture doing that, especially since she had come to enjoy the girl's company. Originally Thisbe had only been a necessary piece of this transaction for a short time. She'd been disposable. But the Revinir had never actually planned out the disposing part. The dragon-woman closed her eyes and sighed.

Maybe it was better that they'd broken off their budding friendship in this way. It would save a step in her process. Because Thisbe was not now, nor would she ever again be, trusted. Fifer or Thisbe or some combination of her people had killed four of the Revinir's prized red dragons.

The anger that welled up now was exactly the medicine needed to jump-start the Revinir's quest for revenge. She would fight like she'd never fought before. On land. The way fights were supposed to happen. And nothing would stand in her way. She had all the dragons and all the people of this

LISA McMANN

land. Some might die doing her bidding, but they'd kill off the humans and creatures of the seven islands in the process, and that was all that really mattered. When it was over, the Revinir wouldn't care one bit.

With that reset to her line of thinking, she started feeling better, and soon she had given the dragons their orders—to stake out all the ends of the land and figure out just how many of Thisbe's people were in this world, sneaking around. It couldn't be many . . . but still. Four dragons down. It made her uneasy.

Before she dismissed the dragons, she called a group forward. "Pan, the ruler of the sea!" she shouted. "Arabis the orange! Ivis the green! Hux the ice blue! And Yarbeck the purple and gold!"

The five assembled before her.

"You five," she said, "are going to be my new team stationed at Ashguard's palace. Your instructions are to kill anyone from the seven islands who crosses the property's boundaries, whether they're coming in or going out." The dragon-woman's brow furrowed. Then she added, "Just keep at least one black-eyed person alive, please. I'll need them to get this job done right, once and for all."

The mind-controlled group agreed.

Drock, toward the back of the crowd, felt his throat tighten. The Revinir hadn't called his name in that group with his mother and siblings. But he knew it wasn't because she'd forgotten him—indeed, she'd stared hard at the dark purple dragon as she dismissed the others to their duties. Drock felt the weight of her stare. He kept up his charade of being mind-controlled and slowly turned away with the rest of the dragons. But fear grew in the pit of his stomach, and a chill rippled down his spine. The Revinir was pitting the dragons from the seven islands against the people from the seven islands. She was telling them to attack their friends, knowing that the people of Artimé were too good to fight against the dragons they loved.

But she hadn't included Drock. Which could only mean one thing.

She knew.

Family vs. Family

From the side of the castle entry archway, standing very still, Matilda and Kitten watched what the Revinir was doing, but they couldn't hear everything she was saying, especially when she pulled the five familiar dragons aside. Kitten tried to sneak closer to hear, but there were soldiers with big boots everywhere, and Kitten wasn't sure how many lives she had left, so she had to abandon that plan.

When the Revinir turned, apparently finished with doling out duties, Kitten skittered back behind Matilda's feet. The dragon-woman came thundering past them, harrumphing and coughing and clawing at the metal star that stubbornly refused to be expelled from her throat.

The two remained stationary until all soldiers and dragons were out of sight. Then they followed the noise. All the while, Matilda was transmitting bits of information to her dearest companion, Charlie, who was still with Carina on a ghost dragon as they rounded the vast land. But because she hadn't heard everything, Matilda didn't fully grasp the gravity of what the Revinir had just done.

"That seems suspect," Carina said after she interpreted what Charlie had to say regarding Pan and her young. "They'll be heading to the same place we are, but they won't recognize us or be friendly. I don't trust the Revinir—she's not doing this to be nice. We should avoid confrontation and just go straight to the village like Florence told us to do." She turned and called to her ghost dragon. "Did you hear that? We're still planning to go to the village beyond Ashguard's palace."

"Heard," called out the dragon, though he would soon forget. Carina was used to that by now.

Charlie signed some more. Carina stared, then sighed. "Matilda thinks we ought to be very cautious and not enter

Ashguard's property at all—not even cross it to get to the village. There will be dragons on the lookout for us. We should hide inside the houses so passing dragons don't detect us."

"That sounds like the best way," said Lani from one dragon over. "We want to keep our element of surprise at all costs. It could mean the difference between success and failure."

Carina sent a message to Florence to alert her to what was happening.

Around nightfall, Carina and the rest of her army descended on the vacant village and filled the homes as quietly as possible, eager to be on solid ground for the night. They would learn more tomorrow once everyone had rested up. Carina transported Ol' Tater to stand under the cover of trees, and Sean draped a tarp over him. Then she sent the ghost dragons to roam as they pleased, which is what they would have done anyway. Finally she let Florence know they had arrived without incident. Exhausted, she and Sean and their kids found a vacant house and settled in.

While they slept, the skies around the formerly vacant village became filled with the Revinir's mind-controlled dragons.

» » « «

Inside Ashguard's palace, Florence spread out on the floor by the east window and remained stationed there throughout the night, watching for the dragons they all knew and loved to show up. She wasn't quite sure what would happen, but she, like Carina and Matilda, didn't trust the Revinir to do anything kind. This was most certainly a trick of some sort.

Fifer woke up in the middle of the night, ready for a dose of pain medicine, and joined Florence by the window. "Have they arrived?" Fifer asked, her voice crackly with sleep.

"Not yet. I'm hoping . . ."

Fifer looked at Florence with a hint of pity. "Hoping what?"

"Never mind."

"Hoping they'll somehow recognize us?"

Florence was quiet. "Yes, I suppose so."

"It's normal to feel like that. You haven't seen them under her mind control. But let me assure you that they will not know us, and in fact, they will very likely attack us. It's hard to think about, but it's true."

"I'm sure you're right," said Florence, though she seemed unconvinced. "After all we've been through, it is hard to think that. I want them to see us and . . . remember. Somehow."

"If it were that easy, we might not be in such a terrible predicament right now," said Fifer. "It's been rough here. And . . . Thisbe has had a harder time than anyone. Don't you agree?"

Florence stared out the window, ruminating over it. "I don't know," she said gruffly. Like she didn't want to admit it. "She seems to be doing pretty well."

Fifer glanced sidelong at the warrior trainer. "She risked absolutely everything for us. She knew everyone would hate her for it. She knew she might never get your trust back. And she did it anyway. For all of us."

Florence dropped her gaze.

After a while, Fifer went back to bed.

By dawn, when Fifer and Thisbe rose, the five familiar dragons had arrived. They stationed themselves around the property in a similar way to how the red dragons had been. Arabis and Hux at the front corners, Yarbeck and Ivis at the back, and Pan, spreading across the side boundary between the palace and the orchard. It was startling to see them. Even more startling were the additional dragons that circled the skies all around them and above the orchard and village.

LISA McMANN

The twins watched out the window. "Pan's eyes are dull," Thisbe said. "They're definitely still under the Revinir's mind control."

"It's hard to see them like this," said Sky.

"Is Drock here too?" Fifer asked. "I would expect she'd send him as well. Maybe he's on the other side of the palace. If he is, perhaps we can find out more about what's happening and when the Revinir is planning to strike. It can't be long now. She's not going to forgive Thisbe or let any of this go."

"Drock isn't here," said Florence. "Simber checked from all the windows in the base of the turret before you got up."

Thisbe frowned. She and Florence had talked things through the other day, but the air was still uncomfortable between them, and even worse between her and Aaron. Being at odds with those two kept them all from moving past the distrust that still hovered all around, and without trust, things weren't going to go smoothly. Thisbe knew that she'd been the one to create the issue and bring it into their lives by doing what she'd done. But she'd fully proven she was only trying to do what was best for the people of the seven islands.

Still, it was harder than she'd imagined to sew things back

LISA McMANN

together. Feelings were complicated, and the whole experiment had taken a shocking turn when Ishibashi had died, which changed things in a much bigger way than expected—Thisbe realized that. She couldn't force everyone to just get over it, especially when Thisbe was struggling so much herself.

Being in this library with Aaron and Florence had been hard. And it was probably going to get worse before it got better now that they had mind-controlled dragons guarding them again. What were their orders? They'd find out soon enough. Meanwhile, Thisbe was stuck in close quarters with two people who were having trouble forgiving her.

But people's lives were at stake—many people's lives. And many dragons' lives too. Thisbe couldn't let the bad feelings between them get in the way of the serious situation they were facing. They had to work together to come up with a foolproof way to save everybody who was left.

Maiven Taveer came up the stairs past Simber and caught Thisbe's eye. She smiled. At least Thisbe's grandmother's anger and distrust had faded. Thisbe flashed her a grateful smile in return.

She moved to the south window to study Pan. "I don't like this at all," she said. "We have no idea what orders the Revinir

LISA McMANN

has given them. They could attack us, even be programmed to kill anyone who just walks out of the palace."

"Kill us?" asked Dev from his sleeping couch. His voice had the roughness of morning in it, and he slowly eased up to a sitting position and reached for his canteen. His hands were steady this morning after a good sleep. "That's a far step beyond what the red dragons were told to do."

"I don't know that's the case," Thisbe explained. "But the Revinir is vengeful and she's angry. After what I did to her, I wouldn't be surprised if she commanded all dragons to kill me. If not everyone."

"Oh, Thisbe," said Fifer. "You've got to take tremendous care. All of us do. And one of us ought to go outside just to see what they do." She turned sharply. "Definitely not Dev, though," she said.

He held his hands up in surrender. "Don't worry. I've had enough of dragons for now."

"I'll go," Florence said. "I'm the least vulnerable."

"Especially if you're standing on the ground already," said Fifer, thinking of the warrior's fall from Astrid's back. "Thank you, Florence. I agree. You're our best option."

"I won't fight them, though," Florence said. "I can't. I don't care if they don't recognize us right now. They are our friends. No matter what they try, I will not kill them."

"Fair enough, and we're all feeling the same way, I imagine," said Fifer.

Florence hesitated, then murmured, "Maybe I can get them to see that it's me."

Thisbe turned sharply toward Florence. "I'm telling you—"

"I told her too," Fifer said, throwing her hands in the air.

"I know," Florence said sharply. Then she checked herself and softened her voice. "I know you're right about it. Both of you. Wishful thinking, I guess."

"Trust me," Dev piped up. "They will not know you. I fed them every day for years, and they don't know me, either. It's hard to understand until you get used to it."

Thisbe caught Dev's eye and nodded. He'd jumped right into having her back, just like before. He'd really turned out to be worth the trouble, and she nodded to show him she appreciated him.

Dev nodded back, then tested his muscles and slowly stood up to have a look.

LISA McMANN

By now Aaron had woken up too. He joined Florence at the east window, where he could see Hux and Arabis. "It makes me sick to see them like this," he said. He glanced at Thisbe, and his expression darkened. The two still hadn't really had it out. He knew he was overreacting—being unreasonably harsh on her, now that she'd explained everything. But Ishibashi's death stood between them like a roadblock in their relationship. He was trying to forgive her for making such a grave mistake that led to Ishibashi's death, but it wasn't easy. And he was certain there was still something she wasn't owning up to, which made him so scared—because that's what he'd done himself when he was her age. He *knew* back then that he was keeping himself from the truth, but he continued doing bad things anyway. So what was Thisbe hiding?

Thisbe looked coolly at Aaron. She'd apologized. And while she was sick with sorrow over it, she refused to harbor the blame that Aaron seemed to want to assign to her. She'd had no idea that Ishibashi would suffer for her actions at the time. Why hadn't Aaron protected the 110-year-old man instead of the other way around?

Thisbe refused to hurt her brother further by asking that,

but she also wasn't about to let it all go. She would do everything in her power to defeat this enemy, and then after it was all over, she'd work on making amends with whoever was still standing.

Oof. That was a hard thought, and it softened Thisbe slightly. They'd lost a lot of people over the years, and she didn't want to lose any more. It was almost enough to make her go groveling to Aaron and Florence and Simber and beg them to forgive her, just so all of this uneasiness would go away.

But every time she began to think that, she stopped herself. Because she'd done more than anyone to try to take down the Revinir. If only she hadn't messed it up.

Friend vs. Friend

Florence descended the stairs, leaving her quiver of arrows and bow behind. She stepped out of the tower onto the pavers of the courtyard. Then she slowly walked out to the side yard toward Arabis, trying not to make the ground shake.

All five dragons detected her immediately and turned to face her. Florence kept her arms at her sides, but called out, "Pan, it's me. Florence. From Artimé. Remember?"

Smoke rose from Pan's jowls and nostrils. She crouched as if ready to leap. Her ropelike tail swished through the long grass behind her.

Florence stopped for a moment to check the location of each dragon but was unable to see the two in the corners behind her who were now hidden from view by the palace. She kept going, talking to Pan again. "Pan, it's Florence from Artimé. We're friends. Remember? We helped you when your babies needed wings—both times."

Pan hissed, and smoke curled up from her nostrils. Arabis and Yarbeck advanced from their corners. Florence still couldn't see the other two. She stopped again. But the dragons kept advancing.

"Pan, please—don't you know me? Think hard! I know you're under the Revinir's mind control, but we want you back on our side. We're desperate for your help."

"She needs to stop saying things like that," Thisbe muttered from the library window. "They'll tell the Revinir everything. Besides, Pan isn't going to recognize her! I wish she'd believe us."

"She will soon enough," said Dev, and Fifer nodded.

The black water dragon, ruler of the sea, let out a horrible roar. As Arabis and Yarbeck took flight, Florence turned and started running back to the palace. But it was too late. Pan pounced on Florence. She knocked the huge statue flat and roared again, sending fire enveloping the warrior's head.

Florence rolled and squirmed out from under the dragon as Arabis and Yarbeck descended, claws outstretched. Pan whirled around and used her tail as a whip. She lassoed Florence around the legs and tugged, lifting the heavy statue up off the ground like she weighed nothing. Arabis and Yarbeck bit down on her.

Florence fought to free herself and landed hard on the ground, shaking the palace. Luckily, she didn't break this time. She got up and stumbled for the center tower, but Arabis grabbed her and knocked her flat again. Hux and Ivis reached them and joined in the fight, and no matter what Florence said or did, they didn't stop attacking her.

Finally, Florence collapsed facedown on the ground as the dragons bit and clawed and breathed fire on her until they decided she was dead. Pan lifted her face to the sky and roared in success. Flames shot up. Then the dragons took one final sniff at the slain warrior and retreated to their posts.

Everyone in the library crowded around the windows and watched the whole thing, some in various stages of incredulity. Their friendly dragons had attacked Florence—even Pan, who knew her so well. "Is Florence okay?" Dev asked, worried. "She's not moving."

"I'm . . . not sure," said Fifer, horrified. She'd known this could happen, but seeing it had been awful just the same.

"I think she's fine," said Aaron, peering over everyone. "She's faking dead."

"I mean, she's all in one piece," Thisbe mused. "She said she'd be fine."

"She's holding very still," Sky said.

"Like . . . a statue," said Thisbe.

Maiven, despite her concern over Florence, gave Thisbe the tiniest hint of a smile.

"This is sickening," said Seth. It was hard for those who loved Florence to see her face-planted and unmoving. She was the toughest Artiméan they had. "How could they do that to her?"

"They don't realize anything they're doing," said Rohan. "Isn't that right, Dev?"

Dev looked startled to be singled out, then realized Rohan was talking about when he'd been under the Revinir's mind

LISA McMANN

control. "I certainly don't remember a thing that happened while I was being controlled."

"I hope she moves soon so we know if she's okay," said Maiven. "But I'd hate for her to be attacked again if she does."

They heard Simber coming up the stairs. He poked his head up in the library, halted by the size of his wings. "Has she moved?" he growled.

"Not yet," said Rohan.

"I'm going out therrre." Simber was tired of doing nothing. He was fierce and able, and his abilities weren't being used.

"Simber," said Fifer, turning. "No. Please don't. She'll be fine, and you'll just put yourself in danger of the flames. Florence insisted we all stay put."

"It would be horrible to lose you, Sim," Aaron said. "I don't have an entire day to bring you back to life if you get melted into sand again—and I wouldn't be able to get to you, anyway."

The cheetah reluctantly accepted that logic. "If she doesn't move in five minutes," he warned, "I'm going to check on herrr."

"That's fine," said Fifer, turning back to the window. "All the dragons have gone back to their stations." She paused, then

LISA McMANN

sighed. "I know it's so hard to comprehend how they don't recognize us at all, or have any memory of us. It's actually painful after everything Thisbe and Seth and I did for them."

"It was so hard to see Dev like that too," Thisbe said quietly. "It feels strange when someone you know so well has no idea who you are. It . . . hurts. Badly."

Rohan glanced at Thisbe and gave her a warm smile. "I'm glad we've made it past those days. You were so smart to figure out the antidote."

They all watched Florence for another moment. "She moved!" Maiven said.

"Are you sure?" asked Aaron. "I didn't see anything."

"I think so. Yes! Look—she's wiggling her fingers. She's about to get up."

Sure enough, the warrior trainer made the slightest movements to position herself in such a way that would allow her to spring upward.

"She's moving!" Aaron called to Simber.

"I can hearrr you, like always," Simber reminded him. Fifer was the only head mage that had truly grasped that Simber's hearing was impeccable. It was nice not having to explain it

LISA McMANN

to her constantly. He backed down to the fifth-floor landing, which was wide enough to allow him to turn around.

"She's up!" cried Fifer.

"And running!" said Seth.

"Oh no!" said Maiven, pointing. "Look!"

"The dragons are coming in again!" Sky shouted, and then she gasped. "Ugh, no!"

"Florence made it to the pavers!" Dev reported, and they all rushed to the other windows and some to the railing because they could no longer see her below them. Dev stayed at the window to give a play-by-play of the dragon movement. "Dragons still advancing!" he said. "Pan's coming in fast!" The tower began to shiver, and the people could hear loud footsteps entering the base of it. Simber growled one floor below them.

"The green one is right behind!" cried Dev. "Brace yourselves for impact!"

Florence's thudding footsteps continued, and then a crash knocked everyone back from the bannister, as well as several books off the shelves.

Simber roared.

When the shaking slowed, Thisbe got up. She darted unsteadily around Aaron to the stairs, then flew down them, hanging on to the railing in case it happened again. She slipped past Simber before anyone could do anything to stop her. As she went, she let the fire build in her throat until it had nowhere else to go but out. She let out a dragon roar.

Rohan's and Dev's scales vibrated in response. Dev felt the pressure in his aching chest, and he couldn't control it—this was a life-or-death situation, and his instincts took over. His roar merged with Thisbe's, big and loud and rattling the windows. Rohan began to feel the rumble in his own throat, and he joined in, more like a softer echo of the others, for he was made up of only a small amount of dragon. Still, every bit of it helped.

The shaking of the tower stopped. Fifer ran to Dev's window and scanned the grounds below. "Pan is retreating!" she reported. "Keep roaring!"

The three part-dragon humans continued, letting their instincts guide them, until all five full dragons had gone back to their corners. The standoff ended.

Dev slumped to the sofa, exhausted. Fifer went to the bannister and joined Seth and Aaron looking over it. Thisbe, Florence, and Simber trudged up to the library in silence as they all realized they had an enormous problem on their hands.

A Terrible Plan

They checked Florence over, finding scratches and teeth marks over her body, and they also discovered that she'd somehow lost the tip of her pinkie on her left hand. But nothing hurt, and she was fine.

Thisbe crossed her arms over her chest. "Are you okay?"

"It was hard to see our friends come at me like that," Florence said, pointedly not looking at Thisbe or Fifer. "I fear we're stuck here. In this tower, I mean. I doubt they'll allow us to go to the river to fish. I'm not sure how we're going to carry out our mission." Finally she turned to the twins. "You were right about the dragons."

Thisbe pinched her eyes shut and sighed. "Thanks," she muttered. She was glad Florence acknowledged that, but she was upset that this was happening, and the realization of what it meant was really starting to hit her. They couldn't go to the river. No fish, no apples . . . Could they even make it safely to the courtyard water pump? "This is my fault," she said quietly. "I'm so sorry, everyone. I'm sure the Revinir put these rules in place with our dragons to punish me. And now everyone will suffer."

"Perhaps we can still get water from the pump," Fifer said, trying not to panic. "If we're careful, maybe they won't notice." She'd been through a lot with dragons recently, and she'd already been stuck on this property for an endless amount of time. The thought of being held in this tower indefinitely without access to food or water was giving her heart palpitations.

"I'll get you some water," Florence said. "Don't worry. And we have a few days' worth of food from Artimé left, I think. So we're fine, right?"

"What about everyone else?" asked Sky. "I heard from my mother—they're all camped out in the village. No issues."

"They'll have food with them," said Florence.

"But they can't safely get it to us," Fifer pointed out.

"I'll let Carina know not to even attempt to come over here," said Aaron, pulling out a send component.

Thisbe's face was drawn. She turned and went to the east window and stared out it. Rohan followed her, and Seth frowned and went as well.

"It's not your fault," Rohan said to her.

"Well, but it is," said Thisbe matter-of-factly. "And I accept responsibility for it." She glanced side-eyed at Florence, but the warrior was deep in conversation with Maiven, Fifer, and Sky. "I have totally put everyone from the seven islands in grave danger. I wish I knew what would make this stop, but I'm not sure. I fear that even if I give myself up, the Revinir will just keep going after everyone anyway."

"You're not going to give yourself up," said Seth. "Sheesh, Thisbe. We're going to fight her. We have to."

"Under the current circumstances," Thisbe said wryly, "she won't even have to fight. These dragons will kill us, or we'll starve to death."

"We'll figure something out!" said Seth, more harshly than

LISA McMANN

he intended. But Thisbe's negativity was really bothering him. "What is wrong with you?" he demanded.

"What?"

"You're not acting like the Thisbe I've known all my life." Seth didn't normally confront either twin for fear of being accidentally smote, but the twins had grown out of that hazardous trait. And Seth was as eager as anyone to get this right.

Thisbe wasn't used to him challenging her either. Taken aback, she stared at him, her lips parted. "How do you want me to act, Seth?" she asked, and not in a nice way. Her eyes sparked, and one of the sparks sizzled on the windowsill and burned out.

"Like *you*." Seth took a small, cautious step backward but didn't retreat. "You know. Brave, smart, fearless." He paused, then went on. "Like you taught me to be."

Thisbe sucked in a breath. She studied Seth for a long moment. Then she turned to the window, trying to calm her anger. She didn't want to hurt anybody, least of all Seth. He was right, she knew. But how was she supposed to act brave and fearless, when her smarts were telling her that the Revinir was the most dangerous thing in all the worlds? The more knowledge and wisdom Thisbe gained in life, the less brave and fearless she felt. Those things seemed so naive now. And Thisbe had failed to kill the Revinir when she'd had the chance, which had put a severe damper on her bravery and fearlessness. But . . . she didn't want Seth to think that she'd lost anything.

She pressed her forehead against the windowpane. Her breath fogged up the glass. Arabis and Hux, with their dead expressions and the listless curves of their necks, remained in their corners to keep watch over this strange, broken-down palace that had belonged to someone who had disappeared years before. These dragons were forced to make sure nobody made it out of this place alive. What was Thisbe supposed to do about that? Bravely march out to the lawn to her death? Smartly stay up here and starve? Fearlessly try to scare these big, real dragons with her small roar, knowing that even though she'd gotten them to retreat after they'd tried to destroy the tower, they wouldn't go any farther than that? The Revinir's instructions were infinitely stronger than anything Thisbe could say to them. And then there was the added fact that these dragons, in a different situation, were their friends. There was no way any of the statues and people here would

183 « Dragon Fury

LISA McMANN

kill one of them. Placing them here had been a brilliant move by the Revinir—she had to know how it compromised them.

A rapid succession of bad ideas passed through Thisbe's mind: They could try to make a run for it, which totally wouldn't work for all the same reasons it wouldn't have worked when the red dragons had been guarding the property—it would take few steps or wing flaps for the dragons to catch up. They could try using magic carpet components high up in the sky, but that would also fail spectacularly for the same reasons, and besides, Florence wouldn't be able to fit on one or even several. Perhaps the ghost dragons could help, but it wouldn't stop the command the Revinir had given the mind-controlled dragons. Eventually they'd get past every barrier or temporary solution Thisbe could configure.

Her mind returned to the magic carpets. What if they used invisibility paintbrushes along with them? Then some of them could get away. It would be tricky, though. But Fifer would insist that no one should be left behind. Florence could try to walk out, but her thundering footsteps would be a dead give-away, and the dragons would only attack her again.

Thisbe sighed. She'd need more time to work through

everything. "It would be easier to just figure out how to break the mind control spell," she muttered. Which translated to: not easy at all.

"That would actually be ideal," Seth said. He'd gotten tired of standing and had sat down on the floor nearby.

Thisbe looked down. She'd forgotten Seth and Rohan were still there, waiting for her to be brave and fearless. "What would be?"

"Breaking the mind control spell on our dragons," Seth said. "Then we'd have their help fighting the Revinir. It would be a game changer."

Thisbe blinked. "Well, sure, but we don't know how to do that," she said. "No one does. I think the Revinir has to die for them to be freed."

Seth frowned and scratched his head. "But she didn't have to die for the black-eyed people to get their minds back."

"Right," Thisbe explained, "well, the ancestor broth only works on the black-eyed people. Because it uses the bones of our ancestors."

Rohan turned his head sharply. "Wait a minute . . . ," he said, thinking hard.

LISA McMANN

Thisbe looked at him. "I honestly don't think our ancestor broth will work on the dragons," she said firmly.

"No," said Rohan slowly. "Probably not. But, Thisbe, what about the dragon-bone broth? Because that is made from the *ancestors* of the *dragons*."

A Dangerous Idea

Thisbe stared hard at Rohan. She narrowed her eyes, thinking things through. "So you think that giving the dragons some dragon-bone broth might actually work the same way our ancestor broth works on us? That it might break their mind control?"

"That's exactly what I'm saying," said Rohan. "The ancestor broth works for us. Why wouldn't the dragons' ancestor broth work for them?"

"It seems logical," said Seth as Fifer joined them.

"What's going on?" Fifer asked.

Seth filled her in.

LISA McMANN

Thisbe was quiet for a long moment. Then she sighed and turned back to the window. "Even if it would work, how are we supposed to get dragon bones to make enough broth to feed these dragons? They'd need gallons of it. A few vials isn't going to work on those beasts. Unless . . ."

"Wait," said Seth. "Could the ghost dragons retrieve the bones from the red dragons you just slayed?"

"No," said Rohan. "They aren't ancestor bones. I wouldn't want to waste time testing them. If we're going to try it, we need the ancient ones."

"From the catacombs?" asked Seth. He shuddered, remembering what had happened the time he'd gone down there. Alex had breathed his last.

"Yes," said Rohan. The young man studied Thisbe, who'd been extraordinarily quiet in the past few moments. Then he said, "I don't see how we can get away from here safely, though. Florence just proved that the dragons will attack ruthlessly."

Thisbe lifted her head. "I know how we can do it," she said.

"You do?" asked Rohan. "How?"

"But I don't want to do it that way."

"What way?" asked Seth.

"What are you saying?" asked Fifer.

"Okay, look. We're trapped here," Thisbe began. "But the rest of our team is in the village."

Aaron looked up and called over to them. "Carina says there are mind-controlled dragons circling above, looking for movement, so everyone is sheltering in place. She says she thinks they have not been detected."

"Thanks, Aaron," Fifer called back.

"Oh." Thisbe frowned, then continued. "All right. So as far as we know, the Revinir isn't aware that our entire world is over here. And it doesn't sound like there are dragons stationed over there—they are just circling and observing."

"Right," Aaron confirmed.

"Still dangerous," Fifer remarked, "especially if they've been given orders to attack."

"True," said Thisbe. "But . . . I can think of a handful of people who know exactly where to find the dragon bones."

Rohan smoothed his component vest thoughtfully. "You mean Asha and Prindi and the others."

Seth flushed at the mention of Prindi, but nobody noticed. Thankfully. He'd just started getting to know her when he'd

LISA McMANN

had to go on this mission. But he thought about her sometimes.

"Ugh," said Thisbe. "But yes."

"Why 'ugh'?" asked Seth, almost worried Thisbe had read his thoughts.

"Yeah," said Fifer. "Is that such a bad idea to ask them to go get bones? They can use invisibility paintbrushes and sneak out on a ghost dragon."

"I'm sure the catacombs are the last place any of them want to return to," Thisbe explained. "It won't be safe—there could be soldiers down there who wouldn't treat them kindly. And they could be spotted at any point along the way and followed or even captured or attacked."

Seth imagined what it would be like for the former slaves to return to the place they'd been imprisoned for so many years. "That does seem awful," he said gravely. "They've been through enough."

"They're our only hope," said Rohan. "We should at least ask them. I can't speak for them, but I'm desperate to help."

"I'm not sure they're our only hope," Thisbe muttered, "but they might be the best option." Fifer, Seth, and Rohan continued to debate the plan, while Thisbe fell silent again, deep in thought. After a while, Fifer called the rest of the team to order so she could explain the recent developments. While she laid things out for Maiven, Sky, Florence, and Aaron, Thisbe slipped down the stairs to Simber's side. "You heard the plan, right?"

Simber rolled his eyes and put his chin on his paws. "Obviously."

"And what do you think?"

"I think the black-eyed forrrmer slaves should trrry it. It's ourrr best bet."

Thisbe tapped her lips. "Do you want to know what I think?"

"That you should tell me why you think of the Rrrevinirrr as Emma?" Simber asked.

"I don't know what you're talking about," Thisbe said, lying to his face and not really even caring, because this was a big moment. "Do you want to know or not?"

"The suspense is killing me," said Simber dryly.

Thisbe rested her hand on the cheetah's forehead. "I can't let the others from the village go alone and face danger while I

LISA McMANN

sit here in relative safety. Besides, there's not enough of them to carry those huge bones and the cauldrons we'd need. So I think you and I are going to sneak out of here and lead this mission."

Simber gave Thisbe a side-eye. His ears twitched.

"Are you ready to go invisible and do something dangerous?" Thisbe asked. When he hesitated, she added, "There's a very good chance we could die."

The stone statue lifted his head. And then a small, snarly smile tugged the corners of his mouth.

Mission
Improbable

Thisbe wrote a message pitching the plan to Asha, Prindi, Reza, and the other black-eyed people, and soon the reply came. Despite the dragons circling overhead, they were all in and willing to risk it. They had plenty of invisibility paintbrushes and were already feeling pent up from being in hiding. And while they'd all been keeping busy making weapons as they waited for word from Matilda that the Revinir was on the move, there were plenty of others to do that job. So the details were arranged: That evening, Gorgrun the ghost dragon would transport them to the square and remain there—if he didn't forget—to bring them back.

LISA McMANN

"But where will they make the broth?" Fifer mused. "It needs to be inside the boundaries of these palace grounds to lure the dragons into drinking it. I don't think things would go well with anyone bringing cauldrons in from the village."

"I've already thought of that," Thisbe announced. "Simber and I are going as well. Please don't argue. I can't let the others go alone. There aren't enough of them to carry the bones and cauldrons we need. And they also need a seasoned spell caster in case the catacombs are still manned with soldiers."

"Great plan," said Rohan. "I'll join you."

"That's not safe!" said Fifer as she and Dev looked up, startled. "How—"

"Invisibility paintbrushes," Thisbe said before Fifer could get the question out.

"But—"

"We'll fly up through the roof hole and head out high above the dragons' heads," Thisbe explained. "They probably won't detect us, and even if they do smell us, they won't be able to find us easily."

"Did Simber—"

"He's excited to have something to do," said Thisbe. "And

LISA McMANN

he has excelled at being invisible in the past, if you remember. He quite likes it."

Simber harrumphed from the stairs.

Fifer closed her mouth. Then: "All right. I'm going too."

"And me," said Dev. "It's only right for all the young generation of future rulers to be part of this. We're making history. Maybe someone will write about us in a book someday. And I . . . I mean, whoever owns this palace . . . could put a copy here in this library."

"I'd like to go along too," said Maiven, "but it seems there are no seats left on Simber's back, so I will sit this one out."

"You need to stay safe, Grandmum," said Rohan, who still called her the affectionate nickname even though she wasn't really his grandmother. "You're our leader—you'll have other things to do soon enough."

Seth seemed about to speak, but then he closed his mouth. There wasn't enough room for him, either. But it was all right. This was the black-eyed people's mission—it meant something especially important to them. He didn't need to elbow his way into that.

Thisbe eyed Dev and Fifer. "Are you two sure you're feeling

195 « Dragon Fury

LISA McMANN

up to this? It'll be a lot of walking and carrying heavy things."

"I'm fine," said Fifer, who was probably telling the truth.

"Me too," said Dev, who was likely lying, but wasn't about to be written out of the history books.

"All right," said Fifer, taking out the send spell so she could reply to the others in the village. "Both teams will leave after dark and meet in Dragonsmarche if we don't see them along the way. We'll all bring invisibility paintbrushes for getting us out of dragon range as well as for our return trip. We'll also need other spells to handle the soldiers, if there are any of them left down there." She scribbled a few sentences, then looked up. "Anything else?"

As they stood without comment, a send spell came soaring in. It stopped at Florence. She opened it and read aloud:

Florence,

We've heard from Matilda. The Revinir's army and dragons are receiving orders, and she is getting restless to make a move. She's only waiting for the dragons that are guarding you to take at least one of you down, so that she can use that to bolster her troops as well as give the dragons fewer targets. *She doesn't seem to know our large group is here in the village. Yet.*

Are you sure you want to try this dragon-bone mission tonight?

Lani

Florence looked at Fifer for guidance. Fifer nodded. "We need our dragons back."

Florence pulled out the pencil.

Lani,

We're sure.

Florence

LISA McMANN

After Dark

Thisbe, Rohan, Fifer, and Dev stood on the stairs just above the fifth floor while Simber crouched below them on the landing. The humans swiftly finished painting themselves invisible, then did the same to the flying cheetah and climbed onto his back. Simber didn't waste a minute. He stepped gingerly out onto the fifth floor until his wings cleared the entryway and the boards began to give way beneath him, then took flight. Simber glided around the room to gain speed, then soared up to the ceiling. "Coverrr yourrr heads and hold on," Simber said in a whisper. They'd have to push through some debris between the two holes.

"We'rrre going to make some noise, but it can't be helped."

With their heads down and bodies shielding one another the best they could, the four held on as Simber's head pushed through the ceiling and the rotted wood fell away. Their near-invisible expulsion into the air above the palace wasn't as loud as they'd expected, for the roof pieces broke away easily. But without a doubt it was loud enough for the dragons to hear. Simber shook, trying to get the bits of debris off him, and the children swept the rest of the dust off his back and each other so it wouldn't give the dragons anything to see. It was dark, with only a quarter moon, and the stars were mostly covered by clouds, so that helped.

Simber lifted higher and higher, and the four gripped each other tightly so they wouldn't slide right off his back end. None of them spoke or made a noise. Thisbe's stomach wrenched and fell inside her as they soared to a dizzying height, but she pinched her eyes shut and held on, trusting the others to tell her if she needed to do anything else.

After a moment, Simber leveled off and started to move horizontally. Thisbe dared a peek. They glided toward the dragons, who were acting restless and concerned because of the ruckus. But they stayed on the ground and stared at the palace roof where the debris had exploded. Pan, whom they could hardly see in the darkness because of her pitch-black scales, began to move toward the palace to check out the noise from the roof. But no one came after them.

Simber flew like a bullet, trying to get as much distance between them and the dragons as possible before the invisibility spell wore off. He knew dragons not only had incredible eyesight, but their sense of smell was keen. Rohan kept track of the minutes going by and whispered to the others when the spells were about to wear off. "Shall we reapply? Or risk it?"

"One more dose for good measure," Fifer said, and the rest agreed, reaching down in mid-flight to cover as much of Simber as they could.

By the time that second spell wore off, they'd left the palace far behind them, and all agreed they were safe to fly high over this no-man's-land without being invisible. They'd employ the spell again once they drew close to Dragonsmarche in case soldiers and other mind-controlled dragons were in sight.

Feeling a bit more at ease now that they were flying straight, Thisbe leaned forward to pat the cheetah's neck. "You did great, Sim. I've been thinking about what happens once we get there and you drop us off at the elevator. If you want, you could try to fly around and peek inside the cave opening to the catacombs. You might not be able to come in very far before the turns become too narrow, but it'll give you something to do if you get bored. I'll send you a seek spell when it's time for you to come back to the square and pick us up."

"Would that be a better way for us to go in too?" Fifer asked. "Through the cave entrance? Because Simber can't apply the invisibility paintbrushes to himself, which means he'll be visible in Dragonsmarche."

"No," said the other three in unison—they knew the catacombs much better than Fifer did. "It's way too far from the kitchen," Thisbe explained. "It would take us hours to get there and back to Simber on foot. It's not ideal because it's so exposed, but we need to enter and exit from the elevator in the square."

"Got it."

"There shouldn't be many people prowling around Dragonsmarche at this hour anyway," said Dev. "Aren't the soldiers all called up for duty and stationed around the castle?"

"We hope they are," said Thisbe.

"Indeed," agreed Dev.

As the smell of the still-smoldering forest grew stronger, and Dragonsmarche came into murky view, Simber detected Gorgrun and his team not far away. Fifer sent a send spell to Asha, noting that it didn't go far before it stopped. The reply came swiftly. All seemed well.

"Drrragons cirrrcling in the distance," Simber reported.

"It looks like they're still putting out flare-ups in the forest," said Rohan.

"I hope that'll keep them occupied," said Thisbe, feeling a pang of anxiety. She pulled out her next invisibility paintbrush, wanting to apply it now but knowing they'd have some time on the ground they'd need to account for, and she didn't want to start too early. Luckily, Simber gave the order.

"We'rrre about five minutes frrrom landing," Simber said. "Let's go invisible beforrre those cirrrcling drrragons detect us."

The four complied, then covered as much of Simber as possible. They couldn't reach all of him, but he certainly wasn't recognizable as a dangerous or threatening flying cheetah. The darkness helped hide what still showed of him.

Within minutes, Simber landed as gently and quietly as he could on the Dragonsmarche pavers and came to a stop near the spot where the elevator control was. Dev slid off and started searching the bricks for the right one that would raise it and allow them access to the catacombs.

The other three followed and accidentally mowed him down, causing a bit of confusion and alternating fits of annoyance and stifled laughter in their invisibility. Once they got themselves sorted out and Dev found the proper brick, they waited and watched for the other team, not wanting to bring up the elevator until it was absolutely necessary. Soon enough they saw a foggy wisp coming toward them. While they waited for the ghost dragon to land, Thisbe, Fifer, Dev, and Rohan searched the skies, worried as dragons circled above the smoldering forest. There were a couple of soldiers patrolling the streets nearby, but the wide-open square was completely empty.

"How much longer before we're visible?" Thisbe whispered to Rohan.

"A couple of minutes."

"This place is cleared out," Dev said under his breath. "It makes me think nobody's working in the catacombs anymore."

LISA McMANN

"Why do you think that?" whispered Fifer.

"If the catacombs were fully staffed, they'd have a few people posted out here, or at least wandering the square and protecting the elevator. I wonder if they've abandoned everything. It's not like the Revinir needs more broth made, and without us being held captive down there, what else is there to protect?"

"Let's hope you're right," said Thisbe. "But be ready with spells anyway."

When the patch of fog came to a stop and the soft thud of feet hitting the pavers could be heard, Thisbe called out to the other team in a whisper. "Asha! Prindi! Are you all here?"

"We're here. Ready to go. We've only got a couple minutes of invisibility left."

"We're almost out too. Simber, I'll send a seek spell when we're ready to be picked up. Everything looks clear, though. We'll see you in a bit. The dragon bones are nearby in the crypts—it's the broth cauldrons that'll take some time to get to, but Rohan and I will run for them. Don't go too far."

"I'll stay nearrrby," said Simber.

"Good. Hit it, Dev," said Thisbe.

Dev moved the brick lever, and soon the elevator rose from

the square. While Simber kept watch on the soldiers in the nearby streets and the dragons circling above, Thisbe and Fifer and the others drew magical components and other weapons. They all got in and waited impatiently for the elevator to disappear from view. They stood, slowly growing visible, poised to fight the moment the elevator door opened underground.

Simber, gradually appearing now that his invisibility spells were wearing off, watched them leave. Then, after a thoughtful moment, he turned toward the path across the road that would take him into the forest to Alex's grave. With a quick glance all around, he headed for it. But he didn't notice the two pairs of dull yellow eyes peering over the rocky hill that separated the square from the crater lake. And he didn't see the dragons take flight, heading for the Revinir's castle.

A Familiar Face

The elevator door opened to a dark, empty hallway. None of the sconces on the walls were lit, which seemed odd. Still, the team of black-eyed people entered with expertise, caution, and stealth they had acquired since training under Maiven and Florence.

They moved up the hallway, fully visible now. Someone lit a highlighter to help them see. With a start, Dev noticed one black-eyed girl right away—she was the one who looked like the painting he'd found in the desk in Ashguard's palace. The resemblance was striking. And even though it probably wasn't her—the painting was too old for that to be possible—it could

LISA McMANN

be her mother. She was no doubt related to Ashguard. Which meant she would take over the palace, and his library. Dev's expression flickered, and he tried not to let his heart sink. They had other more important things to attend to. But that little dream inside him, the one that said he belonged somewhere, was dying. And it refused to go quietly.

"Stop," he muttered to himself, and double-checked his weapons. He needed to pay attention now more than ever. The future of this land was dependent on this small group of people, and they all needed to be quick and smart to get this mission completed without casualties.

They could all wield weapons and do at least a little magic by this point. Some, like Rohan and Prindi, were quite advanced with their spells. Everyone had been given component vests by Florence after their training. Only Dev didn't have one, and that was an oversight Thisbe wanted to correct as soon as possible if Florence or Carina had thought to bring along any spares. The rest of them lit highlighters, peered down passage-ways, and advanced toward Thisbe's old crypt, which was just down the hallway from the elevator.

While the others stood back, Thisbe used powerful fire

bolts from her eyes and fingertips to blow out the door to her crypt. When the smoke cleared, she checked to make sure there were still plenty of dragon bones and reminded the others they could get more if needed by going through the tunnel she'd created, which led into Rohan's crypt. Thisbe took a lingering look at that passageway and remembered the sweet times she and Rohan had spent together, curled up. Talking about life. Sharing their first kiss. The two glanced at each other. Rohan gave her a small smile. "There were a few nice moments down here," he said near her ear. "But I'd still rather be anywhere else, as long as you're with me."

Thisbe's face grew warm. "Come on," she said, and took Rohan's hand. "Let's run to the kitchen so we can get far away from here as soon as possible. And never return." They started for the kitchen.

The passageways appeared safe except when coming to an intersection or a curve, which wouldn't allow them to see very far ahead, so they had to slow down and be cautious. But, like them, no human could navigate the catacombs in pitch darkness, and there weren't any lights to be seen except for their own highlighter, so they assumed they were alone. Thisbe and

Rohan peered around corners and down side halls, but they became increasingly sure the place had been abandoned completely after their escape. And it made sense. With no one left to guard, it seemed silly to have soldiers down here. Finally, with increasing confidence, they reached the kitchen, finding the stove fires extinguished and cold. Two cauldrons sat atop the ashes, empty.

"Let's see if there is any broth left over from before," Thisbe whispered, her stomach twisting in knots. Being here was giving her flashbacks. The two moved cautiously into the attached storage room where Thisbe had spent so much time juggling vials of broth, trying to keep Dev and the others from drinking more of the dragon-bone kind. She'd risked so much down here, seen so much pain. Dev sobbing on the floor, feeling lost and alone. So many of her now friends who'd been walking around like zombies under the Revinir's mind control. The Revinir forcing her to work harder and harder each day, dragging bones. Very little food and water.

The sound of glass crunching under their feet dashed their hopes of finding anything intact. They pointed their highlighters at the shelf where the two kinds of broth had been stored.

Vials were smashed. Everything had been destroyed. Rohan double-checked each slot just to be sure and cleaned off the lone vial that sat in its slot, unbroken.

"Which kind is it?" asked Thisbe, peering at it. "Ancestor? We could use an extra backup, just in case. We only have a handful of them left."

"No," said Rohan, holding his light close to it. "It's dragon-bone broth. I'll take it with us anyway, even though it won't make much of a difference."

As Rohan put the vial into his pocket and the two returned to collect the cauldrons, a faint light appeared outside in the hallway, growing brighter. Thisbe gasped and pointed, and she and Rohan quickly doused their highlighters. Could it be one of their team members? But why would they come all the way down here? They quickly realized it couldn't be one of their friends, for the light was coming from the direction of the castle, not the elevator.

Together in the dark, the two could only crouch silently together as footsteps approached. The light flickered, as if it were fire from a torch. Soon, whoever held it stopped walking and stood outside the kitchen doorway.

Thisbe and Rohan shifted, making shards of glass crunch under them. They held their breath as a man appeared, his face illuminated by fire.

Mangrel, the crypt keeper, stepped into the kitchen toward them.

Enlisting Help

Thisbe stared at Mangrel as mixed feelings pounded her. He had kept her and the others imprisoned in this underground maze of bones. He'd branded the back of her neck with the Revinir's symbol, like he'd done with all the other black-eyed children. But he'd softened over time as the Revinir kept doing more and more horrible things to her. He'd started slipping her extra food, especially toward the end of her imprisonment down here, and he'd looked the other way more than once when Thisbe had exploded things in her crypt. When she and the rest of the group had escaped, he'd surprised them all by helping distract the other guards at the last minute, and he told them to make a run for it. That was worth something to Thisbe.

She also worried about what would happen if Mangrel continued on down the hallway and discovered their friends stealing ancient dragon bones. Would he hurt them or try to put a stop to their bone gathering? They could take him out if they knew he was coming, but they were preoccupied and might not see him until it was too late—he could lock at least a few of them in a crypt. And Thisbe didn't have time to deal with that kind of problem right now.

While Rohan watched Thisbe in the darkness, trying to read her mind, Thisbe teetered about what to do. Mangrel sniffed the air and took another step inside. The light from his torch fell on Thisbe's and Rohan's shoes.

"Who are you?" he demanded. "Show yourself!" He pulled a dagger from his belt and brandished it, then charged into the room.

Rohan squeezed Thisbe's arm—either in fear or in warning. But Mangrel kept coming for them. Thisbe disregarded Rohan's signal and slipped her fingers into her vest pockets.

LISA McMANN

She grabbed and flung a handful of scatterclips at the man. The clips stuck through the crypt keeper's clothing and slammed him against the kitchen wall, pinning him there. "What? Who?" he yelled in surprise. "Hey! Put me down!"

"Not sure that was entirely necessary, but okay," Rohan remarked under his breath.

"I didn't want him to do anything he'd regret," replied Thisbe with a smirk. It felt good to use her magic again on a real target . . . and not miss this time. She stepped closer to Mangrel's torch so he could see her. "Hi, Mangrel. It's me, Thisbe. And Rohan is here too. Where are all the guards?"

Mangrel's mouth dropped open in surprise; then his face clouded as he figured out what had just happened to him. He tried to point his torch at them so he could see the two better, but his pinned arm wouldn't allow for much movement. "What are *you* doing down here?" he snarled. "Don't you know what you've done?"

Thisbe and Rohan exchanged a confused glance. "What *we've* done?" repeated Rohan. "What do you mean?"

The crypt keeper stared. "I have orders to kill you if I see you, just like the dragons. Why did you come back to this place? You know the Revinir has put the other catacomb guards to death because you all escaped!"

Thisbe's heart sank. She hadn't heard anything about it. The two of them instinctively edged toward the door. "I didn't know she'd done that," Thisbe said, feeling a bit numb. "I feel bad about it. But . . ." She gave a quizzical look, as if realizing what she was apologizing for. "Wait a minute. You mean the soldiers who actually tried to kill me and Rohan before? The ones who treated us and our friends like dirt? Who went along with the theory that certain children should be used as slaves?" Fire flashed from her eyes. "Those are the ones you want to lecture me about?"

"Thisbe," Rohan cautioned, but she wasn't going to stop now.

"Honestly, Mangrel," Thisbe continued. "You have no right to be yelling at me about this. I should be lecturing you after what you've done. And I will not take the blame for what the Revinir decides to do to the people who serve her. I'm the one trying to get her out of power. I'm the one trying to help people like you by saving this land of the dragons and restoring it to what it used to be. I don't see *you* doing anything like

LISA McMANN

that!" She hesitated, then dropped her voice. "It's true I feel a bit sorry for you because you helped us get away. And I'm very grateful for that. But you didn't try to free us. You didn't try to stop the Revinir—you went along with it. You stuck a burning-hot iron against my neck, Mangrel. That's *terrible*! You were almost as obedient to the Revinir as the guards were. So don't try to pin any blame on me and my formerly enslaved friends."

She reached inside her vest for a few heart attack components, feeling a bit reckless. "And don't even try to make a move once those scatterclips disappear, or you're dead. I'm not really afraid of anyone anymore. Least of all, you."

Mangrel stared for a long moment, then dropped his gaze. He was helpless to do anything but hang his head. "I did what I could. You don't understand."

"I understand that you allowed a dictator to imprison children and use them as slaves, and you participated in that for years."

Mangrel didn't respond. He kept his head down.

"We should go," Rohan whispered to Thisbe. He lifted up a cauldron to remind her.

LISA McMANN

Thisbe flipped her highlighter on and shined it on Mangrel's face, revealing the remorse the man felt. "I'm not lying when I say I can take you out of this world in an instant, Mangrel," said Thisbe. "And so can Rohan. And while we don't want to do that, precisely because you've done the absolute bare minimum of a few nice things for me, I'm not afraid to." She stepped back. "Drop your dagger."

The crypt keeper seemed fully deflated. He dropped his dagger, and it went clattering to the floor. Thisbe kicked it over to Rohan, who picked it up.

"Give me your torch." Thisbe stepped forward, rolling one of the heart attack components between her fingers, ready in case he tried anything. But Mangrel did what he was told and didn't even attempt to pull from his restraints.

"I'm going to release the spell and let you down so you can give me any other weapons you're carrying."

Thisbe did so, and once his limbs were free, Mangrel pulled a knife out of a sheath around his leg and dropped it onto the floor near Thisbe's feet. She kicked that one back to Rohan too.

"I wouldn't have hurt you," Mangrel muttered. "I didn't

know it was you at first. And . . . I'm sorry. You're right. I should have done better, no matter what the cost. I knew it all along."

"Then why . . . ?"

"It's . . . complicated. And I was in a bind. But basically, I gave up trying."

Rohan grimaced. He was starting to get worked up now. "You giving up meant I was a slave since childhood," he said. "It meant I lost everything. It meant I don't have anyone left or a place to go. My fellow black-eyed former slaves and I hardly know how to act in public because we spent more time down here than out there. You participated in that."

The man blanched. "Yes. You're right. I'm so sorry."

Thisbe looked at Rohan, glad he'd finally said something and feeling the emotion lingering in the air—she knew he'd feel better later for having done it. "Anything else?" she asked him.

He shook his head and blew out a breath. "No. That's all. I accept your apology."

Mangrel couldn't look the boy in the eye. "Thank you."

Thisbe pointed down the hallway toward the elevator, indicating Mangrel should start walking. "I will keep your apology in mind," said Thisbe, less generous but fair enough under the circumstances. "Now grab a cauldron from Rohan. We're going to try to make life better for everyone, even you. So a little help now will go a long way to redeeming yourself."

Mangrel's face was conflicted, but he did what he was told. Thisbe made him go ahead of them on the long walk back toward the elevator.

Rohan raised an eyebrow at Thisbe as the man shuffled along in front of them. Thisbe shrugged, but she couldn't hide her feeling of triumph. After her encounter with the Revinir, she had apparently ceased to give in to people who were trying to take advantage of her. It worked out all right in this instance.

As they walked, Thisbe began thinking about their pending escape from here. Not only did they have to get all of the people out, but all of the bones and cauldrons, too. She began calculating the number of invisibility paintbrushes they'd need. None of them had thought to account for paintbrushes for the bones and cauldrons, but that was the last thing they wanted the Revinir's dragons to see, even if the humans were invisible. If the Revinir heard about a bunch of bones and cauldrons

219 « Dragon Fury

LISA McMANN

waltzing away on their own, it wouldn't take long for her to figure out who was behind it and speculate what they were doing with them. Plus they'd have to cover them when they approached Ashguard's palace to hide them from the dragons there, too. She checked her vest pockets, but that didn't help much when she didn't know how many everyone else had. It was a potential predicament to worry about later. But she had other questions now. She took the cauldron from Rohan for a while so he could rest his arms.

"Tell me, Mangrel," said Thisbe after a time. The heavy cauldron, on its thin metal handle, thudded against her legs, and her arms strained to carry it. "What's the situation with soldier and dragon activity in the square at this time of night? And what do you know about the Revinir's plans?"

Gathering Bones

I don't know much about the Revinir's plans," said Mangrel. "I'm down here alone. I was only given strict orders to keep an eye out for you, Thisbe, and kill you if I saw you. I never expected you'd come back here." He paused, then asked again, still wondering, "Why would you? Or perhaps you don't want to tell me." He glanced over his shoulder and added, "I won't tell anyone you came. I promise. It's the least I can do after . . . everything."

"Thank you," said Rohan. "And what about the soldiers and dragons in the square?"

"No soldiers there anymore. There's nothing to keep watch

LISA McMANN

over—just a big empty square. The market ended weeks ago. People are beginning to starve. The food isn't being transported to the people who need it, and the farmers are throwing it all away. It's really horrible."

Thisbe frowned. "You mean like when we were slaves?" She'd gone a few days without food down here.

"I . . . yes. Only bigger. And endless." He continued where he left off. "All the soldiers are assembled in camps around the castle, waiting for orders to go after you."

"We saw dragons overhead when we arrived," Rohan said, trying to keep the conversation helpful.

"They seem to just circle about. Mostly they're focused on putting out the fire the last couple of days, but they'd notice you in the square if they were overhead. But," Mangrel said, "they all go down to the crater lake around this time of night to fish and eat. You should be able to slip away easily if you head out soon."

"Hmm," said Thisbe, not sure if she trusted the man. But the story rang true—this was similar timing to when the red dragons had gone to the river to eat. "Maybe we won't have to use our invisibility paintbrushes," she whispered to Rohan.

"*You're* definitely using one," Rohan said, alarmed. "She's out to get you. We're not taking any chances."

"Well, but maybe we can leave Simber and the bones and cauldrons alone after all."

"I hadn't thought about them," Rohan said, checking his stash of components to see how many invisibility paintbrushes he carried. "It would look suspicious to see unaccompanied bones flying through the air, wouldn't it?"

"That's what I've been worrying about. I didn't think about how many extra components we'd need to cover a bunch of giant bones and two enormous cauldrons."

Rohan frowned. "We don't want to use up everything we have—we'll need them at the end of the journey. That's even more important."

"Right," said Thisbe, calculating.

Mangrel didn't have a clue what the two were talking about, though he remembered them using something to make them invisible before—they'd done it in the elevator, and it had been shocking to witness. He had other things on his mind, though. "I'm grateful you didn't kill me," he said after a time of silence.

"Just remember: If you try anything against us, I will not

hesitate to do so," said Thisbe. Still, she felt a pang. Mangrel was stuck down here all by himself, carrying a torch and wandering the empty hallways, watching over bones. Why was he even still here?

The crypt keeper nodded. "I know."

Eventually they passed the hallway that led to Rohan's old crypt, and they could hear the others dragging bones to the elevator. Soon they rounded the corner to the main hallway where Thisbe's old crypt was, and the others came into view. They had one side of the elevator halfway loaded up, leaving just enough room for the team to fit inside if they could manage to lift the cauldrons above their heads.

Everyone but Fifer shrank back, visibly shaken at the sight of Mangrel, but Rohan explained what had happened as he helped load the last bones into the elevator.

"This should be enough," said Dev. "Shall we pile in?"

"Aren't we all going invisible?" Rohan asked Thisbe with a challenging look in his eye. He plugged Mangrel's torch into one of the sconces on the wall.

"I—" Thisbe wavered. "Yes, I suppose we should. We can't take any chances. Everyone, please make sure you save enough paintbrushes for the end of our trip so we aren't detected. It's more important not to be seen back at our camps than it is here." They all began to paint themselves, starting from their feet and moving up.

Rohan looked relieved as he began applying his. "Bones and cauldrons too?"

Thisbe bit her lip before completely disappearing. "No. I think we should chance it and not waste the components. It's dark. The dragons are likely feeding at the lake. There are no soldiers stationed here anymore, according to Mangrel, and I believe him. The important part for now is that the dragons here don't see humans looking suspicious."

"Okay," said Rohan, trying not to sound doubtful, but it seemed to him like the sight of dragon bones moving on their own would be cause for all-out panic. But there was no time to argue now that the clock was ticking on their invisibility. "Shall we head up?"

"Wait," said Thisbe, finishing painting her hair. "I forgot to call Simber." She quickly sent a seek spell to him, which startled Mangrel with its zooming ball of light that took the fastest path it could, down the long passageway to the cave exit, since the elevator was still down here, plugging that route. After waiting a few anxious minutes to give Simber time to return before bringing the elevator up into full view, everyone squeezed in alongside the giant stack of bones.

Thisbe looked out at Mangrel, who was still just standing there, looking a bit forlorn. "Rohan," she said, "can you give him his weapons back, please?"

"Are you sure?" asked Rohan.

Thisbe narrowed her gaze and studied the crypt keeper. "Yes," she said. "He may need to protect himself. I wish him no harm—we have enough enemies."

Rohan hopped out of the elevator and handed the man's knife and dagger back to him.

"Thank you," Mangrel said. "And good luck. Whatever happens, I wish you all well."

Thisbe smiled, then realized he couldn't see it. "You too. Once we take over the world, I'll come and let you know so you can get out of here."

Rohan returned to the elevator, and with that, Dev pushed the button. The elevator began to rise, and everyone strained on tiptoes to see if anyone was around and watching.

The square seemed empty, and there were no dragons circling above, which was a great relief. It was exactly as Mangrel had said. Simber hadn't arrived yet, but Thisbe had no doubt he'd be coming shortly. He was probably trying to round up Gorgrun for the ones going to the village. The group filed out of the elevator, then began stacking the bones on the pavers while they waited for their rides.

As they piled the last ones, a roar filled their ears, and everyone froze. From up over the nearest row of houses outside the square came the Revinir and two other dragons, flames exploding from their throats.

A Very Close Call

The children were invisible standing in Dragonsmarche, but the bones, cauldrons, and elevator weren't. "Run!" Thisbe whispered harshly to the others. "Hide behind the hills. We'll find you there." She unsheathed her sword and heard the zing of at least one other.

Some of them scattered, but no one quite knew who else was running. The rest stayed to defend their very important mission, knowing they still had a few minutes left of invisibility. But the invisibility feature had its drawbacks, and a sense of uneasiness took over them as they lost track of each other and began to step carefully about, trying to connect with other people without banging into them full on or getting sliced by their weapons. It was impossible to determine how many of them stood against the three roaring dragons.

Thisbe and the others who'd stayed knew their cargo was crucial, but if they moved it now, they'd be discovered because of that movement. Still, there was no way Thisbe was leaving here without the bones and pots. If they couldn't make dragon-bone broth, Artimé's top fighters, including their Magical Warrior trainer, would remain trapped by their own dragons. But if they could deliver the bones as planned, they might end up with some dragons on their side again, and that could tip the scales in their favor. There was no better way to fight the Revinir than with her own weapons. They needed this.

The Revinir kept flying toward them. Thisbe could see that the two dragons accompanying her were the last of the red ones that had been hiding in the sea near Artimé's jungle when the Revinir had abducted the twins. Riding on the Revinir's back were several castle workers, including Zel, who had been Thisbe's personal assistant for a time. Thisbe narrowed her eyes and took a few steps back, bumping into someone but

LISA McMANN

not knowing who, and sending that person tripping over the pile of bones, knocking a few of them clattering to the ground. "Sorry!" she whispered and moved over behind the elevator so there wouldn't be another collision like that.

As she went, Thisbe touched the last obliterate component inside her secret vest compartment. She was sorely tempted to remove it and use it, but then she let it go with a grimace. Obviously the Revinir knew Thisbe well, because she had ensured that the mage wouldn't try to obliterate her again by surrounding herself with servants. Thisbe knew the Revinir needed to be removed from power at all costs. She knew that the dragon-woman wouldn't stop harming others, and that there was no choice except to take her down. But she didn't want to hurt anyone else in the process. And the Revinir seemed to have figured that out. Not to mention that Thisbe wasn't exactly sure where all of her friends were at the moment. Just because they were invisible didn't mean they couldn't be injured or killed by the detonation of such a powerful spell.

Where is Simber? Thisbe thought as she scrambled to figure out what to do now.

"I can smell you, Thisbe Stowe!" shouted the Revinir. The

dragon-woman landed in the square near the elevator, her nostrils flaring. She let a spray of fire sweep across the pavers in front of her. Someone muttered and threw a metal star at the monster. It struck her in the neck, and the dragon-woman let out a telling yelp of pain that surprised Thisbe—she'd never witnessed the Revinir expressing physical pain or discomfort before. Thisbe peered around the elevator and saw that her neck was swollen right below her jaw. Had something happened to her? Was she injured?

Thisbe's confidence grew. If only she could get the people off the Revinir's back so she could take a clean shot! *Fifer?* she said in her mind.

I'm by the bones, Fifer replied.

I'm behind the elevator.

Just then a message spell reached Thisbe, revealing her hiding place. She grabbed it and shoved it inside her vest, trying to hide it. The Revinir roared and stepped toward her. Reluctantly Thisbe left her post and ran, arms outstretched and feeling around for others, out into the open square.

"I know you're here!" the Revinir roared again, and several of the mages launched heart attack spells at her, revealing just how many of them had stayed to fight off the dragon. But, as before, the spells didn't work on her.

Sudden movement against the dark sky caught Thisbe's eye, and she knew instinctively it was Simber and Gorgrun finally returning. Could they get here before the invisibility spells wore off? They didn't have much time. She wished she could communicate with Simber, but surely he saw by now that the Revinir was here and the elevator was up in the square, even if he couldn't see the humans standing there.

It didn't matter, though, because Rohan and Dev were just starting to appear. Their invisibility was wearing off.

I'm going visible, Fifer said to Thisbe.

Me too. I won't hide from her. I won't back down.

We'll face her together. Simber is coming.

The rest of them had a decision to make without having a chance to consult with the others: Do they reapply their remaining invisibility brushes now, or save them for when they went back? Run for the hills, or would that only cause the Revinir to chase them down?

Thisbe knew that if she used a fresh paintbrush but the others didn't, they'd be targeted. That didn't sit right. This was Thisbe's mess. Thisbe's battle. She left her brushes alone and hoped she'd chosen correctly. They'd need the remaining ones anyway to get past Pan and the others if they made it out of this mess alive. Besides, Simber needed to know where she was—and not just her. She took out the obliterate spell and vowed to use it if the Revinir tried anything, no matter who went down with it. She had to. She cringed and released the latch on the tiny box so she'd be ready.

As Thisbe's body slowly appeared, Simber and Gorgrun drew near, but stayed out of the Revinir's sight behind her. Thisbe moved toward Fifer, Dev, and Rohan, who, like her, were fully visible now, though still entrenched in darkness. She glanced at Dev, who hung behind the other two, and remembered that the Revinir still thought he was dead. What would she do to him if she saw him alive?

The dragon-woman's beaklike snout was sniffing all around, trying to figure out where everyone was and if there were more who hadn't reappeared. To distract the Revinir from making out Dev's features in the darkness, Thisbe shouted out to her. "I'll use this spell, and I won't miss this time," Thisbe warned. "We will take this land back. We're not stopping."

233 « Dragon Fury

LISA McMANN

The Revinir seemed mildly startled by Thisbe's threat. She reared back before recovering and putting on her usual snide expression. "Sure. Sure you will," said the dragon-woman, her confident words sounding a bit hollow. She motioned to her red dragons to stand down. "You wouldn't hurt Zel. And what about my other slaves, who must still be hiding from me? They might be a little too close to me for you to use that thing—it's such a powerful spell, as you've already proven. Knocked me down. Then your weak little grandfather tried to take me out with his baby-size metal star weapons. What a failure. Of course you already know that."

Thisbe quickly glanced around. Fifer stepped forward to line up with her. "Is that why your neck is swollen?" she asked. "From Ishibashi's throwing star?"

Rohan and Dev stayed in the shadows, but Thisbe still gave Dev a frantic look—it was best for the Revinir to believe him to be dead. What was he doing? He flashed a defiant look in return. Fifer lit a highlighter to draw attention to herself and away from Dev.

"Why don't you go ahead and kill us all, then?" Thisbe called out. "If you don't think I'll use the spell, what are you waiting for?" She paused, then added, "Oh, wait. I know. You need at least one of us to stay alive in order to complete your takeover plan."

"No one will join you if you hurt any of us," said Dev, who was apparently tired of hiding. He and Rohan raised their weapons.

The Revinir did a double take, and her mouth gaped when she realized it was Dev standing there. In the darkness, a metal star zinged through the air from an invisible source, aiming for the dragon-woman's open mouth. It slammed into her teeth, breaking off a few. The Revinir roared in anger and lunged toward the direction of the throw.

Thisbe raised her arm, poised to cast the obliterate spell. Her hand shook. "I'll use it, Emma," she shouted. "Don't even think about coming any closer."

"Stop. Calling. Me. Emma!" the Revinir roared, but then abruptly clutched her neck. She coughed and choked and tried to clear her throat. Then she shoved her claws deep into her mouth and fished around. Wincing in pain, she withdrew them, slime covered and dripping, but had no success in removing the source of discomfort. "I told you before."

"What's going on with your throat?" asked Fifer, trying again to get information. "Are you injured? You seem . . . weak."

"Be quiet!" the Revinir said as she shook the goo from her claws. "I'm not speaking to you." She sniffed hard, then muttered under her breath. Something rotten-smelling wafted from the dragon-woman.

Fifer made a face and let out a little snort. Dev gagged, while Rohan stood firm, doing his best to keep Dev protected behind him.

"What do you want?" asked Thisbe, frustrated. She'd expected the Revinir to attack—after all, the dragon-woman had put a kill order on her with all the dragons and soldiers and even Mangrel, so why wasn't she carrying it out? Thisbe rolled the pebble between her fingers, ready to cast it . . . she thought. But not if the Revinir didn't come at them. Thisbe eyed Simber, who was still hovering with Gorgrun behind the Revinir, unnoticed by any of the three opposing dragons. Was he planning something? She certainly hoped so. "Well?" Thisbe demanded. "Tell me!"

"I want to know why you betrayed me."

Thisbe felt like she'd been punched in the stomach. She

didn't want to talk about this, especially in front of the others. She glanced at Fifer and saw her sister was watching Simber too. *Time for a distraction?* Thisbe said to Fifer using her mind.

Yes. I'll give Simber a signal.

"Why do you think I betrayed you?" asked Thisbe, stalling for time. Maybe the Revinir would answer the uncomfortable question herself.

The Revinir was quiet for a long moment. Fifer flicked her wrist and Simber and Gorgrun advanced. Finally the dragon-woman said, "I don't know," in a quiet voice. "I thought we had a special friendship." She cut off the last word sharply, as if she hated herself for speaking it. With a growl, she asked, "What are you doing with those dragon bones? Are you trying to become like me?"

Thisbe sucked in a breath at the idea of that. A rush of pity and horror mingled together inside her. "I would never, ever want to do that," she said, and she meant it.

The Revinir's face curled in anger. Before she could reply, Dev stepped in front of everyone else. "No one would ever want to be anything like you."

"Dev!" the Revinir cried, fire curling up around her jowls.

LISA McMANN

"Why won't you die?" She lunged at the young man, who swung his sword, nicking her chin and making her rise up in anger. Thisbe moved to place the obliterate spell square at her head, but now the dragon-woman was too close to the boys. Thisbe's face contorted in frustration, and she brought her arm down to her side. "Blast it!" she muttered when Dev didn't shrink back, and the four charged with weapons drawn.

"Simber! Now!" Fifer shouted.

Simber and Gorgrun slammed into the red dragons, knocking them for a loop, then crashed into them again, making them hit the pavers with a thunderous impact. The Revinir whirled around to see what had just happened, and as she turned, she let loose a shower of sparks over the crowd. "Hold the red ones back, Gorgrun!" Thisbe instructed, while Simber came veering down to the square, clipping the Revinir in the jaw with his wing. She whirled, dazed and yelping, and sprayed a line of fire at the children that ended in a plume of smoke and a hacking cough. She clutched her throat.

Meanwhile, Simber landed next to the bones, and Rohan and Dev began loading them on his back.

"Let's go!" Fifer yelled, loud enough so the others who were hiding could hear. "Gorgrun, one last push, then pick up your riders near the hills behind us!"

Gorgrun took a hard swipe with his mighty tail at the two red dragons, cuffing them and knocking them into the Revinir, who tipped and spilled her servants. As Gorgrun took off for the hills to collect his team, Thisbe clawed at her pocket, scrambling to get the obliterate spell while the Revinir had lost her riders. But the mind-controlled people climbed right back on, and the moment was lost.

"Hurry!" Fifer commanded. Thisbe gave up the plan and turned sharply to figure out their escape. She, Dev, and Rohan dove to grab what they could of the bones and cauldrons. Fifer jumped on Simber's back and steadied the load, and the other three scrambled up behind her. Simber scooped up the remaining bones. Before the Revinir and the red dragons could figure out what was happening, Thisbe, Fifer, and the rest of the team were heading back to Ashguard's palace and the village with all of their necessary goods intact.

"That was close," Fifer said. "Well done, Simber."

"I wonderrr why *Emma* isn't following us," said the cheetah, looking back and catching Thisbe's eye while narrowing his own.

LISA McMANN

Thisbe shrugged.

"Why do you call herrr that?"

"It's her name." Thisbe looked away from Simber's suspicious glance.

As they caught their breath and checked their injuries, all she could focus on was how messed up the Revinir must be to think Thisbe would ever want to be like her.

Out of Sorts

The Revinir and her two red dragons didn't follow Simber and the ghost dragon. Instead the dragon-woman watched as her former protégé and the rest of the black-eyed rulers left the area. She wondered how they'd managed to get past the five vicious dragons she'd sent to guard them, and then she realized with a pulse of concern that maybe they'd had no qualms about slaying their dragon friends after all. After the way Thisbe had treated her, it wouldn't be too surprising that they all were just coldhearted.

She wanted to feel angry—the same kind of anger she'd felt when the betrayal had happened. She almost sent the red

LISA McMANN

dragons after the group, but then she would be alone except for the mind-controlled servants she'd brought with her. They were not stimulating conversationalists. Nor were the red dragons, for that matter, but their presence was large, which somehow made up for something.

"Might as well be alone," she muttered. Every last one of her servants and dragons had been stripped of any sort of intelligent banter after the Revinir had taken control of them. It had only bothered the Revinir a little before Thisbe came along. But now that the girl was gone, it was painfully obvious that smart conversation in the castle was severely lacking.

How could Thisbe not be missing it too? They'd really had a connection. Was she only playing a part with her people to keep them from attacking her? The thought was absurd, yet . . . it was enough to keep the Revinir from acting immediately. Was it possible that Thisbe had *purposely* missed her with that obliterate spell? She wanted to believe it.

With a shake of her head, the Revinir turned away and started toward the castle. She didn't have the heart to go after them tonight. She needed to get her anger back so she could do the job once and for all with the proper amount of vengeance it would take—and with the dragon and soldier backup—to slay them all and be done with it. She didn't think she'd have to work too hard to take them all out. There were fewer than twenty of them from Artimé according to the last report from her dragons patrolling the skies. She realized the statues would likely be difficult to do away with. It didn't matter, though—they couldn't really hurt her. If they took down some soldiers and dragons in the effort, so be it. That didn't affect her.

No, those statues weren't dangerous like that grandfather had been. She winced and tried to swallow. Her throat injury, where the metal star had embedded, was getting worse as time passed. She was glad she'd killed him for it, but that didn't lessen the pain.

As the Revinir continued to ruminate on the recent incident, trying to build anger, she wondered why she hadn't just eliminated all the children in the square when she'd had the chance. Dev had been there too—the nerve of him somehow surviving! That was downright embarrassing.

But Thisbe. She had been rude, and that was frankly hard to get used to, so it had startled her a little. It seemed

LISA McMANN

243 « Dragon Fury

uncharacteristic. Maybe the Revinir had hesitated in retaliating because she held on to the hope that Thisbe would return . . . and they could try all of this again. The girl was still the best option, believe it or not. It wasn't likely that the Revinir could convince another black-eyed person to join her after everything that had happened.

Truth be told, it didn't seem likely with Thisbe, either, now. Obviously because she'd tried to kill her—though there were still some lingering doubts in the Revinir's mind about how the girl had missed. And she'd threatened her again just now but hadn't acted on it.

Still, things seemed bleak. It was the tone of Thisbe's voice, the disgust she spat out that guided the Revinir's thoughts now, whether she'd intended to show those stark emotions or not. Especially after she had thrown that last verbal barb, saying she would never, ever want to be like her. What had the Revinir done to deserve that? Especially the "never, *ever*" part. Why did Thisbe have to say it like that?

None of this was turning out the way the Revinir had hoped and dreamed it would. And now, with her massive army camping out, stretching from the castle along the road almost all the way to the square, waiting for the command to fight, the Revinir wasn't sure what to do.

Actually, no. That wasn't true. She knew what she had to do. Kill them all except for one of the black-eyed slaves, then force that one to comply. But she'd lost her drive after Thisbe had left. And she had to find it again.

The pain in her throat muddled her determination. It shouldn't be hard to hold on to the anger she'd felt after Thisbe had tried to kill her, but it was. Because for the first time in her life, the little girl named Emma, buried deep inside her, had felt like she'd had a kindred spirit. A friend. Someone who'd understood her. And it didn't make sense that Thisbe had been faking it all. It couldn't be possible! They'd had moments together that the Revinir was certain were authentic. And now all she wanted was more of that. But Thisbe had turned cold on her in an instant. With no warning. Had she been playing her the entire time? It felt awful.

The only way the Revinir knew how to get angry again was to think about all the times people had betrayed her in the past, ending with the moment that Thisbe had turned and thrown

LISA McMANN

the component that was meant to destroy her. No—ending with her saying she'd never, ever want to be like her.

After a few hours of tossing and turning in her sleep, the Revinir rose and went to the ballroom. The pain in her throat had worsened and was helping her anger increase. Another day or two like this and she'd be back to her normal furious self. And then? Thisbe and Fifer and their friends had better be on their toes, because the Revinir was coming after them.

Making Connections

Gorgrun and Simber flew side by side over the uninhabited space between Dragonsmarche and Ashguard's palace, which allowed their riders to talk about the plans moving forward. The ones staying in the village had heard Fifer's theory that water was important to use against the Revinir, but they hadn't gotten the full details. Fifer, Rohan, Thisbe, and Dev updated the rest with everything they could think of so they could pass it along to Carina and Lani and the others.

As they rode, Thisbe suddenly remembered the send spell that had come flying in at that terrible moment. She reached

LISA McMANN

inside her vest and pulled it out. While Fifer lit a highlighter so they could see, Thisbe read:

Thisbe,

Matilda alerted Charlie that the Revinir is on the way to Dragonsmarche! Apparently some dragons saw the elevator rise up and went to report it to her. Be careful!

Carina

Thisbe looked up and laughed sardonically. "Well, that arrived just a few minutes too late." She penned a response letting Carina know they were safe and on their way back.

"It's nice to have the gargoyles as spies," said Asha.

Dev nodded. He'd officially met all the others during the bone gathering in the catacombs. When everyone fell silent, he spoke up. "Hey, Asha, I found a painting of someone in the palace. It's a girl who looks like you, but it's old. Could it maybe be your mother? Are you . . . related to Ashguard by any chance?"

Asha's eyes widened. "Yes, he's my grandfather!"

"O-oh," said Dev, nodding while his heart twisted. "I . . . yes. I see."

"Please save it for me until I can take a look. I'd recognize her if I saw it." Her eyes shone in the night. "Thank you, Dev."

Dev nodded. "Of course," he said quietly, then turned away before his expression could betray the sudden sadness that had come over him. But Fifer and Thisbe noticed. They exchanged a curious glance.

What was that about? asked Thisbe.

Not sure, Fifer replied.

Before they could mind-discuss it further, Simber cleared his throat. "Drrragons cirrrcling ahead," he said, looking back at Fifer. "We'rrre coming up to the prrroperrrties. Time forrr us to split up and go invisible."

The two parties said a hasty good-bye, and soon Gorgrun turned into a puff of fog with his riders invisible, heading for the village. The four with Simber landed so they could be sure to reach all parts of the great winged cheetah with the paintbrushes, from the tip of his tail to the ends of his wings. Then they returned to the air and glided high toward the two front corner dragons just as the sun rose behind them.

Arabis's neck snapped to attention as they flew over. Then she took flight and bumbled in the air as if trying to figure out where to go.

"She smells us," Rohan whispered.

"It's the bones," Dev muttered.

"Hurry, Sim!" Fifer urged, but the cat was going as fast as he could, while still trying to make the sharp turn to maneuver into the hole in the roof.

From the side yard, Pan got up and watched Arabis sharply. She sampled the air.

"Keep moving," Thisbe said under her breath, watching them. She bent forward to hug Simber's neck, staying close so they'd make it back through the hole without incident. The others wrapped their arms around each other and leaned forward, trying not to exclaim or cry out as Arabis rapidly gained on them.

Thisbe closed her eyes and clung to the statue.

With Arabis on his tail, Simber banked in the air, then put on the brakes with his wings until the last second. He folded his wings and soared down through the roof. Before they crashed into the floor, Simber caught himself and reversed course. He circled the room, then came to a stop as near to the fifth-floor landing as he could reach. Bits of the floor crumbled beneath his hind legs.

"Hurrry," Simber told them, bending his neck and lowering his head to allow them to crawl over it. The four quickly unloaded the bones and cauldrons. "Get to the steps! I can't see you and I don't want to crrrush you!"

As Fifer ran to obey, she looked up through the hole and saw a flash of orange go by, but Arabis didn't attempt to come through the roof or even look inside the hole. "I think we made it," she said, feeling breathless. As the floor began to cave in beneath Simber's back feet, the children leaped up the stairs and Simber scrambled to the stone landing. A large chunk of the fifth floor broke off and slammed down onto the fourth floor. It stopped there.

Dev glanced back through the doorway, realizing there was no longer a way to get to the secret nook without leaping over a gaping hole. He was glad he'd taken the painting out of there and put it in the library. This place was getting destroyed by the minute.

Aaron, Sky, and Maiven peered over the library railing to see what the noise was, and by now the invisibility spells were wearing off.

"We'll explain everything in a minute," Fifer said. "But in the meantime, can you give us a hand with these bones?"

Memories and
Reminders

S oon all of them were back inside the library—or in
Simber's case, sprawled on the steps leading up to it.
While the nighttime travelers dozed, Aaron and
Sky watched for the dragons to settle down so they
could attempt to fill the cauldrons. Maiven prepared breakfast
for everyone using the scant remaining supplies Florence had
taken with her from the kitchen in Artimé. When Arabis and
Pan were back in place, Aaron and Sky made themselves and
the cauldrons invisible and snuck down to the water pump
with the cauldrons. They filled them as quickly as they could
and hurried back to safety in the tower before the dragons

came to see why the pump was running on its own but leaving no water pooling on the courtyard.

Florence, Simber, Seth, and Maiven continued to plot their attack on the Revinir and were soon joined by Aaron and Sky. The four black-eyed children got up from their naps and started back to work.

Fifer and Rohan joined the plotting committee, while Thisbe and Dev took up the task of making the dragon-bone broth—just like old times. And it felt really strange to be doing it. "I hate this," Dev muttered to Thisbe as he stacked dragon bones into his cauldron. "It feels terrible."

"My stomach is sick," said Thisbe. "All the times we did this—I didn't think it had affected me, but doing this brings back all of those bad memories. The Revinir making us drink this stuff . . ." Thisbe closed her lips, lost in the horror of it all. The Revinir had done terrible things to them—to all of the black-eyed children here, and to all of the ones gathered in the village nearby. She remembered sitting on the floor of the catacombs kitchen with Dev sobbing in her arms. She remembered those first dragon scales that had painfully popped out of her skin, and the rush of images that had been so confusing when she'd been forced to take her first dose of ancestor broth. The Revinir had done some very bad things to them.

Thisbe had to keep remembering that what the Revinir had done to her and others was not normal, and it was not okay. And she had to move beyond the pity she'd felt for the horrible creature. Because there was no doubt that the Revinir would end them all in an instant if she wanted to. She had no soul or heart left, or at least not enough to make a change. The Emma inside the dragon was gone. Erased. Thisbe closed her eyes at the sting of smoke and sat back on her heels.

"Why do you think she didn't come after us?" asked Dev as he stoked the fire. They wanted this broth done as quickly as possible. "She saw me."

"I noticed," said Thisbe. "You could have kept back in the shadows, you know. And . . . I'm not sure why." But she'd seen the look on the Revinir's face. She'd heard the vulnerability in her voice. "Maybe she thinks there's still a chance to get me to join her."

"I was tired of hiding." Dev covered his cauldron and turned toward her. "Is there?" he asked carefully.

"Is there what?"

"A . . . chance."

Thisbe hesitated an instant—long enough to be telling. "Of course not."

Dev looked hard at her. "Thisbe?"

"What?"

"Something's on your mind."

Thisbe's lips parted. She closed them again.

"It's okay to tell me," said Dev, glancing over to see the others gathered around the desk, deep in conversation. "Believe me, I understand how complicated everything is."

Thisbe blew out a breath. Did she dare confide in him about how conflicted she was feeling?

"I remember when you helped me," Dev said, trying to sound casual. "Back in the kitchen. After Princess Shanti was killed." He turned fully toward the fire so Thisbe wouldn't feel like he was being intense. "You said some hard things to me back then. And . . . I'm ready to do the same thing for you if you want me to."

Thisbe pinched her eyes shut and pretended to wave smoke away. She got up and opened the nearest window, then returned, hoping Dev had mercifully dropped the subject.

"The hardest part was being willing to hear it." Dev sat back on his haunches but kept his gaze fixed on the fire. "It's okay if you're not ready."

Thisbe let out a small groan of frustration and felt fire coming to her throat. Her scales fluttered against her skin. She didn't want to do this. She wasn't even sure what specifically was troubling her, so how in the world would Dev know? It made her ill-tempered that he seemed to think she needed his advice. It was so annoying. And now they were stuck here together to monitor the broth for hours.

"I don't know if I want your advice," Thisbe mumbled. "I guess it depends what you're going to say."

Dev laughed. It was nice to hear laughter, and Fifer, Seth, and Rohan looked over from their meeting with Florence and smiled at the two. Maybe one day they'd all laugh together once all of this was over.

Thisbe smiled back at them uneasily, then lowered her voice. "I'm just conflicted."

"About what?"

"About the Revinir."

LISA McMANN

"What part of her? She's complicated."

Thisbe glanced sidelong at Dev and nodded. "Yeah. She really is. She was a kid like us once, you know? I read her journals, and we talked a little when I was over there. Obviously I don't like her and nobody should. But I feel . . . sympathy for her, I guess." She tapped a stick on her cauldron as wisps of steam began to curl above it. "I feel like I'm a bad person for not hating her universally like everyone else does."

Dev was quiet for a moment, and he didn't look at her. "I think that just proves what a complex person—and a good person—you are," he said.

Thisbe was quiet. "Then why do I feel like Florence is constantly staring at me? Judging me?"

Dev glanced behind them.

"She's staring at me right now, isn't she?" said Thisbe.

"Yes."

"See? I can feel her eyes boring into the back of my head."

Dev gave a lopsided grin. "She'll never really understand everything you went through for the sake of Artimé. None of them will."

"Do you understand?"

"I think so. And Fifer does too. You made such a huge sac-rifice."

"Too bad I biffed it."

Dev leaned in. "Why did you biff it?"

Thisbe closed her eyes and scoffed. Why, indeed? She couldn't put into words all of the complicated feelings she was having. Could she confess to Dev that she'd had certain urges, thinking about how it might actually be fun to join the Revinir's side? Not that she'd ever actually do it—but did other people think that way sometimes? Was everyone so plain and simple that they never had bad thoughts just for the sake of imagin-ing what things would be like if they carried out something unimaginable? Wasn't that what creativity was—constantly imagining what-ifs? Wasn't that the heart of what Artimé was?

Maiven glanced over and caught Thisbe's eye. She gave her a warm smile and a nod, then turned back to the group.

Thisbe's heart clutched. She looked sideways at Dev. What would he think if she confessed she'd really enjoyed the Revinir's company a couple of times—that they'd actually had a few good moments together? Could Dev, who'd been thrown out the window by the dragon-woman and left for dead, still

LISA McMANN

see Thisbe in the same way if she said something even a little bit positive about her?

She didn't dare. All she could answer was "I guess it was hard using such a powerful spell on someone who had once been a kid like us."

"Hmm," Dev said thoughtfully.

After a while, when the old familiar, sickening smell of dragon-bone broth wafted into their faces, Thisbe turned to Dev. "I thought you were going to give me advice."

Dev shrugged, then picked up the stirring stick to move his dragon bones around. "I can't."

"Why not?"

"Because you haven't actually told me anything for real yet."

Thisbe froze, then took the stick when Dev was done with it. "Maybe I don't know which of my feelings are real."

"I think all feelings are real," said Dev thoughtfully. "But we just have to work through some of them. When you figure it out, I'll be here."

They fell silent, lost in the flames. After a while, Thisbe spoke again. "What did I say to you that day in the catacombs kitchen?"

"You don't remember?"

"I mean, it was a rough day all around for both of us."

"Fair enough. You told me that Shanti was not my friend."

"Oh." Thisbe blew out a breath. "Wow. That was probably a bit harsh."

"True, though."

"And it . . . helped?"

Dev nodded. "Not right away. But eventually."

"So now," Thisbe deduced, "you're prepared to tell me that the Revinir isn't my friend."

"If necessary, yes. But I think . . ." He didn't finish his thought.

Thisbe pursed her lips. "I *know* that already," she said.

Dev didn't answer. The defensiveness hung in the air around them and wouldn't go away.

Tempting Dragons

ow are we going to get them to drink this stuff?"
Fifer asked after another nap. The sun was set-
ting, and for a minute she wasn't sure how long
she'd been down. Her voice roused Dev, who'd
fallen asleep on the floor next to the fireplace, and he sat up and
blinked, bewildered. Thisbe had been monitoring both pots of
broth during his rest. Dev had been looking peaked after their
journey. He'd done a little too much, and they needed him to
continue healing.

"Hmm," said Thisbe, handing them both a round of medicine that Florence had put on the table nearby for when they

awoke. She lifted the lid off one cauldron and took a big sniff. Fifer wrinkled up her nose as the smell wafted her way. The odor of ancient bones soaking in boiling water wasn't exactly appealing. She reached for her canteen and swallowed her magical meds. Dev obediently did the same.

Seth came over from where he and Florence had been discussing his role in the upcoming attack. "Do you need any help with those cauldrons, Thiz?"

"Yes, please—they're about done now," said Thisbe. Dev struggled to get up to help too, but Thisbe waved him off. "We've got this." She and Seth placed the steaming cauldrons on the hearth to cool for a few hours.

"Add food to it," Rohan said, answering Fifer's initial question. "Something they'd like. They'll ingest the broth along with it."

"We have no food," Thisbe muttered.

"Do you think the broth will give them more scales?" Dev asked. "Like it would for us?"

"I don't know," said Thisbe. "I imagine it's more likely to give them visions, since it's their ancestors' bones that made the broth."

"And most importantly," said Fifer, "it should break the mind control."

"We hope," said Thisbe.

Florence looked up from the giant desk area of the library where she'd been scribbling notes and drawing diagrams. "Is it ready?" she asked.

"Yes," said Thisbe, sounding a bit stiff. She and Florence hadn't fallen back into their old friendly ways. Despite Florence's apology, it still seemed like she didn't trust her, and that wasn't something Thisbe could fix in an instant . . . or maybe ever. The trust had been broken on both sides, and it would take some real work to repair it. But for now Thisbe had other vital things to accomplish. She turned away from the warrior trainer. "Simber, do you think you can carry these cauldrons down the stairs without spilling them? Not yet—tonight, I mean. Also, how many invisibility paintbrushes do we have left, Seth? I need to go fishing without being seen."

"I'll check," said Seth, going to the components supply bag.

"Fishing seems dangerous," Rohan remarked. He knew better than to oppose anything outright, because Thisbe did what she wanted anyway. But there had been a lot of risk lately,

LISA McMANN

and it was exhausting him with worry. He blew out a breath that held all the words he wanted to say.

"I'll go instead," said Fifer. "You've worked hard enough today. I've had a long rest, and I'm actually pretty good at fishing these days."

"I'm going too," said Dev. "I'm the best with the net." He glanced sidelong at Fifer. "And I'm feeling good."

"Don't worry about using up our stash of invisibility paintbrushes," Florence said. "Aaron and I are going to make more components later with the rest of the supplies I brought."

"We didn't expect to use so many," Fifer explained. "But we had to cover the bones and cauldrons, too. The other group has a lot more, so they should be good."

"Great," said Florence. "Why do you need fish, though? We still have a little bit of food left from Artimé, don't we?" Florence didn't fully understand the ways humans needed food all the time.

"We need something to put in the broth to make the dragons eat it," Thisbe said curtly. "And I want to get this stuff down there for their overnight dinnertime. The Revinir knows we have the bones—she saw them and decided that we

LISA McMANN

were trying to be like her." She scoffed. "It's only a matter of time before she figures out what we're really trying to do with them."

Florence watched Thisbe curiously, but Thisbe refused to connect their gaze.

"Oh!" said Fifer, as a thought came to her. "By the way, Aaron, I've been meaning to ask—did you and Ishibashi use throwing stars as weapons to fight the Revinir? Because she's been injured. She keeps tugging at her throat, and her neck is swollen. She muttered something about Ishibashi."

Aaron was taken aback at the mention of the scientist, and it took him a minute to find his voice. "It all happened pretty fast," he said. "But he sent off at least two throwing stars before she retaliated. Perhaps he got one in a tender spot when her mouth was open."

"It sounds like Ishibashi might have helped us out more than he knew," Sky said. "If she's injured, she might not be able to fight with her usual gusto."

"Let's hope it gets infected," Dev muttered. "She deserves it." He shuddered, then turned to Fifer. "Ready?"

"Let's do it."

"Be careful out there," Florence warned. "Are you sure you can run fast if you have to?"

"We're both fine now," said Fifer. She didn't want anyone thinking she was still too weak to do things. And she really just wanted to see how Dev was doing. They hadn't had any time alone since they'd recovered from their injuries, and she missed him. "We're getting good at this by now."

"How are you going to hide the fish once you catch them?" asked Thisbe, worried.

"Inside my robe," said Fifer. "Don't worry."

"I'll bring a spear, just in case the dragons come at us," said Dev. "But the darkness helps too."

"All right," said Thisbe, throwing her hands up. She plopped down on a sofa. The rest of the team scattered to take care of other things. But Maiven came over and sat beside her.

"How are you?" Maiven asked. She studied her granddaughter.

Thisbe glanced over. "I'm fine."

"Is there anything you want to talk about?"

"Why?" Thisbe asked suspiciously.

"I'm just curious. You seem to be struggling. And as a fellow

LISA McMANN

leader of this land, I want you to know you can talk to me. Or ask me questions." She settled in.

"Thanks."

When Thisbe didn't say anything, Maiven smoothly continued like she hadn't noticed. "You know, I was in prison for decades."

Thisbe blinked, unsure where Maiven was going with this. "Yes, I know." But it got her thinking. "What was that like? Why aren't you more . . . ?"

"More what?"

"More angry?"

"Oh, I'm very angry," Maiven said. "I'm furious. But I'm saving it for this fight." She glanced at Thisbe. "Anger is a gift from your body. Did you know that? It's a sensor that tells you when you are being treated unfairly. Are you angry too? Because I would expect you to be, after all you did. And how that was received. And . . . how your brother is handling it."

Thisbe's mind whirled. She turned sharply. "I'm not an evil person."

Maiven's gaze sharpened. "Anger and evilness are far from the same thing," she said. "Don't confuse the two."

LISA McMANN

Dragon Fury » 268

Thisbe considered that. "But I think evil things some-times." She clamped her mouth shut. Maiven and the others didn't need any more reason to worry about her.

"Let me tell you about thinking evil thoughts," Maiven said with a chuckle. "When I was in prison, I planned out the deaths of everyone I came in contact with. From the king to the guards to the palace servants who happened by."

"Even Dev?"

"Especially Dev!" said Maiven. "He was the easiest because he actually came into my cell every day."

"But you never really wanted to hurt him, did you? He was feeding you."

"Exactly," said Maiven. "And I never would have. He was always very cordial to me, and I held him in high regard—I knew he was a slave to the king's family. But when a queen is trapped in a place with nothing else to do, sometimes she must plot revenge to keep her mind active. Now," she added, "understand I didn't plan to carry out any of those plots. But it was totally normal for me to think them. And that doesn't make me an evil queen, does it?"

"No, of course not." Thisbe pressed her lips together, not

sure what else to say. She'd been so guarded for so long that it felt wrong to somehow agree with Maiven, yet she was flooded with relief that the queen thought that way too. Despite her worries, Thisbe knew it had to be part of creativity to imagine evil things. Like Maiven, she'd never intended to carry them out. Maybe that wasn't actually being evil after all. "Samheed writes plays with evil characters," she mused.

"But he's not evil himself, is he?"

"It depends who you ask," Thisbe said slyly. "But no. Not in the slightest."

"His imagination for creating villains on the page makes him a complex person. And an imaginative one. Just like my thoughts make me. Those traits are very important for a queen or any other ruler to have."

Thisbe took a deep breath and glanced around, then said quietly, "So if I had a thought about what it would be like to join the Revinir and rule the land of the dragons, but would never really do it, that's not a bad thing? Would you still trust me?"

Maiven leaned in. "I've thought it myself."

"About me?" asked Thisbe.

"No. About me."

Thisbe's eyes widened. "What? *You've* thought about joining the Revinir?"

"Like you, I would never do it. But a queen must imagine all scenarios and think about every possibility for the sake of her people. It's my duty to consider everything, and look a few steps ahead of that idea to understand where it would lead. And obviously ruling alongside the Revinir would be horrible for my people, but I had to at least think it through in order to know that. Right?"

Thisbe nodded thoughtfully. She was more like Maiven and Samheed than she'd realized. If thinking evil thoughts made her more like them than the Revinir . . . well, that was all right. After a while she looked up at her grandmother. "I'm not sure how you did it, but you've made me feel better."

"I'm glad," said Maiven. "And once this is all over, I'm looking forward to having you in the castle with me. I am pleased to know you think like a queen."

"I hope we see the day when that happens," Thisbe said. But she knew how powerful the Revinir was.

"We will," said Maiven. "And soon. The Revinir's own evil

that she acted on—mind controlling everyone in sight—will be her downfall. Mark my words."

"I really want you to be right, Grandmother," said Thisbe. But while she'd been comforted by the conversation, deep down an uneasiness remained, because she still felt sympathy for the villain who had caused so much pain. And the thought of everyone looking to Thisbe to use the last obliterate spell gave her a stomachache. If she confessed all of that to Maiven, would the queen still accept her? Thisbe was too afraid to find out.

Once the broth had sufficiently cooled, Thisbe and Rohan removed the bones from the cauldrons and set them aside in case they had to use them again for another batch. Then they lugged the cauldrons over to Simber, who carried them down one at a time and left them at the bottom of the stairs.

Fifer and Dev went down too with the net and a spear. At the base of the tower they painted themselves and their items invisible. Catching hands so they wouldn't lose each other, and maybe also because they just wanted to hold hands, they moved swiftly but quietly to the riverbank halfway between two dragons. The beasts hardly stirred, though their nostrils flared as they seemed to pick up some human scent.

Within minutes the two had their first fish, which would have looked to an observer like a fish flopping up out of the water onto the shore. Fifer and Dev reapplied the paintbrushes to themselves and all the items before they became visible, then caught another fish.

"That should be enough," Fifer whispered. "We can make it back without reapplying. Let's go." She slipped the two squirming fish inside her robe, and she and Dev climbed the bank and moved swiftly across the lawn. Fifer nearly lost one of the fish along the way but heroically managed to keep it from flopping and sliding out her robe's armhole. When they reached the stairwell, Fifer dropped the fish into the cooled broth, one in each cauldron.

"Whew," Dev whispered.

"We did it," Fifer said. "Ready for step two?"

"I . . . yes." Dev was winded, but they were in this now, and they needed to keep going. They painted the cauldrons and themselves once more, then carefully lugged the giant pots back to the riverbank where the dragons gathered at night to fish for their food. The cauldrons would become visible in several minutes and hopefully entice at least one of the dragons to ingest enough broth to snap them out of the Revinir's mind control.

As they set the cauldrons down and turned to go back to the palace, they didn't see Pan, black as the night, with her nose twitching in the wind. She began sneaking toward them, low to the ground. Her long, ropelike tail switched back and forth through the long grass behind her as she noted how the grass also bowed enticingly in front of her, beneath invisible footsteps.

A Kiss in the Dark

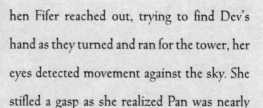

When Fifer reached out, trying to find Dev's hand as they turned and ran for the tower, her eyes detected movement against the sky. She stifled a gasp as she realized Pan was nearly on top of them. Her hand struck Dev's shoulder, and the two silently, frantically, found each other's hands. They squeezed hard, knowing better than to speak, acknowledging that they both saw the ruler of the sea coming at them. The dragon's normally coiled tail was fully extended, and it whipped toward them through the grass.

Fifer leaped over it, but it caught her ankles as it switched back the other way, curling around them. She gripped Dev's hand tighter and kicked, freeing one ankle. Seconds later she was airborne anyway, pulled by Dev, who'd apparently been caught by the tail too. "Put us down!" Fifer shouted, abandoning silence. "We've left you some food!"

Dev let out a small roar as Fifer struggled against the thin black tail, trying to kick free. She pulled out her dagger and stabbed at Pan's tail, wanting to connect just enough between scales to shock the dragon into letting go. The creature roared in pain and dropped them. They tumbled over the ground, then got back up and ran for their lives to the center turret, tripping and falling onto the stairs and climbing up to the first landing before finally coming to a stop in a heap, out of breath but uninjured. Safe. They lay stunned for a moment, arms and legs tangled together, as their invisibility wore off.

"Are you okay?" Dev whispered.

"Yes. Are you?" Fifer strained to see. His face was inches from hers.

"I'm fine." He stayed close, their bodies breathing hard together, and for a moment they stared into each other's eyes as they clung to one another. And then Fifer reached up to touch Dev's face. She slid her hand over his cheek, and then she leaned in and touched her lips to his.

Dev sucked in a breath. Then he kissed her back. And for a moment they lay there entwined before pulling away.

"I'm . . . sorry?" said Fifer, not sure what to say after kissing someone without asking permission first. She moved farther back so she could see him better.

"It's okay—I liked it," said Dev. And then both of them grinned. Their hearts were still pounding from the chase and the kiss, but they got to their feet with stars in their eyes, nearly forgetting about how Pan had almost just thrown them across the yard or squeezed them to death.

"You held on so tightly," Dev said, flexing his fingers.

"Did I hurt you?"

"No, I mean, that probably saved us. Since we couldn't see each other."

"I . . . didn't want to let go. Of you. Like, I couldn't."

Dev pressed his lips together to stifle his grin. He knew Fifer wasn't really someone who talked about romantic feelings or things of that nature. In fact, it was clear that she really didn't like touching people she didn't know very well. So this

LISA McMANN

seemed . . . momentous. "I like you," he began, as if he were going to say more, but there was nothing more to say. "I . . . I like you."

A flicker of a frown crossed Fifer's face. She wasn't sure how to answer. The truth was that she liked Dev, too. It was just . . . she'd never experienced feelings like this before with anyone, and they seemed weird. Especially when there were so many other things going on. So it was confusing. "We should watch the dragons," she said, straightening her robe.

"Of course," said Dev, and he took a step away. He was getting to know her cues pretty well by now. "Let's check the window."

They went to the window together. Fifer's cheeks were hot, and her stomach had butterflies. In the dark tower, she touched her finger to her lips where Dev's lips had been and remembered how soft and warm they'd felt. Warmer than she'd thought they'd be. But then she shook the memory away and peered out, looking for Pan.

The dragon had gone to the riverbank.

"Can you see the cauldrons?" Fifer whispered.

"Too far away and too dark," said Dev. "But they're sitting

right about where Pan is. And look—Arabis and Hux are coming to check it out too."

"Simber, are you watching this?" Fifer whispered, knowing the cheetah would be able to hear her from just about anywhere.

"I'm watching," he said in a low growl. "*All* of it."

Fifer froze. She and Dev looked at each other wide-eyed, then slowly turned their gazes upward to look through the spiral staircase. They could see Simber splayed on the steps a couple of floors above them, looking through the space. Fifer stifled a laugh, and then Dev hid his face in his sleeve.

They heard the statue chuckle softly.

"We're very intent on watching the dragons," Fifer declared in a serious head mage voice.

"And look," said Dev, turning to the window. "All five of them are gathering by the river now. Simber, can you tell if they're checking out the cauldrons?"

The staircase creaked as Simber moved back to the window, and Fifer and Dev exchanged a silent, mirthful glance. They leaned out their window, trying to see in the dark. All they could make out were the outlines of five large bodies.

"They've noticed it," Simber said softly.

The three continued watching, and up in the library Aaron, Sky, and Florence were gathered at the south window, and Maiven, Rohan, Thisbe, and Seth were at the west window to watch as well.

After a while Pan broke away from the others and headed back toward her assigned spot. Fifer elbowed Dev and pointed her out. They watched in silence through the open window as she stopped in her tracks. She shook her head, then looked all around, her nostrils flaring and her throat emitting a low grumble. She swung her neck around to look at the palace, and the light coming from the windows illuminated her face. Her eyes were open wide.

"She looks confused," whispered Fifer.

"She still looks terrifying," Dev replied. He'd never known Pan before she'd been put under the Revinir's mind control. The ruler of the sea was twice the size of her young dragons.

"Simber," Fifer whispered. "Call out to her. She knows you best of everyone."

"You rrread my mind," said Simber. "Pan," he called out. "Pan, it's Simberrr."

The dragon turned toward Simber's voice.

"That's different," said Fifer cautiously.

"Right!" said Dev. "The dragons haven't been doing that even when someone calls their name."

Simber lumbered down the stairs. "I'm going out therrre," he said.

"Be careful!" Fifer said. "We don't know if any of them will attack you or if their fire is hot enough to destroy you. At the very least, it can harm you."

"I'll be fine," the cat grumbled. Fifer and Dev squeezed up against the wall of the landing to let him pass. "Whateverrr the case, the brrroth seems to have had an effect."

With Simber slinking across the pavers in the courtyard, Fifer ran up to the library. "Pan seems to have been affected," she said, out of breath. "Can you get ready to start another batch of broth? There's no time to waste!"

"The fire's already going," said Thisbe. "Tell Simber to grab the empty cauldrons so we can fill them with water!" She and Rohan followed Fifer down to the ground level, where they joined Dev. Seth trailed behind. They all peered around the doorway.

Simber had crossed over to the lawn to approach the black dragon. Pan had smoke rising from her nostrils, but she didn't go after him. "Be careful," Fifer muttered, crouching in the tower doorway so the others could see over her. The last thing they needed was a fire-destroyed pile-of-sand Simber blowing around the lawn with no way to fix him because their own friendly dragons were trying to kill them.

"Please, please," Thisbe whispered under her breath. Rohan peered over her shoulder, watching intently.

Simber kept talking to Pan as he slinked toward her, throwing out memories to calm her down. "The people of Arrrtimé arrre herrre," he said. "The ones who made wings forrr yourrr childrrren."

Pan lashed her tail but still didn't attack or retreat.

"Move toward the cauldrons!" Fifer whispered. "We need them to make more broth!"

Simber switched his tail, signaling he'd heard her. He glanced to the right, toward the river, to gauge what was happening there with the other dragons. They were congregated at the cauldrons. "Pan," he said. "Yourrr mind is being contrrrroled by the Rrrevinirrr. But we'rrre trrrying to get you back.

You arrre the rrruler of the sea, but the Rrrevinirrr has you worrrking for herrr like a slave. That doesn't seem rrright, does it? You should be in charrrge."

Pan seemed even more confused. "What's . . . happening?"

"Yes!" Fifer and Thisbe whispered together. Rohan and Dev bumped fists. They knew that if Pan was asking questions like that, she was teetering on the edge of mind control. She needed just a little more broth to return solidly to them. It was working!

"See if you can salvage a little more of the broth for Pan!" Fifer whispered.

Simber turned toward the river and began walking slowly. He eyed the younger dragons carefully, knowing that any of them could attack at any time. "The antidote to yourrr mind contrrrol is forrr you to drrrink the brrroth we made forrr you. You've been underrr the Rrrevinirrr's contrrrol forrr quite some time now. It's been harrrd to watch, my frrriend."

Pan walked behind Simber, uncertainly at first, then more willingly. Then she noticed the other dragons and let out a low growl.

"Those arrre yourrr childrrren," Simber said gently, then named them. "All but Drrrock arrre herrre."

LISA McMANN

"Drock," said Pan, thinking hard. "The dark purple."

"Yes," said Simber, trying not to scare her with his excitement that she'd remembered.

"Is he . . . alive?"

"Verrry much so," said Simber. "He's the only one who withstood the mind contrrrol. He's been exceedingly helpful. He'll be thrrrilled to know you arrre coming back to us." Simber hesitated, then added, "Therrre's one thing you could do to help you rrrecognize all of us a little betterrr." He glanced over his shoulder at her as they approached the other dragons.

"What is it?"

"Drrrink a little morrre of the brrroth."

The other dragons stepped back when the ruler of the sea approached. They seemed to be in various stages of confusion as well, and two of them roared at each other before settling down.

"Is this what made me confused?"

"It made you rrrecognize me," said Simber. "If you trrrust me as yourrr frrriend, you'll drrrink morrre."

"I . . . trust you, Simber." Pan bent down over one of the cauldrons and began to lap up the dregs that remained.

LISA McMANN

As she did so, Hux the ice blue, who'd been the second one to get at the cauldrons, looked at the stone cheetah statue with confused recognition on his face. "Who . . . who are you? I know you." He looked to the others as if startled to see them. Then: "Mother!" he cried. "Mother, what has happened to us? Where are we?"

Pan looked up from the empty cauldron. "Hux," she said with a hint of wonderment. The two embraced, and the other three, not quite there yet, wandered in distress. Simber grabbed the empty cauldrons and loped back toward the palace, promising to come back with more as soon as he could.

While Florence hurried to update the people in the village of this new development, the five in the doorway erupted in cheers. Finally, finally. Pan and Hux were with them again. Something was going their way.

Once and for All

The Revinir was in a foul mood, partly because she'd wasted time feeling sorry for herself. Thisbe had gotten inside her head and taken up residence there, but the Revinir was kicking her out. Dev being alive and working with Thisbe had somehow helped her snap out of it and come to a stark realization—that there were no black-eyed children that could be trusted. She needed to change her goals.

It was time to get over it and take charge again. She didn't need anybody anymore. This life she already had, ruling her land while surrounded by mind-controlled people and dragons, was going to be just fine after all. It was a lot easier to deal with everyone and everything when there weren't any feelings involved. Whatever had happened there, when she'd allowed Thisbe to see her as a real being with emotions, had been a grave mistake. But that was over now. Dev, Thisbe, Rohan— they could all go die together.

"I don't need you, Thisbe Stowe," she muttered as she sipped warm dragon-bone broth. It was the only thing she could swallow now that her throat was so swollen from the infected wound. She couldn't even feel the sharp edge of the star anymore—the tissue of her throat had grown so inflamed that it had enveloped the weapon. It made her sound hoarse, like she had a very bad cold. "I don't need anyone. I've already got this land under my control. Sure, it's not quite how I wanted it. But I've changed my mind after that whole mess with the partnership. What was I thinking? It's going to be much easier on my own. The only thing standing in my way are those black-eyed children and magical intruders who think they own a piece of this place. They are sorely mistaken. And we are about to prove it to them." She turned and looked around, suddenly aware that she'd been saying all of this out loud to . . . no one.

A few glazed-eyed servants stared at the floor. A gray statue of a gargoyle looked out with dead eyes. The Revinir frowned at it. Why hadn't she noticed its ugliness before? When this was all over, she'd get rid of it.

Things were dead lonely in the castle. Now that the Revinir had been vulnerable and let someone in, it was hard to go back to this. But she convinced herself that it was the only way it could be now. She turned to Zel, whom she'd decided to add to her staff—she'd taken a sort of comfort in knowing that Zel had been Thisbe's servant for a time here.

"Zel," she said, "tomorrow we go to war."

"Yes, Revinir," said Zel.

"I want you to alert the staff and have the soldiers prepare the dragons. Send messengers to the other villages to let them know that it's time. We're going to march all the way to Ashguard's palace and take it over. And this time, none of my enemies will be allowed to survive. No black-eyed people, no mages or ordinary people, no statues—we must destroy them all."

"Tomorrow," said Zel.

"First thing," said the Revinir. "Tell everyone to gather outside the castle. We'll go together as one. People and dragons, and . . . me." She was her own category. The thought made her even lonelier.

Zel started to leave the room to do as she was told, but the Revinir stopped her. "One last thing," she said. "Have the soldiers and other dragons track down Drock the dark purple dragon. Imprison him in one of the dungeon cages, where he belongs. He's been tricking me, and I've had enough of it."

"Yes, Revinir."

"We'll execute him later," the Revinir went on, feeling a swell of excitement for the first time in days. "Yes. We'll execute him once all of his friends are disposed of. Or . . . maybe we'll just let him live and wallow in the sadness of losing every last one of them."

Zel nodded and left the room. There was no argument, no discussion. No one to suggest that the Revinir was making a series of bad decisions. It was refreshing in its own way.

Maybe she really could get used to this way of life again.

LISA McMANN

A Sky Full of Dragons

By morning, Thisbe and Dev had finished making the second batch of dragon-bone broth. Pan and Hux helped them corral Arabis, Ivis, and Yarbeck so they'd each ingest enough to bring them fully back to their own minds. Once that happened, they divvied up the rest equally to give them all an extra boost of safety against the Revinir's roar. For they would soon need it.

Matilda kept Charlie and Carina abreast of what the Revinir had said about changing her plan and wanting to do away with all the black-eyed children, and resigning herself to living with the fact that everyone in her kingdom would be glassy-eyed and dull until the end of time. She also told them the frightening news that the Revinir had called for Drock to be taken captive, which was met with anger and shock among all the dragons, humans, and statues. It reignited Thisbe's burning anger—when would the dragon-woman stop this madness? How low would she stoop?

Later, Matilda reported that whenever the Revinir left the ballroom, Kitten would chase after her to see where she was going, then run back to help Matilda find her when the coast was clear, so they weren't missing much, if anything. Charlie let Matilda know that the two were doing a great service that would certainly help the seven islands in the end. Carina passed everything on to Florence or Fifer in the library.

Shortly after the dragons had taken in the last of the broth, the Revinir began roaring. Matilda reported it, though the humans who'd drunk the dragon-bone broth didn't need anyone to tell them that. They and the dragons felt the effects—visions for the humans and an urge to join the Revinir for the dragons. But they'd all had enough of the correct broth to keep them on the right side of things. Still, the roaring made them restless. They knew the time to fight would soon come,

LISA McMANN

and no one knew who would end up victorious.

Fifer and Dev had been healing quickly, and they insisted they were up for the imminent challenge—not that they had a choice. This confrontation was going to happen when the Revinir decided it would happen. She was going to be in for a shock when she finally made her move, though. Would it be enough?

While Florence, Maiven, and Fifer were going over the minute details of their mission, including trying to come up with a solution to every possible thing that could go wrong, the inevitable word came from Matilda: The Revinir was on her way to Ashguard's palace, preparing a tremendous attack. Matilda and Kitten were hitching a ride in the back of one of the chariots, hoping to keep Carina updated on their progress.

Now all that remained for the army at Ashguard's palace and village was to step up to take the Revinir head-on. No longer needing to hide and not caring who the overhead dragons reported their existence to now, the giant group from the village vacated their homes and hiding places and organized on the streets, ready to march when they received the order. Carina called up the ghost dragons, who came in droves, while Lani, Samheed, and the black-eyed future rulers began moving to the palace.

Meanwhile, the team inside Ashguard's palace came down to the yard to prep the newly friendly dragons. Florence had already caught them up on the Revinir and all she'd been doing since they'd fallen under her mind control. Now they needed to lay out the plan to see if the dragons were agreeable to helping carry it out.

Fifer explained that over the past several days, she, Florence, Simber, Aaron, Seth, Sky, and Maiven, with input from the rest of them and the leaders in the village, had come up with a detailed plan that would hopefully take the Revinir by surprise and leave her defenseless. It was a plan that would involve the forest and hills, the square, and the underground tunnels, among other landmarks. And water, of course. They'd use magic and metal stars and spears and small rafts, all of which the people in the village had been feverishly working to build under Copper's direction during their time of hiding and waiting.

Fifer reiterated to them that water was such an important part of the strategy, and she explained why. Once she'd laid out the entire plan to the dragons, she asked their opinion of it.

"I think it's a fine scheme," Pan said. She and her children offered suggestions on how the dragons might help improve it. "We would be highly honored to assist you after all you have been through. After all you have done to free our minds. We only hope to see Drock freed soon and have him join us."

Seth piped up. "I hate imagining Drock in that dragon stall. It was horrible for him back when we fixed his wings."

Fifer nodded. "We'll get him out as soon as we can. Once we take care of all of this, we'll be free to rescue him."

The dragons were somber. They remembered their confinement all too well. And they felt terrible that they'd been fighting against their brother during these months under the Revinir's control.

The villagers arrived through the orchard, with ghost dragons flying in overhead. They spread out on the property, leaving room for the dragons to land. Fifer climbed up onto Florence's shoulders to give instructions.

She caught Dev's eye and smiled. He was wearing a new

component vest, which looked smart with his brown wool skirt. He smiled back encouragingly.

As Fifer watched the army assemble, hundreds upon hundreds of them, all giving up everything to help take down this enemy, she felt her chest tighten. This reminded her of the stories Lani had penned about Alex, when all seemed lost and he was trying to inspire his people in Artimé. She understood his emotion now. She was deeply moved by the people's generosity and vigor. Their abilities and their good cheer in the midst of this terrible time. She held her hand up to greet friends from Artimé she hadn't seen in a long time and watched as Seth reunited with his mother and the rest of his family. Kaylee and Daniel found Aaron—and Aaron all but collapsed in their arms. He'd been through so much. They all had.

When the personal reunions were over and the group quieted, Fifer signaled for attention. "Thank you all for coming," she called out. Her head mage robe fluttered in the morning breeze. "It's so good to see everyone again. You have all been given your assignments, and you know what to do. Team forest, raise your hands!"

Part of the army raised their hands and gave a shout.

LISA McMANN

"Hill fighters, where are you?" shouted Fifer, feeling something inside her chest swell up with pride and getting caught up in the spirit of things.

"Here!" cried another part.

"Leaders for the square, are you ready?"

The leaders of Artimé, Quill, Warbler, Karkinos, and the land of the dragons all gave a shout.

"And, Talon, you know what to do."

"Yes, indeed," Talon said sincerely.

Fifer nodded and turned back to the group. "I want you to know that this will be a difficult battle, but we *will* prevail. We will overthrow the Revinir because we must! Our lives and futures depend on it! And every one of you has a crucial part in this plan. Do your best," Fifer said. "And . . . do your *worst* against the Revinir."

A cheer rose up.

When the crowd grew quiet, Fifer's eyes misted. She tapped her chest and shouted, voice cracking with the memory of her fallen brother, "I am with you!"

"I am with you!" the crowd shouted back, tapping their

chests too, many of them looking teary-eyed like Fifer. They were doing this for their futures, but they were also doing it for Alex. He'd paved the way through the darkness and led the people of all the islands to peace. Now Fifer was following in his footsteps, and they felt a sense of calm and confidence. She had gone from being a dangerous child to a strong leader, and one they wanted to follow for decades to come.

Fifer stood overlooking them, taking one last moment to move her gaze through the ranks, to give the people and statues and creatures a nod and an encouraging smile.

"All right!" she announced. "Florence, we'll be looking to you. Lead the way!" Fifer climbed down from the warrior trainer's shoulders and jumped to the ground. Any tiredness or weakness from her previous injuries had disappeared. They had a job to do. The most important job any of them had ever faced. Were they strong enough to do it?

Most of the army had participated in previous battles, so it didn't take much work to turn them confidently in the direction of their most egregious and elusive enemy. They had one goal in mind, and that was to make it to Dragonsmarche before the Revinir did. And to take advantage of the dragon-woman's weaknesses. She was the only target, and they needed to destroy her. If others got in the way, so be it.

Thisbe's thoughts strayed often to the conversation she'd had with Dev the other day, and he caught her eye now as they went to find their dragon. "Are you doing okay?" he asked.

Thisbe nodded. "Yes. Thanks. I'll check in with you if I have any doubts."

He smiled encouragingly, which gave Thisbe strength. But it also reminded her of how much Dev had changed since he'd become one of them. He was like Drock—one of the unlikely heroes of this terrible time to rise up and give their all when no one expected much of anything from them. Not to mention, Dev making himself available to talk things through with and challenge Thisbe had been the kindest thing Dev had ever done for either of the twins, Thisbe reckoned. He didn't judge her or shame her for feeling sympathy for the evil monster, even though it might have seemed irrational and alarming to hear that she'd felt that way. She and Dev were similar, too, she realized with a start. They'd both experienced unhealthy relationships with terrible people. But they were going to come out of it together. And help each other.

Over the past few days Dev had gently reminded Thisbe of the horrific things the Revinir had done to her and other people throughout the years. And he was sure to press the truth—that the dragon-woman wouldn't stop. In fact, from Matilda's reports, it seemed she'd only continued to grow worse and more destructive since Thisbe had left the castle. Especially because Thisbe had deceived her.

Soon the army had climbed up on their various dragons. Simber paused next to Thisbe as she waited her turn to board a ghost dragon. "Arrre you all rrright now?" Simber asked her.

At first Thisbe didn't know what he meant. "Meaning . . . ?"

"About Emma."

"Oh." Thisbe studied the cheetah. He'd figured out her secret too. He'd probably heard the entire conversation she'd had with Dev from his perch on the stairs. "Yes. I think so. Thanks, Simber. I—I appreciate that you cared enough to ask."

Simber nodded. "Of courrrse I carrre." He hesitated; then

it was Thisbe's turn to board. "If you'rrre strrruggling, I'm always herrre for you."

Thisbe nodded, too choked up to respond . . . and too worried that she was lying to him about the Revinir.

"See you out therrre." Simber turned to get in position in front of them, and Thisbe climbed up the dragon. Simber was on her side. It was a good feeling, but it didn't shake the uncertainty Thisbe felt.

The dragons took flight. Simber and Talon led from the skies, watching out for the Revinir and her oncoming army.

Fifer, Dev, Seth, Rohan, and Thisbe greeted the others on board their ghost dragon, and eventually located Charlie near Samheed and Lani. They reunited with everyone and confirmed that all plans were in place. After a while, Fifer turned to Charlie. "Where are they now?" she asked him.

He was still for a moment while he communicated with Matilda. As Fifer waited for an answer, she realized that what she and Thisbe had with their mind conversations was similar to the gargoyles. Fifer would have to ask them for advice on how to strengthen the connection once things were back to normal. Charlie looked up, then used sign language to respond. "They're nearing the Grimere neighborhoods."

Fifer glanced ahead at Simber and called to him. "How close are we?"

"We might want to pick up the pace," said Simber. "I can't see them yet. Still too farrr off."

At Fifer's command, the front line of ghost dragons began to move faster, prompting the rest of their party to speed up too. "Anything else you can tell us, Charlie?" asked Fifer. She was antsy for information.

During another lengthy pause, Charlie's face turned serious. He signed rapidly, which caused Fifer to miss some of what he was saying. "What was that?" she signed back to him. "I'm sorry—I didn't understand."

But Lani had caught it all. She looked at Fifer. "He said that Matilda and Kitten have stealthily snuck all the way to the carriage closest to where the Revinir is walking, within listening distance to her. She's been ranting and raving, getting more and more heated as they travel. And they just overheard her giving orders to some of her soldiers."

LISA McMANN

"What were the orders?" asked Thisbe. Her voice was sharp with concern, and everyone nearby turned to see what was going on as Charlie began signing again.

Some of them gasped at his answer. Lani interpreted it so that Simber could hear. "The Revinir told her soldiers that she wants a team of them to turn around and march back to the castle. Down to the dungeon. To put Drock to death immediately."

A Side Trip

W hat?" cried Dev. "No! We have to save Drock!"

"She can't do that!" Seth said. "This is sick!"

"We must save him," said Carina, eyes hardening. "Drock was the only one holding us together for so much of this time. That the Revinir would do something this horrible proves there is no other option. We must end her reign forever, and make it so she can't reappear anywhere like she did before."

Thisbe clutched her stomach and cringed. She knew Carina was right. But she hated all of this.

303 « Dragon Fury

LISA McMANN

Simber heard what the Revinir was planning, and he immediately flew over to inform the other dragons from the seven islands that the Revinir was sending a team to put Drock to death. Word spread quickly, and the rest of the army was horrified, especially those who knew of Drock's amazing bravery. He'd saved them and their friends so many times and had been the only one to stave off the dastardly mind control. The Revinir must have discovered that he'd been faking it all this time.

"We have no choice," Fifer declared. "We must stop this right away! Drock is the heart and soul of this land. He was the only real representative of the dragons for months, until yesterday. And he has served all of us with dignity, respect, and bravery. We cannot let him down. Who will go after the soldiers to stop this?"

Seth, who'd been sickened by this news, didn't hold back or wait to be noticed. This was too important. "It should be me and Dev," he said with conviction. "We'll go on one of Drock's siblings. Dev and I both know the area well, and we can be spared from our assignments in the rest of the mission."

Dev nodded. "I agree. Drock is really special to me," he said. "He saved my life. Seth's right. We're the best ones for the job." He stood straighter. "And if you're not upset about this, you should be! Without Drock, many of us wouldn't be here." The leaders of Artimé and Drock's family all seemed thoroughly enraged.

"We must do everything in our power to end this madness," said Claire. "Once and for all. Now's the time for bravery from all of us."

"I'm going to grab a few extra components before we go," Seth said to Dev, reaching for one of the many component sacks.

Dev glanced at Fifer, part of him not wanting to leave the group . . . or her. But Seth's plan made sense. Dev knew the castle like no one else. Seth was familiar with the dungeon, and he had magical abilities that would put them at a huge advantage against a group of soldiers. Dev's fingers brushed Fifer's, and their pinkies entwined for a moment.

Fifer thought through what it would look like for them. Two of her closest friends leaving the safety of the group—was this what a true war was like? Side missions that would put some of her favorite people in grave danger? It made her more determined to end this tumult forever. Today. "All right," Fifer said decisively. She squeezed Dev's hand and gave Seth a solemn look. "Be careful."

"Let's not waste any time," Dev said, letting go of Fifer and picking up his spear and sword. "They have a large head start, but they're on foot. I think we can reach the dungeon first if we go swiftly. Arabis, will you take us?"

The orange dragon was anxious to save her brother. Once the troublemaker of Pan's five children, Drock had become the hero of all dragons, even if most of them didn't know it yet. They couldn't let him down when he was most vulnerable. "It would be an honor." The dragons landed to exchange passengers. The orange dragon looked over the people, creatures, and statues around her, and her eyes landed on Fox. "You come too," she said to him.

Fox blinked and looked behind him. Seeing no one else responding to the dragon, he turned back to face her and put his paw to his chest. "Me?" he asked.

"Yes. Come along."

Fox felt a wave of fear, but then he beamed. He'd been chosen for something important. He leaped into Seth's arms and waited to be taken aboard the dragon.

Dev looked at Thisbe. "Be strong," he said.

Thisbe nodded. She knew he meant with her conflicted feelings about the Revinir. "I will." A lump rose to her throat.

"Please stay safe," Fifer said to Dev and Seth. "We'll need your help when you return." Whatever her friends faced was unknown and dangerous, especially for Dev, since the Revinir had decided all of the black-eyed people should die. "Come back to us as soon as you have Drock safe and sound. You know the plan."

Seth nodded solemnly to the head mage, the girl he'd known since he was a toddler. "We'll be careful," he said. He checked his vest pockets and counted his components, even though he'd just counted them and grabbed extra a short time ago.

"We'll see you before you have time to miss us," Dev said, trying to sound lighthearted, but feeling a sense of dread. He hadn't imagined a scene where he and Fifer wouldn't be fighting together. What if something happened to her?

Fifer reached out and squeezed Dev's arm, looking him in the eyes. She felt a rush of warmth coming to her face, but now was no time to hide her feelings. "Come back to . . . us."

Dev nodded. "I will."

Seth looked on with a raised eyebrow. Something there seemed more intense than he'd ever seen. He turned to go, but then Prindi, one of the black-eyed girls, touched his sleeve. "Stay safe, Seth," she said.

Seth's face turned bright red. "Oh," he said, then tripped on a tree root in the road and nearly face-planted in the dirt. "Yeah." He fled to where Arabis had landed along the side of the road, and somehow he and Dev climbed aboard.

They took off, with Seth and Dev lying flat so that anyone below them along the route would think Arabis was flying solo. The dragon rose up high so she wouldn't be noticed as easily by any of the dragons that were coming this way. And off they went, disappearing into the clouds. The rest of the army took flight again, and Simber urged them to go faster now that they'd lost precious time.

"That was a sudden turn of events," Thisbe said, turning to Fifer. "But I think we can safely fill in the jobs Dev and Seth were going to do."

"I'm worried about Drock," Fifer said. *And Dev.* She knew that Seth would be okay—he had magic and was so much stronger as a mage compared to when they'd first entered the castle dungeon to fix the dragons' wings. He'd be able to take down any average human enemy, and mind-controlled soldiers weren't exactly quick thinking. But Dev only knew a few spells, and he was much more vulnerable. He could wield his weapons, of course, but he didn't have the armor of one of the Revinir's soldiers. She thought about the kiss they'd shared on the steps, and her insides twisted. She cared about Dev. A lot more than she'd thought. How had that happened? The progression of their friendship, their . . . whatever it was . . . felt slow and quick all at the same time.

"The boys will get there quickly with Arabis," said Thisbe, looking carefully at her. "They'll probably beat the soldiers on foot and be out with Drock before the soldiers even show up." She hesitated. "Did something . . . *more* happen with you and Dev?"

Fifer's face grew hot. "Why would you ask that?"

"It's just a feeling."

"I mean," Fifer said, "we're very good friends now, you know. Especially being stuck together for so long when you were away." She didn't look at Thisbe.

"I seeee," said Thisbe, tapping her chin. One corner of her lips tugged upward, but she worked to straighten it.

309 « Dragon Fury

LISA McMANN

"What's going on?" asked Rohan.

"Nothing," the two said sharply in unison. Fifer smiled at Thisbe. She knew that she knew, and *she* knew that *she* knew. It felt good for that to be out in the open between them, even if neither of them had said it expressly.

Fifer thought about how she'd never expected to like someone in that way, the way Thisbe liked Rohan. She'd really needed to know Dev extremely well before she'd even begun to think of him in that way. She knew from books and real-life stories that sometimes people had an instant attraction to each other, but that didn't seem to be the way it worked with Fifer. She hadn't felt one romantic thing about Dev until she actually trusted him, confided in him. Shared stories and really got to know him well. But now she and Dev had somehow transcended the friendship level, and it was a whole new set of feelings for Fifer. It was very confusing. But . . . good. Probably.

Too bad she didn't have time to process those feelings now, because they were heading straight into the biggest battle Artimé and the rest of the seven islands had ever faced in their existence. It would be nice if she and Dev would both get through this and share another kiss.

As the Dragonsmarche square came into view, Fifer's romantic thoughts were blown apart by Simber's deep growl. "The Rrrevinirrr is a thousand yarrrds ahead!"

The head mage's stomach flipped for a different reason this time. She blew out a breath, focused on the task. "This is it, then," she said in a low voice to Thisbe as the army landed near the square and came to a stop. Fifer slid down a dragon wing and met Florence and Maiven. The two moved swiftly out in front of the army and turned to face them. "All right, everyone!" Maiven shouted. "Disembark. It's time to take your places!"

Ambush

Half of the army from the seven islands, armed with components and capable of doing freeze spells, disappeared into the forest across the road from the square. A large group of the remaining ones, with components and nonmagical weapons like spears and swords, went to hide behind the hills on the opposite side. Then Kaylee and Sean, along with children Daniel, Ava, and Lukas, and several other mages who'd trained under Henry's medical direction, took magic carpets down to the lakeside. They carried small rafts and medical supplies with them. Once there, they set up a safe space and triage area in the cave where

Sky, Thisbe, and Rohan had hidden out. And they stationed a number of their people at the shore with the rafts.

Pan, Hux, Ivis, Yarbeck, and all of the ghost dragons flew down below the cliff near the crater lake to hide and wait for their cue. And Talon flew away, due east, on a mission of his own. The only ones who remained in the square were those whom the Revinir already knew were in the land of the dragons: Thisbe and Fifer, Rohan, Florence, Simber, and Aaron.

The minutes went by agonizingly, but Fifer didn't want to advance any farther toward the Revinir. The square was the perfect spot for the beginning of the fight they needed to have in order to beat the dragon-woman.

Nobody was sure exactly how many of their plans would have to be enacted thereafter to do so. Or if they'd lose anyone in the process. Perhaps, with all of them against her and her dumbed-down army, this would take a matter of an hour or so. They could only hope! The seven islands had never been more prepared than they were now, and they had covered absolutely every scenario they could think of in their planning. But nobody was counting on this going easily.

They could see the Revinir's dragons flying and swooping

LISA McMANN

in the distance, and soon her soldiers appeared in the road. The Revinir was a good distance behind the front line of soldiers, walking down the center with people and chariots all around. In the back of one, Matilda and Kitten were constantly communicating with Charlie and Carina behind the nearest hill.

"Seems typical," Thisbe muttered to Fifer as she eyed where the Revinir had planted herself in the group. "Sending her soldiers out in front to get attacked. That's very like her."

"Well, it's better for us," said Fifer.

"True." Thisbe glanced toward the hills. Carina, Sky, Lani, and Samheed were controlling things over there. Reza, Prindi, Asha, Crow, and several others were keeping the ghost dragons from forgetting what they were doing and meandering back to the cavelands. Henry, Thatcher, Scarlet, and other top spell casters waited, hidden by trees and giant rocks around the square. Carina rose up and gave Thisbe an *okay* signal, then slipped out of sight. All was well.

Thisbe turned and searched the forest. She couldn't detect anyone, but she knew hundreds of them were only a few feet back in the shadows and ash, behind the scorched trees. She clenched and released her fists, trying to keep her fingers warm and nimble, then touched the pocket where the obliterate spell was.

"She sees us," Rohan said. His hands trembled as they gripped his vest. It was his first battle in his own land . . . and the pressure was high. "Oh dear gods. Here she comes."

"She looks flusterrred to see us standing herrre," Simber said in a low voice. "She expected to surrrprrrise us at Ashguarrrd's palace."

The Revinir halted everyone, then took flight to get a better view of who she was facing. After a moment of looking around, she laughed. "That's it? No allies? Keep marching!" she ordered, and started toward the small group in the square.

"Everyone stand firm," Fifer commanded the people with her. "Florence, we're right behind you."

"Heads up, everyone," Florence called out in a soft voice to alert the hidden ones in the forest. Simber spread his wings, ready to fly or pounce or do whatever was necessary in case the Revinir struck.

"She won't attack," Thisbe murmured, almost as if she could sense the Revinir's thoughts—something similar had happened before in this very spot, so she didn't discount it. "She's still waiting for me to change my mind and join her. Doesn't she ever stop?" Her mind kept flickering to the conversation with Maiven, but she tried to stay focused.

The dragon-woman soared over the heads of her soldiers and landed in the square in front of them. Her neck was thick and bulging. "What in the name of the High Priest Justine are you trying to prove?" Her voice was raspy and sarcastic. She laughed hard, then winced in pain. "You lot look ridiculous. Did you come all the way from Ashguard's palace to fight me and my soldiers and dragons? I know you've been hiding out there. What a joke." Her gaze landed on Thisbe, and her eyes narrowed. "You're first."

Thisbe felt her lungs freeze. The eyes of hundreds in hiding as well as the leaders of Artimé were on her. She took a step forward and pulled out the last obliterate spell. "Are you sure about that?" she asked.

The Revinir scoffed but revealed her uneasiness by backing up closer to her soldiers. "You won't," she said breezily. "You're imperfect after all, aren't you? 'One of the most powerful mages Artimé has ever seen,'" she mocked. "If that's true, you're all a bunch of sorry weaklings. You can't even take out a single large target without mucking it up." She let out another laugh, then clutched her throat in pain and blew out a breath. "Come closer so I can blast you this time, Thisbe. You owe me. Let's get this over with."

Thisbe narrowed her eyes suspiciously. The Revinir was in serious pain; they could all tell. "You can blast me from there if you really want to," she said, holding her hand steady in the throwing position. "But you'll go down with me if you do." She pinched the obliterate component easily between her thumb and forefinger. Her heart raced, but her confidence soared. She had a theory. "Or maybe your throat is too injured for you to breathe fire. Is that it? Is that why you haven't tried to torch us already?"

"Yes," said Fifer, stepping in line with her twin. "We heard that Ishibashi really nailed you with a throwing star. What a shot, right into your big mouth. And is that a goiter in your neck? Very swollen." Fifer turned to Aaron, Rohan, Simber, and Florence. "You know, I think if we just leave, she'll die of the infection soon anyway. A matter of days. We could wait it out."

"I'm not dying!" the Revinir roared. "I'm stronger than

ever!" She winced again, and a bit of pus oozed from the corner of her mouth and plopped onto the ground. Gingerly she touched her dragon neck with her front claws, running them up and down the bulge there. "I'm perfectly fine and capable of flaming you to ash right now."

"Ah, but you're not doing it," Aaron pointed out. "There's got to be a reason for that. Are you afraid of our tiny army?"

The Revinir cast a look of disgust at the man who looked exactly like the evil mage she'd killed. Twins were the worst, she decided. Thisbe and Fifer. Alex and Aaron. And especially Marcus and Justine.

"Or perhaps you still feel a tiny bit of warmth in your heart for the friendship we had," Thisbe said. Florence gave her a side-eye that went unnoticed, and Simber turned sharply, then relaxed.

"Maybe she's afraid all of the seven islands will descend upon her if they find out she's taken us out," said Florence. "I'm quite sure they would come after you eventually. And they are a powerful lot. They could do you in."

"But she'd be dead by then, anyway, remember?" Fifer said, pointing to her neck and making a face.

"I'm not dying!" the Revinir screeched. The screech ended in a hacking cough that implied quite the opposite.

With the Revinir bent over gasping and unable to signal her army of humans and dragons, Fifer saw the chance she'd been waiting for. She lifted her hands and shouted, "Everyone move!" Immediately swarms of people came up over the hills and out of the forest, throwing spells and spears, not at the Revinir herself, but at her soldiers. The first wave had them laying down soldiers in the streets.

Confusion overtook the ones who remained standing, but they continued forward, not knowing instinctively what they were supposed to do and waiting for a command to halt them. The Revinir's eyes widened mid-cough—she realized what was happening but couldn't stop coughing. She took flight, moving erratically.

Thisbe took aim with her obliterate spell, muttering to herself that she needed to take the first good shot. But the Revinir's movements weren't trackable. She was clearly flying that way on purpose and moving quickly out of range. If Thisbe threw and missed, the spell could land in a group of their own people.

Stay strong, Dev had reminded her, and his words rang in

her ears. But this wasn't Thisbe being weak or protecting the dragon-woman, was it? She was protecting innocent people under the Revinir's control. That was a noble thing to do. With a frustrated noise, Thisbe put the obliterate spell away for a while. It gave her a slight bit of relief to do so, but she knew she'd have another chance later, surely. It wasn't going to be fun. But it was necessary. She had to keep telling herself that.

"Now, Asha!" Florence called out in the direction of the hills.

Seconds later, as the forest team sent another line of soldiers down with magical components, the mass of ghost dragons erupted from the crater lake area, right on cue, as if they'd all remembered what to do. They headed straight for the Revinir's dragons to press them back and keep them from attacking the humans once the Revinir could finally roar out an order to them.

Eventually, when she stopped coughing, the Revinir managed a shout of command, despite the pain that was clear on her face. Then the dragon-woman turned sharply in the air. She flew over the hills toward the crater lake to get out of range of every possible thing her enemies could throw at her. "You can't follow me down here!" she cackled, then coughed again.

"Excellent work, everyone!" Fifer praised as she ran after her. Simber galloped alongside Fifer. Leaving Florence in the square to look after the forest team as they went up against the rest of the Revinir's entire army, the remaining ones dispersed.

Rohan split off from Thisbe and ran to the center of the square to bring up the elevator. Fifer, Thisbe, and Aaron hopped onto Simber's back. Pan, Ivis, Yarbeck, and Hux soared up from their hiding spot behind the cliff, spraying fire at the Revinir before coming to land on the peak of the hill. Hux, with the squad of drop bears on his back, flew over the Revinir's soldiers and gave the signal to his riders. The adorable but deadly gray bears joyfully dropped from Hux's back onto the unsuspecting army, causing mass chaos.

The teams of leaders, black-eyed humans, top spell casters, and traditional fighters who'd been hiding behind the hill rushed up over it. Most climbed onto the backs of the three remaining friendly dragons, and Rohan joined one of them. Simber took off with the three Stowes aboard and set out after the dragon-woman. Hux returned to pick up the remaining fighters, and he and his mother and siblings chased after Simber.

After Rohan raised the elevator, six Artiméan mages from the forest team snuck through the crowd to it. They went inside and maneuvered it down and stationed themselves there, ready to take out the crypt keeper if they saw him. Then they sent the elevator back up so Florence could stack frozen soldiers inside and send them down. Once she did, the catacombs team placed them inside a crypt and directed the elevator back up for the next stack.

High above the lake, the Revinir finally regained enough of her senses to let out a stuttering roar to the mind-controlled dragons. Thisbe, Rohan, and the rest of the ones who'd ingested dragon-bone broth winced as the sound tore through them, triggering the images and urging them to join her side. They fought through it and continued on. Fifer urged Simber to sneak around the Revinir during this distraction and get ahead of her.

All around them, Pan, Hux, Ivis, and Yarbeck, with their riders, completed a circle in the air with the Revinir in the middle and slightly below, so they could pressure her downward toward the water. She'd have to make a bold, unexpected move to be able to break through, but she was outnumbered, at least for now.

Her mind-controlled dragons were being held back by ghost dragons. Her soldiers were being attacked by drop bears and frozen by mage spells. The enemy army would have to tire her out. Their fire didn't harm her, and all but Thisbe's obliterate spell was useless against her. The Revinir's injury would help them, but they didn't know how long she would be able to stay airborne—it could be a very long time.

The Revinir roared in anger and frustration as she realized what they were trying to do. "You won't wear me down!" she shouted, her voice raspy. She moved forward, sideways, and back, constantly darting to stay close to one of the friendly dragons and away from Simber, knowing that Thisbe still had the one spell that would end it all. And also knowing Thisbe wouldn't use it unless she had a perfect shot. Her darting about made it impossible for them to use spears against her too— there was no way to aim it up a nostril like they'd done with the red dragons. And any spear thrown that missed went spiraling down into the center of the lake, virtually irretrievable.

As the Revinir roared again for her mind-controlled dragons, who were still stuck behind the wall of ghost dragons, the volcano in the center of the water shook, then plunged under the water and disappeared, sucking thousands of gallons along with it.

"Hmm," said Fifer to her siblings and Simber. "All right, then." The three knew how unpredictable the volcanos were. Thankfully Florence and their team had also allowed for that. "Put plan B in place, Aaron." Aaron took out a send component, wrote something quickly, and sent it soaring off to the east.

A Sacrifice

Dev, Seth, and Fox flew swiftly on Arabis's back. It didn't matter now if any of the mind-controlled dragons saw Arabis flying the wrong way and snitched on her. They were going to be occupied for the next little while and hopefully detained by the ghost dragons, so they couldn't get to the Revinir anyway. Thus it was highly doubtful anything would be done to stop the orange dragon from breaking ranks. She flew freely, taking the most direct route over the village and hills and meadowland, with the castle in sight, stretching up to the sky atop its needle-shaped point of rocky land.

LISA McMANN

325 « Dragon Fury

Fox chatted along the way, mostly to himself. "Why do you suppose she picked me?" and "Wait until Kitten hears about this."

Dev and Seth were nervous about their task, but excited as well. Both of them had been able to relate to Drock in different ways. Seth had bonded with the dragon over their mutual bouts of anxiety and panic attacks, back when he was trying to free the dragon. Dev and Drock had both been alone against the world at the moment Drock caught him after he was thrown from the window.

The two boys shared their painful stories with each other, going into more detail than ever before. And even though each knew the general gist of the other's tale, going deep with expressing how they'd felt in their darkest moments really made them trust and appreciate each other on a new level. Fox shed a quiet tear while listening, and soon he, too, felt like *he'd* had a special connection with the dark purple dragon, even though he hadn't.

Before Fox had a chance to tell his story of how he and Drock were very close to being best friends, Dev pointed out a group of about ten soldiers on the road ahead of them. "That's what we're up against," Dev said. They were the soldiers that the Revinir had sent to kill Drock.

"Should we stop them? For good?" asked Seth.

Dev winced. "They're under the Revinir's control. I don't want to hurt anyone who might not have done this if they were in their right mind."

Seth nodded. "Good call. But if they attack us, I'm not holding back."

As they neared the castle, Arabis overtook the Revinir's group on the ground. Seth, Dev, Fox, and Arabis wouldn't have much time inside before the soldiers would get to them, but they had some, which was better than none. Certainly, though, with Arabis and the two young men there, it wouldn't be too difficult to keep them from meddling. They weren't sure how many people were still guarding the castle, though. The unknown was making Seth nervous.

Arabis glided straight into the grand entrance of the castle and came to a stop on the malachite floor. The huge room was ornate, and empty of people. Had the Revinir left her entire castle unguarded? That seemed a bit . . . naive. Dev, Fox, and Seth slid off Arabis's back. "Arabis, you lead

LISA McMANN

with Dev and Fox," said Seth. "I'll cover us from behind."

The group turned the corner at the rear of the entry room and entered the downward-sloping hallway that wound around, leading to the dungeon. Both boys felt a wave of nausea as they did so. They'd spent too much time down here—Dev feeding prisoners for as long as he could remember, and Seth attaching new wings to the captive dragons and doing exactly what they'd come down here to do today—free Drock. In fact, Seth's anxiety was hitting him hard right now, being in this place with such horrible memories, but knowing Drock was down here too somehow gave Seth the ability to continue. It had taken that understanding between them for Seth to successfully calm Drock enough to attach his new magical wings and free him. He was hoping they could help each other again.

"Drock has really changed so much since the last time he was down here," Dev said to Arabis as they traveled down the slope. "He's become such a steadying force. You won't believe it."

"I look forward to seeing my brother no matter how he has changed," said Arabis.

"I wasn't exaggerating when I told you he saved my life," Dev said from up front, even though he'd already told them both. "He was watching what the Revinir was doing. Flying around the tower, knowing what she was like, and what she might do. Drock caught me in free fall. He risked his own life to take me to safety in the cavelands." Dev peered around a curve in the hallway and held his hand up for silence. With the area clear, he proceeded and continued the tale. "For the first time in my life I felt like someone cared about me."

"I didn't know all of that," Arabis said softly.

"Drock has always been my favorite color," Fox piped up. "Yellow," he added proudly to prove he knew his colors.

Seth chuckled softly and didn't correct the small statue as he walked backward, following Arabis. He listened intently for the sounds of anyone coming and was ready to freeze them. Or he'd strike them with a heart attack spell if they were aggressive enough. There was no sound at all from behind them, but they could hear distinct banging in front of them, coming from the dragon stalls. Arabis craned her neck around the corner and saw her brother tied up and muzzled as he'd been back when they were all held captive.

"No guards down here," Arabis said as she thundered forward. "Drock! It's Arabis!"

A violent crash was the answer, and once Seth could get around Arabis to see what was going on, he ran to join Dev in front of what used to be Arabis's stall. Drock was tethered inside tightly and muzzled. He had no food or water. The sides of the stall were cracked, as if Drock had repeatedly thrown his back end into them. But even if he could manage to knock down the walls, the muzzle, attached to the ceiling, held his face pointed upward and his neck stuck in place. It kept him from hitting the sides hard enough to make much progress. But he was trying with all his might.

"Drock!" Dev cried. "We're going to get you out of here!"

"Drock," Seth said in a calm voice, climbing up the ladder that was built in between the stalls. "Great news. Your mother and siblings are no longer under the Revinir's spell. We found a way to break it. So Arabis is here with us. And she's back to normal. Isn't that great?"

"I am also here," said Fox, dodging Arabis's powerful tail. "Your friend Fox. Remember?"

"They have him strung up so tightly," Arabis said in a worried voice. "Can you hold still, brother? So the humans can free you?"

Drock trembled, but he couldn't stay still.

Seth climbed up higher and nearly got thrown when Drock slammed into the wall again. "Careful, there," he said, holding tightly and continuing to climb all the way to the top. He leaned toward Drock's head so the dragon could see him. "Hi," he said softly. "Remember me?"

Drock's body seemed out of control, and he slammed the wall again. Seth lost his grip and slipped off the ladder. He hit the top of the wall and, with a cry, fell headfirst toward the floor.

"Seth!" Dev cried.

Arabis coiled her tail and stuck it out below Seth just in time to soften his fall.

"Whoa," said Seth, getting to his feet. He took a deep breath and blew it out. "Okay, let's try this again." After a moment he climbed back up. This time Arabis kept her tail coiled around his waist, just in case.

"Drock," Seth said from the top of the ladder. "Take a few deep breaths if you can. I know it's hard. Just breathe. Remember? We did that together before."

"He's traumatized," said Dev. "Being down here again is a nightmare for him."

"It's not great for me, either," Arabis said anxiously, "and I'm completely free."

"I'm doing just okay," said Fox, sniffing around.

"Come up here with me," Seth said.

"Who, me?" said Fox, looking up.

"No, sorry—I meant Dev. Can you?" Seth slung his leg over the top of one side of the stall and hung on to the ladder to make room for Dev.

Dev set his weapons down and climbed up. He leaned over as Seth had done so that Drock could see and smell him properly. "Hi, Drock," he said. "It's Dev here. Remember how you saved my life? Well, we're here to save yours now." Dev noticed that the dragon's nose was cracked and dry and his skin was more wrinkled than usual. "Arabis, can you find a way to give Drock some water?"

Arabis released her tail from around Seth's waist and went to the far corner of the room, to the well that was used for dragons and prisoners. She sucked some water into her mouth, then returned and lifted her head up to where Drock's was. Her snout could just barely reach his. She let a bit of liquid dribble over Drock's nose and soak in. Then a little more.

LISA McMANN

Drock seemed to calm slightly, though Dev and Seth still had to steady themselves for the occasional slam against the side. The two young men soothed the dragon that had meant so much to them at different times in their lives.

"Keep it coming slowly," Dev told Arabis. He stroked Drock's neck between the chains. "There. Stay steady. You're doing great. We're going to get you out of here." Dev glanced at Seth. "Seth is going to climb up and try to get the muzzle off you so you can breathe better and talk. Then we'll take the tethers off your neck, and we'll work our way down. It won't take long if you can hold still."

Drock trembled, but he tried not to buck at the walls.

"Ready, everyone?" Dev said. "Go ahead, Seth."

Seth climbed carefully until he was standing on top of the wall. He used the ceiling to steady himself as he walked, and Arabis kept her tail at the ready. "Stay still, Drock," he said. "We made it through this last time, and we can do it again. We've got some soldiers on our tail, so we're going to try to hurry, okay?"

Dev looked up sharply at the hallway, having almost forgotten there were soldiers coming. "Fox," said Dev calmly, "will you go up the ramp and have a sniff around to see if anyone's approaching?"

Fox pranced over to the ramp, happy to have a job assigned to him. He started up the ramp hesitantly, sniffing and taking a few steps, then sniffing again and running a good distance. He put his nose to the ground and ran around the first curve, and then he stopped at the sound of boots and froze. "They're coming!" he whispered, but no one heard him.

As Seth reached up to place his hand around the muzzle so he could dissipate it, Fox came tearing down the ramp. "They're coming!" the little statue whispered again.

Arabis turned sharply away, ready to attack, which set Drock bucking against his chains again, knocking Seth off the top of the wall for a second time. Seth hung on tightly to the muzzle and swung as Drock squealed in pain from the extra pressure. Arabis turned back to try to help, and Dev stood helpless, his weapons on the floor.

"Get them, Fox!" cried Dev. "Get the soldiers!"

Fox stood still for a moment, his mouth slack and tongue out. Then he charged wildly and leaped at the first soldier, sinking his claws into the man's chest and yipping like mad.

The man, startled, began flailing to get the thing away from him and set off a mass confusion behind him. He slapped at Fox. Fox clamped down hard on the man's chin and growled. The soldier finally grabbed the creature. He yanked Fox's claws out of his chest and his mouth from around his chin, and flung the carved-driftwood animal hard against the dungeon wall. Fox broke in half and slid to the ground, immediately turning gray and lifeless.

Dissipate

While still dangling precariously from Drock's muzzle, Seth shouted at the sight of Fox breaking in two. With his free hand he swiftly dealt three heart attack spells at the man who'd done it, dropping him dead. Dev stared, frozen in place. Arabis swung her neck around and flamed the rest of the soldiers, knocking them flat and leaving a few running for their lives back up the ramp.

Seth's hand began to slip, and he frantically kicked out, trying to catch the wall with his foot. "Help me!" he yelled while Drock continued to wail in pain. "Arabis, lift me up a little!"

Drock began bucking again, and Dev leaned over and tried to hold Seth up a bit to take some of the pressure off.

Arabis returned and grabbed the back of Seth's vest in her mouth, lifting him slightly and trying not to stab him with her teeth. Then Seth, hanging on to the muzzle but being extremely careful not to touch any part of Drock, took a deep breath, concentrating. Trying to calm down so that Drock would calm down too.

"That's it." Dev soothed the dragon. "Stay still now. This piece-of-junk muzzle is coming off in just a second."

Seth, sensing a quiet moment, whispered, "Dissipate." And the whole muzzle disappeared into thin air. Drock let out a roar and slammed his body around.

"Get his neck chains!" cried Dev, and then, in a moment of recklessness, Dev leaped onto the base of Drock's neck. He held on tightly with his arms and legs, stroking the dragon's neck with his hands, and kept talking in soothing tones. "You saved me when the Revinir threw me out the window, Drock," he said. "You carried me to safety in the cavelands. And you stayed with me. You told me that I'm worth saving, and I'm here to tell you that you are worth saving too." He paused for a

LISA McMANN

breath and noted that the dragon seemed to have calmed a bit. So he continued talking, not always sure what he was saying but knowing the tone of his voice was the most important. "You're worth saving. Every single one of us, no matter what anybody tells us, is worth saving. Especially you. You have been the hero of all dragons, Drock. You've worked tirelessly to try to bring this land back when all was lost. You never gave up, even when everything was so bleak. Even when your own mother and siblings didn't recognize you. And now we're going to get you out of here so you can continue your brave work. Because I have to tell you something: Things are looking up. Your sisters and brother and your mother are *all* back with us, in their own minds. And the rest of the dragons will be soon. I believe it, and Seth believes it too, don't you, Seth?"

"Dev's right, Drock," Seth said smoothly as he secured his grip on the next chain and waited for the right moment to dissipate it. "Things are going poorly for the Revinir for the first time ever. She's already been injured, and we need your help to finish her. Can you stay still so I can take off these chains around your neck?"

Drock groaned, reminding them how hard it was for him. Dev and Seth comforted the dragon, with Arabis doing everything she could to help talk Drock through this procedure. Finally he settled. The boys exchanged a relieved glance. Seth held on to the looser of the remaining chains and repeated the dissipate spell, then swiftly moved to the final one.

When he was freed, Drock bent his stiff neck all the way to the floor. He coughed and snorted and hummed a sorrowful noise. Tears filled his eyes, and his whole body shook.

After a while, with everyone else remaining still, Drock's breath evened out.

"Deep slow breaths if you can," said Seth. "You're going to be okay. Just a few more chains around your legs and tail and we'll blast this door down."

Arabis touched noses with Drock, and that seemed to calm him further. "We're almost there, brother," she said. "Stay with me."

Soon enough Drock was free. Arabis torched the door until it dropped off, in flames. The dragons stomped it out, and everyone exited the stall safely.

Seth, who was exhausted after doing the very intense dissipate spell multiple times, went over to Fox and picked up his front and back halves. "I don't know how to fix him," said Seth, "but a few others do. Aaron or Fifer should be able to. Fox really helped us out after all, didn't he?"

"I knew he'd have a good nose," Arabis said. "He did well."

Dev nodded and petted the frozen fox's head. His fur had turned back to driftwood during this broken time, and the grayness made the poor little fox look like there was no way he'd ever been alive at all.

They were starting to push the soldiers' bodies out of the way so they could hurry back to the battle when they heard a clanging sound coming through the hallway that led to the prison cages.

Seth's eyes widened. "What was that?"

Dev stopped and listened. "There are still prisoners down here." Without consulting the others, he moved to the doorway and peered into the darkness. "Hello!" he shouted. "Is anyone alive down here?"

A few weak, desperate, ragged voices answered.

Dev gripped his head, feeling terrible. These people had

been abandoned. Left for dead. He dropped his hands and turned to Seth, Arabis, and Drock. "Hey, Seth," he said, "is there any chance you can use that dissipate spell a few more times before we go?"

A Familiar Stranger

rabis and Drock couldn't fit through the doorway to the dungeon that held the human prisoners, so they headed outside, carrying Fox's broken body. Drock needed some fresh air, and the dragons could stand watch in case anyone else came back. They stationed themselves at the entrance so nobody else could go after Dev and Seth while they freed the remaining prisoners.

Inside, Dev led Seth through the intricate passageways of the dungeon he knew so well. As they maneuvered their way in the dark, Seth lit some of the torches on the walls with origami fire-breathing dragons so they could see better. The two checked every cell looking for anyone who was still alive. Sadly, some had perished from the smoke back when Maiven had been rescued. Others had died of starvation or ill treatment once the Revinir took over—she clearly hadn't done much to care for the prisoners. They'd been forgotten.

Dev's blood ran cold. "I don't think anybody replaced me," he said, glancing back, as he agonized over the deaths of the people he'd served food to for years. He hardly knew anything about them—yet they were in his life every day. "These people have been brutalized and neglected!" He felt angry tears welling up in his eyes. After all they'd been through, after all the suffering they'd experienced, how could Dev not feel empathy for each one of these people he'd served? They were a lot like him, only much worse off. At least Dev had been free to move about. "It's making me sick."

"Me too," Seth muttered. Was there no end to the horrid deeds of the Revinir? He followed closely behind Dev. Seth was ready with components in case anyone was hiding down here to jump them. He knew well enough by now that nothing was ever safe in this place . . . or anywhere, lately. Would things ever get back to normal?

Seth had come a long way since his first trip here with Thisbe and Fifer on the back of Hux the ice-blue dragon. He remembered all of the strife they'd been through. Crossing the gorge and nearly falling into it ranked up there on the panic charts—Seth had thankfully fainted during the worst of it. And nearly failing to save the dragons had been enough to make Seth never want to come back here again. Yet . . . he'd done it. And he'd watched Alex die. Just the other day he'd watched over Ishibashi's body. It was almost too much, yet there was nothing he could do to stop this. Only fighting together, everyone giving their all, would get them through it.

Seth shook his head. This had become a terrible place to visit, yet he couldn't seem to stay away. It made him more determined than ever to help take down the Revinir so that they could all go home and hang out in the lounge and talk to friends and try to find their normal lives again. But had it all changed permanently? Was there no going back to the way things were?

He thought about his friends. Would Thisbe stay here? Fifer would go home, wouldn't she? She was the head mage,

LISA McMANN

after all, but she had black eyes too, so would she want to stay in the land of the dragons? He hoped not—Artimé needed her. But what about Dev? It seemed like there was definitely something going on between those two. Something that made Seth feel unsettled.

If Seth was being honest with himself, he'd actually thought that Fifer sort of liked him for a while. She'd wanted to dance with him at the masquerade ball, but then she'd acted like she didn't really like him after that . . . which might have been his fault, he thought ruefully. He'd surmised after a lifetime of hanging around with the twins that Fifer just didn't like hugs or touching, and that was okay with him. But she didn't seem to have that same rule with Dev. He'd seen her touch his arm, entwine her pinkie with his. Hold his hand. That was not the Fifer he knew. But if she felt something for Dev? That was cool with Seth. He and Thisbe and Fifer had started off on a rocky relationship with Dev, but Seth had seen the way Dev had been with Drock. And he felt sure that the former slave had the very best things inside him.

Seth had someone different popping into his mind lately,

LISA McMANN

anyway. The black-eyed girl he'd gotten to know a bit during their time in Artimé . . . the one who'd told him to stay safe. Was there something there?

"There's someone here!" cried Dev, jolting Seth back to reality.

Dev spoke to a woman in the common language, too rapidly for Seth to understand. Seth hurriedly dissipated the woman's shackles, and they helped her up. Dev draped her arm over his shoulders to assist her in walking, and they continued searching for survivors. They came across a few more, and they started to wonder how they were going to help them all.

"I've got a component for that," Seth said. He pulled out a wadded-up bunch of moss and separated it into pieces. Then he cast them to make magic carpets and sent the freed, ailing prisoners to the base of the sloping hallway by the dragon stalls to wait.

After freeing two others, Dev turned down the last corridor and nearly tripped over someone. It wasn't a prisoner—just a man sitting on the damp floor, looking despondent.

"Hello?" Dev said uncertainly—it could be a soldier, but he

wasn't wearing a uniform. When the man didn't respond, Dev bent down. "Are you . . . alive?"

"I am alive," the man said in a familiar voice. "I'm . . . fine."

Dev took a closer look. "Mangrel?" he said, incredulous. "What are you doing way over here?"

The crypt keeper hung his head. "I ran away from the catacombs yesterday. I can't be there anymore, all alone, day after day. Just me and a million bones. And then the Revinir sent a message that I had to report to the castle drawbridge to fight with her against all of you, and I just . . . I couldn't do that. So I went as far as I could go until I collapsed of exhaustion, and I . . . I guess I fell asleep here."

Dev was deeply puzzled. "Why in the world didn't you just take the elevator to the square and get out that way?"

The old man was quiet for a moment. "I haven't spent much time outdoors in a really long time. I go up in the elevator but come right back down again. Underground feels safer to me when I'm alone. But this dungeon . . . this place is horrible too. Even worse than bones."

Dev signaled for Seth to go ahead and check the remaining cells while he talked to Mangrel. "Listen, the war that the

Revinir has been threatening has started. The people from the Seven Islands have come to help us. We're all trying to remove the Revinir from power and restore the land of the dragons to its rightful rulership. And we could use your help with rescuing these prisoners. They're malnourished and weak." He gave Mangrel a sharp look. "And, well, you kind of owe us all one, you know?"

Mangrel looked up at Dev and nodded. He eased to his feet. "I do. I know it. I'm glad to help you. Maybe . . . maybe that's all I need." He was quiet. "Thisbe really got to me."

Dev narrowed his eyes. Was Mangrel about to do something right for a change?

"It's been gnawing at me since you all escaped," Mangrel admitted. "I've had a lot of time to think about what she said."

Stranger things had happened. "Let's go, then," said Dev. "We've got no time to waste."

Seth returned with the last prisoner, an old man who was grumbling as Seth tried to help him walk, fighting him off and insisting on doing it himself. As they were near the exit on the other side of the castle by now, the four of them took the shortcut by going up the stairs to the giant entrance. They crossed over to the ramp side of the castle that would lead them back down to where the other prisoners were waiting for them. As they stepped into the dazzling light and paused to let their eyes get used to it, the old prisoner grumbled again and yanked his arm away when Seth tried to steady him. Mangrel turned sharply at the man's voice. He took in a breath. And then he whispered, "Ashguard? Is it really you?"

About a Boy

Dev gasped and stumbled backward, bumping against the wall of the castle entryway and gripping it as if he were about to fall. *Ashguard? The curmudgeon?* Dev had never known the man's name—he'd been the grumpy one who wouldn't even speak to Dev when he'd brought him his food. But was it true that all this time the man whose palace Dev had claimed, and then reluctantly unclaimed because it appeared to belong to Asha, had been on Dev's daily food delivery route? Was there any shred of hope that he was still somehow kin? Maybe a great-uncle or a very distant cousin . . . anything would be better than nothing—which is what Dev had experienced his entire life. Maybe there would be some way to find out. Dev was grasping. But it was all he had to hang on to.

Seth ran over to Dev, thinking he'd gone faint with all the strenuous activity after his recent injuries. But Dev waved him off and stood on his own. "I'm just winded," he said. He watched the old man carefully to see what else he would say and scanned his face. Would he admit to being this person? And did Dev look like him, even a little bit? The man was so ragged and dirty, it was hard to tell. Dev could see his black eyes shining with unshed tears, and his expression violently trying to fight off his emotions after being freed.

The prisoner coughed. "Aye, 'tis me," he said grumpily. "Though I can't imagine anyone would recognize this mess. Blasted king had me chained up these past many years. Barely survived the fire, thanks to being on the far end of the dungeon." He looked up. "Who are you, then? Do I know you?"

Mangrel knelt, his hands trembling. "Sir, it's your servant. It's—"

"Why, so it is!" the man bellowed. "Mangrel. I'd never forget you. Why are you looking so sickly? Get up. Off your knee—I'm nothing to be bowed over!"

"I—I—" Mangrel seemed unsure how to answer. "It's a long story," he said. "And not interesting. Besides, we're at war. These boys are trustworthy. We must go now and get the other prisoners out of here."

"Anyone who has freed me is dependable in my book."

"Right," said Dev, tongue-tied to be in the presence of this legend. "Good." The man hadn't seemed to recognize him as the food deliverer, which left Dev with a bit of a hole in his chest. But it had always been dark down there, so it made sense. He brushed it away and went with Seth toward the ramp. Mangrel, feeling indecisive, took a few steps after them.

Dev saw him coming and motioned him to keep following. "Come help us, Mangrel. You stay here, um, Ashguard," he called as they rounded the corner to the ramp. It felt strange to say his name aloud. "We'll be back shortly. If you need anything, there are two friendly dragons out front."

"Aye," said Ashguard grumpily. "I'm fine to wait. I've waited years. A few more minutes is nothing."

"Great." Seth went first, ready in case any hidden soldiers had emerged—one could never be too sure. But this time there were only the prisoners they'd rescued. They'd helped themselves to water from the well. One was peering anxiously into the prisoner area, expecting Seth and Dev to come from that direction.

"All right, then!" Dev announced. "Let's get you all out of here, once and for all."

"Who are you?" one of them asked.

Dev was taken aback once more. "I'm . . . Dev. Nobody anyone would know."

"I recognize you," said another. "You're the one who stopped coming with food."

Dev's face showed how shattered his heart felt. Seth saw it and jumped in to explain to the prisoners that Dev had also been taken prisoner by the Revinir, and that she was to blame for their ill treatment.

Mangrel helped the boys carry the prisoners up the ramp. They let them down to rest near Ashguard. When they were all accounted for, Seth ran out to tell Arabis and Drock what was happening. Arabis came into the entryway to pick them all up while Dev quickly raided the castle kitchen for food and water. Finally they were all on their way back to the action, with Seth and Dev worrying privately about what they were

LISA McMANN

going to do with their surprise group of guests to keep them safe.

"There's always the cave by the lake," Seth said. "The hospital ward will be set up there."

"Kaylee and Sean should be able to assist them," Dev agreed. "That's the best plan, I think."

"I'll let Sean know we're coming with visitors so they can be ready." Seth penned a send spell and sent it off.

"Hey, Seth?" Dev said as they watched the message go.

"Yeah?"

"Thanks for having my back."

Seth flashed an understanding grin. "Same to you."

Along the way, Dev gave the newcomers a quick rundown of everything that had occurred since the Revinir took over the castle. Then Seth detailed what the people from the seven islands were doing to try to bring the proper leaders back to the world. For many of them, this was a lot of new information. Dev couldn't stop staring at Ashguard, trying to gauge how he was taking the news.

With guilt weighing on him, Dev interrupted. "I— Sir,

w-we've been using your abandoned palace as a home base," he stammered. "There's been quite a lot of damage to it. Not from us—from the weather and from dragons and . . . well, mostly dragons." He searched the curmudgeon's face anxiously to see if he would blow up in anger. Then, before he could, Dev added, "Oh! And your granddaughter Asha is alive and fighting with us. She's quite good at magic, too. You know . . . Asha . . . I presume? You remember her? She remembers you."

The man's face changed from grumpy to incredulous, and then tearful. "Asha," he whispered. "Alive and well? I'm shocked. Are you sure?"

"Yes, she's well, and she speaks fondly of you."

The man's eyes glistened again, and he buried his face in his hands for a long moment before looking up. "And did they ever find her brother?"

Seth and Dev looked at each other. "I don't know anything about that," said Dev.

"She mentioned something briefly about a sibling once in Artimé," said Seth. "I believe he's dead . . . or . . . I don't really know. But it didn't seem . . . positive."

The man sighed. "That is what we all thought—Asha

wouldn't remember him, which perhaps has spared her some pain. When Asha was sold at auction and my daughter killed, I went into hiding. But the king's people found me. They ravaged my palace and village and took me and so many of my villagers to the dungeon."

"Indeed," said one of the others. "I am one of them, sir."

Ashguard gazed at her with sorrow etched in his face. "I am sorry I didn't protect you better," he said. All traces of grumpiness had dissipated for the moment.

"The king spared me from the dungeon," said Mangrel, "but he assigned me to the catacombs to assist the Revinir. That's where I've been all this time."

"Stuck underground, like me," said Ashguard. "Only a few miles away, connected by tunnels. A different world, wasn't it?"

The crypt keeper nodded. "Yes, sir."

Ashguard turned to Dev. "Who else among our people is alive? Anyone?"

Dev listed the black-eyed children, but the man didn't recognize any of their names. "And Maiven Taveer," said Dev. "She's—oh. You know her, of course."

"Maiven?" said Ashguard. "Our dear queen? I can't believe it!"

"Yes," said Seth. "We found her in the dungeon some time ago. We were able to get her out during the fire. Thisbe had a vision about her that led us to go after her. And it turns out that Thisbe, who is partly responsible for these battle efforts, and her twin sister, Fifer, who is the ruler of an island called Artimé across the gorge, are Maiven's granddaughters."

"Literally unreal," murmured the man. "This news has certainly lifted my spirits." He took a breath and let it out, and he seemed to straighten up a bit. "Well, I look forward to seeing my old friend Maiven again."

"We have some work to do before the reunions can happen," said Seth, watching the war scene slowly appear in front of them as they closed in on the village and square. Mages were freezing soldiers, and Florence was hoisting them into the elevator. "Looks like things are under control up here, at least." He called to Arabis. "Can you please bring us down to the cave where Sky, Thisbe, and Rohan lived, near the lakeshore? That's a safe place for our new friends to rest. You should see familiar Artiméans down there waiting to take in our patients."

LISA McMANN

"I will do exactly that," said Arabis.

"And, Drock," Dev called, "are you feeling better?"

"I'm doing all right now, thanks to you," said Drock. "Traumatized. But feeling much more like myself now that I'm free. I'm thrilled about the news of my family, and ready to end this dictatorship once and for all. And burn down that godforsaken castle. If I never go back there, it will be too soon."

Ashguard seemed aghast at what was happening to the dragons. But other shocking things were taking place in front of them. The ghost dragons had formed a wall in the sky to keep the rest of the mind-controlled dragons away from the fight. And when he could see the strange living statue they called Florence and her team of magicians shoveling frozen bodies into the elevator, the curmudgeon didn't know what to think, other than that he'd missed a lot being locked up for years. He was clearly out of his league when it came to fighting styles.

Drock broke off from the group and, carrying Fox's halves, went down to the square to check in with Florence while Arabis swooped down to deliver the rescued prisoners to safety in the cave by the lake.

While Arabis carefully maneuvered to land in the small space at the edge of the water, everyone with her was staring at the sky above the lake. The circle of dragons and Simber slowly closed in and pressed the injured Revinir lower over the water she so feared.

But Thisbe, riding on Simber's back with Aaron and Fifer, watched the cornered dragon-woman dart around in an attempt to stay alert and alive. The memory of her conversation with Maiven returned to her, and this time something stood out. They'd talked about how Samheed wasn't evil despite writing about evil villains in his plays and musicals, but they hadn't mentioned the one person in their party who'd done the most horrible, evil things in real life.

Thisbe turned and glanced behind her at the complicated mess that was her brother Aaron; then she studied the Revinir again. The unsettled feeling inside her grew exponentially. After a moment of thoughtfulness, she pushed the obliterate spell deep inside her pocket and whispered a spell to lock it in place.

The Crater Lake

The line of the Revinir's soldiers kept marching up the road toward Florence in the Dragonsmarche square, for the Revinir hadn't told them to stop. As the soldiers progressed, Florence and the forest crew of mages continued to freeze, capture, and transport them to the catacombs. The crew down there filled up the various crypts and locked them when they were full. Then they went back for more until the elevator was starting to groan from so much use.

Astrid, Gorgrun, Quince, and the rest of the ghost dragons were the saviors of Florence and her team, and they made this task very successful, for they unceasingly got in the way of the mind-controlled dragons so that they were rendered useless. The Revinir's dragons became combative whenever she roared for them to help her, and they fought hard against the ghost dragons, but the huge ghostly creatures were a tough match since they were incapable of being injured. As long as Florence reminded them what they were supposed to be doing, everything went according to plan.

But Fifer, Thisbe, Aaron, and the rest were in a stalemate with the Revinir over the lake. Dozens of Artiméans, led by Ms. Octavia, lined the shore all the way around, and some of the people stationed themselves on rafts in the water in case someone got knocked off their dragon and needed rescuing. The volcano stayed down. Pan, Ivis, Yarbeck, Hux, and Simber kept the pressure on the Revinir, trying to drive her down to the water—to the place they knew she didn't want to go.

A suffocating sense of dread had washed over the dragon-woman when she figured out what they were doing, and the shock at the sight of Pan and the others turning on her had given her quite a fright. How had they managed to do that? Did it have something to do with the bones Thisbe and the others had stolen?

Instead of becoming overwhelmed and fearful, the Revinir only got angrier and more sure that they wouldn't succeed. Now and then, as she darted erratically trying to get past them and keep away from Thisbe and her obliterate spell, she was able to slip through or sneak out below the ring of dragons and Simber. But they always managed to stop her and bring her back to their air cage again, forcing her lower each time.

To them, it was a matter of wearing her down . . . and with any luck, her injured throat would contribute to her finally giving up. She hadn't blasted them with fire yet, but that didn't mean she couldn't. Perhaps she was playing them—time would tell. The job they were doing required stamina and patience as well.

"Be ready with your obliterate spell," Fifer whispered.

Thisbe frowned and didn't take it out, but Fifer didn't notice.

"Cast it now!" Fifer said. "No wait—don't."

"Fife, stop," said Thisbe.

"Now!" Fifer whispered. "No! Dang it! Never mind!"

"If you don't stop doing that, I'm going to use it on you," Thisbe muttered.

Aaron laughed, then quickly stopped, and he and Thisbe exchanged dubious glances. They'd hardly spoken since Thisbe had explained everything. And it was uncomfortable being stuck this close to each other, with only Fifer between them, making things more tense.

"You have to stop doing that to me," Thisbe said to Fifer. "It's making me nervous. Seriously, the pressure to get this spell done right after everything that's happened is overwhelming. There was a reason Alex never wanted to bring this one back. Don't forget that."

"Sorry," Fifer muttered. "You're right."

Aaron scoffed. "You haven't even taken it out of your vest."

"That's beside the point," snapped Thisbe. "The time isn't right!"

Aaron knew he probably wasn't helping the situation, and he felt bad about it. But he and Thisbe were having problems they'd never had before. And it was difficult to navigate them, especially when his feelings were such a mess after Ishibashi had died. He'd been irrational and harsh—he knew that. But everything was upside down in his world. He'd barely had a moment to talk to Kaylee in person about it before they had

LISA McMANN

to go their separate ways. But the one thing Kaylee had said to him was "Be kind to your sisters. They've been through enough."

And the weird thing about that was Kaylee didn't even know that he and Thisbe had been at odds over this. She just had a sixth sense about such things. And she was almost always right. Aaron sighed as they hovered in this endless standoff. "Sorry, Thisbe. You're right. Let's not make the situation even more tense, all right, Fifer?"

"Sorry," said Fifer.

"Thank you." Thisbe breathed a sigh of relief. She'd put off the dreaded moment even longer.

The Revinir was nowhere near total exhaustion yet. She was constantly dodging inside the circle and trying to stay a large distance from Thisbe, and far enough from the other dragons to keep them from spraying fire on her—not that they could harm her that way, unless they got right in her face. But the main thing was to keep away from her former confidant. The Revinir didn't know how many of those rotten spells Thisbe had left, but one was all she needed. And the girl seemed to have gotten her confidence back after her fumble in the cavelands. If she could keep away from Thisbe, she might have a chance to sneak out of this dragon jail they'd created and break free for good.

But why weren't the mages firing anything else at her? Probably because they knew their components would just go to waste. And no spears? She saw that they had plenty of them. If they hit her in the neck just right . . . The Revinir touched the bulge and winced. The scales were sparse and spread apart because of the stretched skin there. That made her vulnerable. She quickly moved her claws away so they wouldn't get any ideas.

Whatever their ultimate plan, this weird game they were playing was working—it was threatening her mind more than anything, and that was a bit frightening. Worse than being physically challenged. After all, the Revinir had flown all the way to Artimé and back in one session before—she could stay in the air for a long time. But she hadn't had a giant infection back then. She growled and roared again for her dragons to assist, though it was fruitless and only hurt her throat more. Still, she could feel the fire there, simmering. She'd use it if she had to.

It wasn't fair that the ghost dragons were keeping her mind-controlled ones from helping her. Those dragons belonged to the Revinir, and she was their leader. They all followed her. It had been an unwritten rule that they must do so. That's why she'd ordered Drock put to death. She'd suspected for a while that the dark purple dragon had somehow escaped from her power, and he'd proven it recently by giving Thisbe and Rohan a lift out of the burning forest. The Revinir had noticed. And now that dragon was going to pay. She would take down the rest of them too, if only she could fight properly and use her army of dragons.

Thoughts like these drifted through the Revinir's mind as she tried to figure out how to get out of this mess. It wasn't like she was terribly worried, now that she'd gotten over the shock of the ambush. Her dragons would push through the wall of ghost dragons eventually, and then the Revinir would show these annoying people what obliteration *really* looked like. It was such a shame Thisbe had turned on her. A deep shame. They could be working together right now to rule everything. Had the Revinir done something wrong to cause her to leave? She couldn't imagine what.

Why the enemy was keeping her flying here over the lake, was peculiar, though. She was still far enough above it to feel only mild fear about the water, but what was more concerning was that they were doing this at all. Did they somehow *know* that she had a deathly fear of it? Had they figured out her trauma related to that? Or did they merely see it as a strategy to tire her out and keep her from landing, now that the volcano was down? That had to be it.

But then she remembered the journals she'd written so long ago and wondered if there was something in them that had made Thisbe suspicious about it. Paranoia began to grow inside the Revinir's mind. But she refused to panic even when things were looking dire.

Arabis and Drock appeared, coming up from the lakeshore carrying Dev and Rohan. The Artiméans cheered as the dragons soared toward the circle, and the Revinir's jaw slacked. How did Drock escape? Had she become delusional? Maybe this painful infection was affecting her in unseen ways too. She did feel a bit weaker than normal, but that was probably just from flying in a small area for hours. Either her mind was playing tricks on her, or this enemy really had a lot of

LISA McMANN

surprises for her. . . . How many more could they have?

Overwhelming anger at Thisbe resurfaced. The girl had thwarted all of the Revinir's plans, hopes, and dreams, unraveling everything over the past days. The Revinir watched as the people and dragons surrounding her reacted joyfully over Drock's return, and with the distraction, she knew it was the time to make a move. She darted at Simber and tried not to hold back as she let out a mighty flaming roar, not caring how much it hurt. Fire shot from her mouth, and while she cried out in pain, she kept the flames coming.

Caught off guard, Simber reared back in the air, trying to protect his riders with his chest and wings, while the three Stowe siblings reacted with their own weapons. Fifer sent sailing one of the spears Dev had made, coupled with a handful of heart attack spells, trying to point them into the dragon-woman's mouth. Aaron shot metal stars at her like Ishibashi had done in hopes that he too could place them in an unprotected spot. Thisbe gritted her teeth and agonized. She knew that the evil dragon-woman had to be stopped, but as much as she wanted to pretend everything was fine, why did she have to be the one to do it?

"Thisbe!" Fifer hissed. "Come *on*!"

Thisbe started. She quickly released the spell on her vest pocket and pulled out the obliterate spell. Then she focused on all the awful things the Revinir had done. Frantically she searched the skies and connected eyes with Dev on Drock's back. He gave her a solemn nod. She had to do this. Trying not to collapse, Thisbe stood up on Simber's back so she could see over his wing.

"Aaagh," Thisbe gargled, leaning over and supporting herself on the back of Simber's head. "I think I'm going to faint." It wasn't the height this time, making her feel sick, but she didn't care if her siblings thought it was.

Fifer was on her feet in an instant, holding her sister's arm. "I've got you. Give me the spell. I'll do it."

Thisbe froze. Then, with a shaking hand, she set the pebble into Fifer's outstretched palm. Without hesitation, Fifer took aim and flung the obliterate component at the flames, shouting, "Obliterate!" Aaron yanked the twins down as the Revinir's fiery blast grazed them.

Simber let out a mighty roar as his ears, nose, and parts of his chest and wings turned to sand and fell into the lake. His

LISA McMANN

flight pattern, largely altered by this and the blinding fire, left him bobbing out of control, trying to right himself.

The Revinir was expecting the obliterate spell, and the fact that it came from Fifer rather than Thisbe threw her for only a split second—not enough to matter. She lunged toward it and deftly deflected the component with her claws, batting it back toward Simber. It detonated halfway between them, throwing both parties backward.

The Revinir somersaulted and dropped a short distance before catching herself. But Aaron, Fifer, and Thisbe went flying off Simber from the force of the explosion, and the three siblings and Simber all fell from a terrifying height to the lake below.

The Battle Is On

Thisbe screamed as she fell, then blacked out. Aaron yelled and threw a handful of heart attack spells at the Revinir, missing wildly as the dragon-woman righted herself in the air. Fifer managed to cast a magic carpet for herself, but her aim was off, and she went plummeting past it and it couldn't catch up to her. Simber tried and failed to stop himself from falling, and he hit the water first with a huge splash and sank.

Jim the winged tortoise, who'd been hovering below, slowly swooped just in time to catch Thisbe, and the army of squirrelicorns soared in and grabbed the other two. Their bodies

LISA McMANN

snapped and whiplashed from the sudden stop, but they might not have survived at all if they'd hit the water at that speed. Drock came to their aid and transferred them onto his back for Dev and Rohan to look after.

Seconds later, when the ghost dragons above the square looked down to see what had happened, the Revinir's dragons took advantage of the distraction and burst through a space that had formed between them. A stream of them rocketed toward the Revinir to assist her.

"Finally!" the dragon-woman screamed. Then she coughed and hacked and cried out in pain.

"Attack!" cried Lani in the circle, ever focused and seeing an opportunity. The people on the friendly dragons set off a round of spears. The Revinir curled her neck and covered her vulnerable parts, and the spears bounced off her and fell into the water. The mind-controlled dragons came straight for the seven-island dragons, instigating an in-air fight between them. The Revinir stopped hacking and started looking for a way out.

In the square, Florence and the rest of the forest team finished freezing and jailing the hundreds of soldiers who'd come along to assist the Revinir. The warrior trainer heard the obliterate explosion and saw Simber and his riders fall, and thought the worst when she saw the Revinir still flying. She rushed over to the hill and ran up it so she could look down into the giant crater. With a relieved breath she realized the three Stowe siblings were being transported by Drock, but the Revinir's dragons were attacking the rest of their team with raging fury. Everything that had been working so beautifully up until now was starting to fall apart. It was time to change plans. Luckily, Florence and the others had thought of that.

"Gorgrun! Quince! Astrid!" Florence shouted. The three ghost dragons landed in the square near the hill Florence stood on. The warrior trainer ordered all the forest fighters to climb aboard Quince and Gorgrun. "Keep away from the dragon-to-dragon conflict if you can," she instructed the dragons, "but try to swoop in now and then to distract them and give our people a chance to throw their spears."

She turned. "Everyone!" she shouted to the rest of her army. "Our leaders are being pummeled and they need our help to drive the mind-controlled dragons back! Time to switch from magic to your spears, arrows, and throwing stars. Try to hit

LISA McMANN

the dragons in their sensitive spots! Inside their nostrils and mouths! Let's go!"

Florence went up to Astrid and climbed aboard, then strapped her legs into a harness she'd created after her fall the last time—she wasn't going to let that happen again. She adjusted her quiver on her back, and once Astrid was in the air, Florence pulled out an arrow and her bow. "Do what you can to point me at the Revinir's face," Florence instructed the ghost dragon. "Let's see if we can end this once and for all before anybody else gets hurt." She was silent for a moment as she nocked the arrow, then mused, "Wouldn't it be something if we came away from all of this without a single death?"

On the Ground

Thisbe awoke on Drock's back to find Rohan's anxious face above hers. "You all right, *pria?*" he asked.

She blinked a few times, then sat up. "Oof." She gingerly tested her muscles, then shuddered as she recalled the fall. "Glad I blacked out for part of it, anyway. Is everyone else okay?"

"We're still waiting for Simber to surface," Fifer said, her voice grim. She checked herself over as well and tried not to grimace with the pain. Dev hung back but watched worriedly.

Aaron rubbed the back of his neck, then touched a sore spot on his head. His fingers came away wet with blood. "I'm not

LISA McMANN

even sure what happened. My memory is a little fuzzy after that."

"I cast the obliterate spell," Fifer said, "and the Revinir charged toward it and batted it back at us before it could detonate. It exploded in the air, but the blast hit Simber hard. I hope he's okay."

"He was in one piece when he fell," Drock said.

Aaron still seemed confused. "But why did Fifer—"

"I had a better angle," Fifer said, clipping the words. "I didn't miss—the Revinir just anticipated it and rushed toward us, which caused her to swat it before it could hit her and explode. It was a really smart move on her part, to be honest."

"So that's it for the obliterate spell." Aaron closed his mouth.

"Yes," said Thisbe, tight lipped. "That was the last one."

Drock brought the rattled Stowe siblings to the shore to get treated for their injuries, collect their wits, and wait for Simber to emerge. Once the three of them appeared to be all right, the dragon took off again with Dev and Rohan to rejoin the battle.

Landing on a winged tortoise wasn't exactly soft, but Thisbe admitted it was preferable to hitting the water in the middle of the lake—especially since she'd fainted. The impact could have made everything worse from that height. And Jim had done his best to use his wings to help cushion the fall. Thisbe waved her thanks to him, for he was back over the lake, taking long, slow flaps as he usually did, waiting for the next mage to fall perfectly onto his back.

Fifer watched the water anxiously until Simber's face broke through the surface. He found his way to the shore and limped onto the sand, tattered wings dragging on the ground. He was so distraught that he didn't even bother to shake the water off. He'd taken the brunt of the damage from the Revinir's flames followed by the obliterate explosion. His face was blackened with soot, and parts of his nose and ears had melted off. He looked a sad and hideous sight compared to his former self, but it was even worse when he took a running leap to test his wings—he could no longer fly properly. Not safely, either, especially with passengers aboard. He jerked and spasmed in the air, then crashed to the ground. After a moment, the giant cheetah got up and went to a patch of shade to lie down and mourn.

Thisbe glanced uneasily at her brother and sister and Simber. She'd failed them at a crucial moment. She hadn't been

LISA McMANN

able to go through with it. And now they were all suffering.

"When this is over, we'll get you home," Aaron told Simber. "Pan can carry you. Then I'll fix you with the proper magical sand from Artimé's shore. It's going to be fine. Better this than have you melt away completely. At least you're not frozen at the bottom of the lake. We'd have a hard time repairing you down there."

Simber grunted.

Fifer knew enough to leave Simber alone for a while. She handed healing herbs to Aaron and Thisbe from the metal container she kept inside her robe, and the three sat awkwardly and assessed the situation as things grew loud in the sky above them.

It was a sickening show and so hard to watch as Drock rejoined with Dev and Rohan, who valiantly threw their spears whenever Drock could get close enough to the Revinir. The three looked on as Seth, Prindi, Reza, and Asha, on Ivis, did the same, seemingly with no fear.

After a moment, Thisbe dropped her face into her hands— this could have all been over, but somehow she'd messed up again. She'd continued feeling sorry for the evil Revinir, despite everything. Despite Dev, despite Maiven, despite her own better judgment. But there was something else, too. Something that seemed to be at the root of all of this, only Thisbe had just begun to realize it. She struggled to stand, then moved gingerly a few steps away from her brother—she just didn't want to talk to him right now. Would he blame her for the cat's disfigurement next? Hold that against her forever too? How hypocritical that would be.

But Aaron didn't say anything like that. In fact, he seemed to be wrestling with his own thoughts. And all three of them really just wanted the medicine to kick in swiftly so they could rejoin the battle.

Thisbe kept her eye on the Revinir, who had nearly broken free. Thankfully some of the ghost dragons had moved in to keep her stationary above the lake, trying to slowly drive her downward toward that water she hated so much.

The girl felt a pang. It was a cruel thing to do. And even though the Revinir had done things a thousand times crueler—she'd killed Álex and Ishibashi, tried to kill Dev, and sentenced Drock to death!—Thisbe was struggling. The Revinir was

LISA McMANN

only getting worse, and many hundreds of people and dragons had suffered because of her. Thisbe had to help the others stop her. There was no doubt about that. But there was still something big that Thisbe couldn't get past.

Because of that, it was almost a relief that the obliterate spell had been used up, and now there were none left. It was so violent and destructive that Thisbe just couldn't handle using it ever again. No one should! It could have destroyed Simber completely! No wonder Alex had said he never wanted to bring it back after *he'd* missed with it. He'd been right, and Florence and the twins had been careless to keep trying. They shouldn't have done it. Although . . . Fifer had managed to use hers properly on the red dragons. That was one success and three failed attempts. Not a good record.

Thisbe felt a rush of painful emotions now that some of her numbness had worn off. She kept thinking of Alex and how she'd disappointed him right before he'd died. And now she had a growing issue with Aaron that she couldn't seem to say out loud. But she knew she had to, or she'd never get past it. She agonized for a while, and then, knowing she only had two siblings left—both of whom could have died in that last encounter—she turned to them.

"I want you both to know the absolute truth," she said. In the distance, Simber's ears twitched.

"I thought you told us that already," said Aaron sarcastically.

"Aaron, stop," said Fifer.

"Sorry," Aaron muttered.

"Everything I told you was true," Thisbe continued. "But there was something I didn't tell you because I was scared for you to know."

Fifer reached out for her sister's hand. "What is it?"

Thisbe took a deep breath. Her heart pounded in her chest. "I messed up the obliterate spell the first time because I felt sorry for the Revinir. And I couldn't use it this time either, for the same reason. It's not because I was afraid of heights."

Aaron and Fifer stared.

Finally Aaron said, "You feel sorry for that monster? How could you possibly—"

"Yes," said Thisbe. "It doesn't mean I think she should

be allowed to do what she's doing. And I don't want to be her partner. But she was a little girl once, with feelings, and people hurt her. And that's what turned her into this monster, I think. So I care about the person she was. And I felt like I saw glimpses of that person when I was stuck in the castle with her, trying to trick her."

"Thisbe," Aaron began, but Simber let out a low growl, and Fifer shushed her brother for the second time.

"Aaron," Thisbe said, "I know you are upset with how I handled things, and you're having trouble forgiving me fully for everything that has happened. I understand that, and perhaps we'll always clash because of our perspectives on this issue, even though we used to be really close."

"That has nothing to do with what you just confessed!" said Aaron. "This dragon-woman killed our brother! She has to be eliminated!"

Now the girls stared at Aaron, who'd used the loaded word that Quill had coined for sending Unwanteds to their death.

But Thisbe wasn't about to challenge him on that when there was so much more to say. "People saw glimpses of something good inside of you once too, Aaron—after you'd done some pretty unspeakable things. So my question for you is: How can you not at least consider pardoning the Revinir after almost everyone pardoned *you*?"

Aaron recoiled. The silence among the three Stowes and Simber was deafening. Fifer flashed a hard look at Thisbe, and Thisbe dropped her gaze and stared stonily at the ground. She'd only said the truth. And it had to get out there, or it would continue to eat at her inside.

After a long moment, Simber spoke up. "Aarrron was worrrth forrrgiving because he was sorrry forrr what he'd done. And the Rrrevinirrr isn't sorrry, and she isn't stopping. That's the differrrence."

Thisbe looked at the statue, and once she'd thought that through, she nodded. "You're right, Simber. I know that in my head. But my heart won't let go of Emma. That's why . . . that's why *I* can't kill her. I'm not saying someone else shouldn't. I'm saying I can't. And if you don't understand that, then what do you have to say for the graciousness people extended to you when you were at your worst?"

Fifer remained silent, seeing that the other two needed to clear this up without her.

LISA McMANN

After a while Aaron looked up. "You're right, Thisbe," he said. "You're right about everything you said, even though it was hard for me to hear it. And . . . I'm proud and happy to have a sister who holds so much compassion and forgiveness. I think I need to beg for you to forgive me now, after how hard I've been on you lately."

Thisbe choked up. "Of course," she whispered. "I just want you to know . . ." She paused, unable to get any more words out.

Aaron couldn't speak either. A trickle of blood from the cut on his head dripped onto his shirt, staining it.

Thisbe took a deep breath and tried again. "I just want you to know that I love you. I really love you so much, like more than anything. And I want us to be close again like we were before."

Aaron's chin trembled. He wiped the blood away and pressed his lips together. "I love you, too."

Thisbe continued. "You might not know this, but Alex and I had been fighting when Fifer and I went to the land of the dragons that first time. I never saw him after that, and I think about it every single day. I'm sick about how we were never able to talk things through. I know he was so disappointed in me, and I feel like . . ." Her voice broke once more, and she took another moment to let the brokenness pass. "I feel like if it happened again, with you, that I could never forgive myself. So I'm turning to you now with the most sincere heart, despite my faults and mistakes, and I'm asking you to forgive me, too. I want my brother back." After that, the tears began to fall freely down her cheeks.

Aaron sat, still stunned, but then he nodded and swallowed hard. He got up and embraced her. The two gripped each other as if their lives were in danger—which indeed they were. Fifer looked on, tears streaming down her cheeks.

Finally they pulled apart. Aaron leaned back to look Thisbe in the eye. "There's more I need to explain here. I've always been stubborn, no matter how hard I try to fight it. And even though you had no part in Ishibashi's death, I wanted to blame someone, and I admit you were an easy target. But not for the reasons you think."

Thisbe blinked. "Why, then?"

"Because I thought your mistakes were somehow *my* fault."

"Whoa, wait a minute," Fifer said, finally barging in. She held up her hand to her brother. "I wouldn't call them mistakes," she chided. "We had a very well-plotted plan that very nearly worked."

"Right, right," Aaron said. "That was a poor choice of words. And now I get what you were doing. But the thing is, I was the 'bad' twin my whole life, and to some people I still am, as you know so well. And I thought that maybe you, too, Thisbe—that you had some level of deviousness inside you. And I felt like that was my fault. So it was more than me judging you, or being mad at you. It was . . . me being mad at me." His tears ran down too. "I felt like *I'd* failed again."

Thisbe sucked in a breath and blew it out, long and low. "Wow," she said. "You said something like that in the moment before I turned to cast the first obliterate spell at the Revinir. But I didn't get it then. And I never understood how hard you were on yourself until now. But let me tell you, I get it now. In a big way." She shook her head. "Sheesh, Aaron. Do you think you'll ever be able to just be carefree and happy?"

"Maybe if you stop reminding him how awful he used to

be," Fifer suggested, and Simber let out a laugh in spite of himself.

Aaron pressed his lips together and glanced from one sister to the other. "I don't know," he admitted. "But a few things have changed recently. And . . . I'm going to try."

Thisbe reached out and took his hand. "So, are we good? Forever and ever? No matter what happens?"

"We are good forever and ever," Aaron said.

"Me too?" asked Fifer.

"Yes. All of us. We are forever bonded together by this moment. And if anything ever happens to any of us, we can all look back at this instant, in the midst of battle, along the shore of the crater lake, and know with full certainty and peace that we are good."

Thisbe smiled, then blew out a breath. "Thank you."

"And do you know what else?" said Aaron.

"What?" asked Thisbe.

"Alex and you are good too."

Thisbe felt her heart thud. She'd longed for those words, knowing she'd never find out the answer. "How could you possibly know that?"

Aaron's crooked grin made a rare appearance, and he tapped his chest. "That's just how it is with twins." He gave his sisters another hug, and then they all got up and signaled to Drock that they were ready to fight again.

The Exact Right Moment

The battle toiled on. Florence shot arrows whenever she could, but just one stuck, and not deeply. They could only hope some of its magical properties seeped in and helped weaken the dragon-woman. Pan and her children, along with their riders, forced the Revinir to separate from the remaining mind-controlled dragons who had fought their way to her, and finally the ghost dragons were able to push the Revinir's dragons back once more.

Seth, Rohan, Lani, Scarlet, and Thatcher were all thrown from their dragons at one moment or another, and there was nothing Fifer or Thisbe could do about it but fight on and hope their friends were rescued by the lake brigade. They wouldn't know until they saw them again.

From a nearby dragon, Carina shouted for her son. "Seth!" But he didn't surface. "Help!" she called down. "Seth's still underwater!"

"There goes Simber," Aaron pointed out, seeing the cheetah limping across land and into the water. "What's he doing?"

"He's going after Seth," Fifer said, fear rising in her throat. "I hope he can find him."

"Don't be distracted," Thisbe warned the others, though she prayed silently that the cheetah would find Seth quickly. The Revinir was acting more and more rash now, and she was spraying fire and ramming into the other dragons, knocking even more mages off their rides.

"Stay focused!" Fifer commanded, though her heart felt like lead. "Stick to the plan!"

Five seconds later, Dev got knocked off of Drock, into the lake.

"Dear gods," Fifer muttered, heart pounding. They were losing fighters, and there was no chance for the good dragons to break away to collect the mages who were still able to fight—or the spears that the lake brigade was collecting.

But there were people down there rescuing the fallen. They'd planned for this. Fifer knew that this time they'd thought of every scenario. But what if there were too many floundering in the lake at once? Dev wasn't exactly a swimmer like the rest of them. "Please be okay," she whispered.

Time languished, and the Revinir's wings grew heavy. Her whole body felt feverish with infection. And with one of Florence's arrows now stuck through the tender tip of her snout like a piercing, she wasn't feeling good at all. She began to struggle to stay up in the sky while still darting this way and that to avoid Florence's dreaded magical arrows, which seemed so much stronger than regular ones. Everyone moved down with her, pressing her toward the lake.

Fifer, Thisbe, Rohan, and Aaron, aboard Drock, circled wide to communicate with their fellow fighters and the other friendly dragons. They came to a stop near Pan, where Maiven was. Aaron began glancing off to the east as if looking for something.

Finally that something came in the form of a send spell. Aaron's face drained. He opened it and read it, then handed it to his sisters.

Aaron,

Any moment now.

Talon

Fifer looked at her siblings. "It's happening. Are you two going to be all right?"

Thisbe turned to Aaron, whose eyes were filled with regret.

"I think I need to sit this one out," Aaron said.

Thisbe's eyes filled with tears. "Thank you, Aaron. Fifer, you're going to have to do this without us."

"I agree you both should abstain," said Fifer warmly. "But for me? It's go time. Stay back—this is going to get ugly."

Aaron and Thisbe moved to the back end of the dragon to keep out of the way as the ruler of Artimé signaled to Florence and Maiven and Pan and the other good dragons, letting them know the time was near. They signaled to Sky, Claire, Gunnar, Sean, Crow, Prindi, Ibrahim, Clementi, and the other fighters who still remained on their dragons.

Everyone nodded, and they pressed forward, pushing the Revinir out over the center of the crater lake and down toward the water.

"Be ready!" Fifer shouted.

The Revinir looked at Fifer, her face masked in fear she could no longer hide. Her eyes sought out Thisbe's, and she was surprised to see the girl sitting back, weaponless, with Aaron. Had the girl turned on her teammates? And convinced her brother to join her? Perhaps there was a shred of hope for her after all.

But the Revinir was losing ground, being pushed very specifically in one direction, and feeling very ill. There was no doubt that the dragon-woman had always worked best when she was at her worst. Hardship was all she needed to fight for her life. She pushed back at Drock as fire boiled in her belly. "You will never defeat me!" she cried, then spat flames at the dark purple dragon and his riders.

Drock dropped and dodged as the fire flew over their heads, singeing their hair and clothes. But the movement had knocked Aaron off balance, and with a cry, he flipped off the dragon and fell to the water below. Drock's dodge was all the Revinir needed to cause a break in the circle of oppressors. She plowed through the space, trying one more time to escape. "Thisbe! Join me! We can still make this work!"

"I will not!" Thisbe yelled back at her. "Hurry, Drock!" Thisbe watched everything begin to fall apart. With Aaron's life in danger again, Thisbe began to doubt herself once more. Pained, she closed her eyes, then grabbed a throwing star, hoping she wouldn't have to use it.

Pan and Arabis charged after the Revinir and forced the dragon-woman back while Drock returned to fill the space. The Revinir sprayed fire again, groaning in pain as she did so. Several on Pan's and Arabis's backs were hit by the flames, with Gunnar Haluki taking the brunt of it. He flipped off of Arabis and fell headlong to the lake.

"Stay on plan!" Fifer shouted, her voice ragged. Maiven repeated the sentiment.

If the dragons left the formation now, their intricate plans would be ruined. All of the ghost dragons were struggling to keep the Revinir's mind-controlled dragons back. Simber was damaged, unable to fly correctly, but he had been in and out of the water for the past while helping out the humans, squirrelicorns, and statues there. His sharp eye caught the former governor's fall, and he left the shore once more and went after him.

LISA McMANN

As the group of dragons pushed back over the lake, painstakingly centering the Revinir once more, they began pressing down again, shielding themselves from her wrath the best they could. But several others were more than singed in the process.

"Hurry up," Fifer muttered.

Florence caught Fifer's eye from Astrid's back. "We can't hold her much longer—our fighters are in danger. We've lost a few more, and our dragons are suffering too." She pointed to Hux the ice blue, whose entire chest was blackened. Simber struggled below them, flailing in the water he hated so much.

"Shall we end it?" Fifer asked Thisbe and Maiven as she felt a flutter of panic. "Call it off?"

"We can't," said Maiven.

"Absolutely not," said Thisbe, knowing the thing she couldn't do still had to be done. "You're inches away! You need to rally!" It was like a switch had flipped. She knew now, beyond a hint of doubt, that the Revinir's days of tyranny were done. They'd tried and failed so many times. The people who'd signed up to fight her were well aware that there was a chance they might not come home. They all wanted to end this, and that meant casualties. It was sickening, yet there was no other way anyone had ever been able to think of to stop the Revinir. She'd only been growing more powerful. And people here and all around their world were suffering.

If they could only hold out a few more minutes!

"Press forward!" Fifer commanded. "It's now or never! Everyone hold steady!"

"Lean in, troops!" called Maiven Taveer. "This is our world we're fighting for! Give it your all!"

"Mages!" cried Fifer. "Code red! Go!" With eyes like slits and teeth gritted, the fighters leaned forward on their dragons, throwing handfuls of heart attack spells all at once at the dragon-woman. They all bounced off her into the lake, but the dragon-woman shook. Had it done anything to her? She roared in discomfort and anger.

"Now code black!" cried Fifer. "Aim for her neck, nostrils, and throat!" Florence took aim and shot an arrow at the monster, and Sky and several others threw their spears at the bulge. Florence's arrow slid between the Revinir's teeth and lodged somewhere that caused great pain. The spears hit and bounced off . . . all but one. Sky's slipped halfway up her nostril. The Revinir squealed and dropped twenty feet in the air, then yanked the spear out and cracked it in half and threw it back at Sky. It whizzed past her ear.

They were getting close to the water. But the Revinir wouldn't go down to it. She fought with all she had to keep from getting anywhere near it. "Stop!" she screamed. "Stop!"

But the teams didn't stop. They pressed harder until they were less than fifty feet from the surface.

Finally the water below them, where the volcano resided, began to churn.

Revenge

I t's happening," Sky shouted. She knew the volcano activities better than anyone after studying them for so many years. "Stay strong! Twenty seconds!"

"Steady now!" said Maiven.

"Eyes down!" barked Florence.

"Code blue!" Fifer shouted. "Ten! Nine! Eight!"

The Revinir could sense what they were doing, but she wasn't sure what these people were thinking. Did they expect a few fireballs from a volcano to affect her? Her scales were fireproof. Dragons had a lot steadier firepower than the volcano did, and their flames had hardly singed her so far.

She spun in the air, finding it harder and harder to breathe with the new arrow lodged in her palate. Everything hurt. But she was not going down into that water.

"Three! Two! One!" Fifer shouted.

The Revinir braced for the impact of burning lava. There was nowhere else to go.

The water shuddered. The volcano shot up below them. Fireballs slammed into the Revinir and all the dragons surrounding her, followed by a huge spray of water.

It wasn't enough.

"Ha!" cried the Revinir, then coughed violently. "This was your grand finale? You'll never succeed!"

"Hold steady!" Fifer commanded.

"Stay strong!" Maiven shouted.

They braced for it—the one part of the entire plan for which they had no backup. Begging it would work as they'd painstakingly mapped it out. For if it didn't work, they might lose it all—everything they'd strived to do.

Thisbe bowed her head.

"Please," Carina whispered from her dragon. But she was looking down at the water.

Seconds later, a huge blue whale with a large bone spike on its forehead came flying out of the volcano. She rose up in the air, her body shimmering in a beautiful curve. And with exceeding grace and form, she found her target and went for it. Spike Furious's spike skewered the gape-mouthed Revinir through the throat.

The Revinir cried out in shock, and then her cry went silent, and her body limp. The whale and the dragon-woman, stuck together, peaked in the air. Then they arced gracefully toward the lake.

"THIS!" cried Spike Furious. "IS FOR!" she shouted. "THE ALEX!"

They hit the water with a tremendous splash. Spike Furious drove the Revinir down deep and drilled the monstrous evil thing into the floor of the lake. Everyone stared in silence, tensed and filled with dread. Waiting for the evil Revinir to come back and get the better of them, like she'd always done. Time after time after time.

But she didn't come back.

"Spike Furious has avenged Alex's death!" Carina cried, her voice catching. "She has ended the rule of a horrible dictator!"

People cheered and some began to chant. "Spike! Spike! Spike!"

Fifer and Thisbe, red with burns, their faces etched with pain, looked at one another.

"I think it's over," Fifer murmured. "Are you all right?"

Thisbe nodded, though she felt horrible inside. "You did what had to be done."

They waited a little longer, just to be absolutely certain.

The other mages began looking at one another, the dread on their faces being slowly replaced with hope. Could it truly be? Had they actually succeeded?

"We did it!" Fifer called out. "Spike Furious did it! And it's all thanks to everyone here who fought for this!"

Thisbe turned to look around at the army from the seven islands, feeling a bit numb. But then she noticed the mind-controlled dragons were acting strange—like they weren't mind controlled anymore. "Fifer, look!" Thisbe cried. She realized what this meant, and what had to come next. Despite her mixed feelings over what had just happened, Thisbe knew she had to act before anyone else could mess it up. She got to her feet and shouted, "Maiven Taveer for black-eyed ruler!"

The other black-eyed people, startled at first by the

LISA McMANN

abruptness of it all, gathered their wits and shouted their support. Even old Ashguard the curmudgeon, who'd left the triage area with Mangrel to assist Simber in the rescue efforts, chimed in with his support.

"I accept your charge," said the queen, and then she called out, "Drock the dark purple, will you join with me as co-ruler of the land of the dragons?"

Drock looked shocked. He turned to his siblings. His mother.

"Do you want to do this?" Pan asked him.

Drock stared. "Yes," he said, like a whisper. "Yes, I do."

"Then it is settled," Pan said, pride evident in her voice.

"Drock for dragon ruler!" his siblings cried.

The rest of the dragons, now no longer mind controlled and thrust into reality, bewildered as could be, did not object.

With a new depth of sincerity to his voice, Drock agreed to take up the honorable position. "With great pleasure I will serve at your side, Queen Maiven Taveer."

"I am well pleased," said the queen, holding his gaze. "We shall work wonderfully together."

The ghost dragons all halted what they were doing and

looked at one another, at first in surprise and then with a knowing sense of calm. They roared in appreciation to Maiven and Drock, and seconds later, Gorgrun, Quince, Astrid, and the rest of the glorious ghost dragons disappeared into the air with a poof.

Florence, instantly losing her ride, fell to the lake. But everyone knew she would be all right.

Their painstaking plans had worked. After years of trying, they'd finally succeeded. The evilest, most horrible being in all the worlds, who'd caused the people of Artimé and Warbler and all of their friends great pain and suffering over multiple decades, had been soundly defeated. The ghost dragons had been freed. The prisoners in the dungeon released. The people of Grimere saved. The seven islands were at peace once more, and the kingdom of the land of the dragons had been restored.

The twin sisters collapsed on Drock's back.

Below them, a battered Simber dragged limp, sodden bodies to the shore. Carina noticed. And then she screamed. "Seth!"

After the Storm

Chaos erupted. All the mind-controlled dragons had snapped out of their zombielike state when the Revinir died. But they had no idea what was going on or even where they were. They'd come from other realms beyond Grimere and had already been under the influence of the dragon-woman when they'd arrived.

"I'll handle these dragons," Maiven called to Fifer. "You go to your friend."

"Take us to Simber!" Thisbe told Drock. "Please hurry!" Was that limp, unmoving body that Simber had set on the shore really Seth? The twins leaned forward as if it would help

Drock go faster. Their best friend . . . could he be dead? It was unthinkable! He was a great swimmer—had he been injured before falling? Or, like Thisbe, had he blacked out?

Carina's dragon beat them to the shore, and the woman leaped off, trying to get to Seth as quickly as she could. Henry was right behind her, and Sean came running from the triage cave after hearing the news. They crowded around. Simber, useless to help, went back into the lake to search for more bodies.

Thisbe and Fifer, feeling numb, slid off Drock's wing and sent him back to the skies to help Maiven handle the new issues with the foreign dragons. They ran over toward Seth, but there was no way to see what was happening with so many people there now. Knowing the healers needed room, they stepped away and went to the hospital cave to see about their other loved ones.

There were several cots arranged around the edges of the cave. Fifer scanned the place, expecting to find Dev sitting somewhere, warming up with a blanket. She saw Thatcher and Lani talking quietly from their beds, looking bedraggled but recovering nicely. Two cots had bodies on them completely covered with blankets. Dev was nowhere.

Fear struck her, and she gripped Thisbe's arm. "Lani," Fifer said anxiously. "Where's Dev?"

Lani looked up. "I haven't seen him. Is Seth all right? Sean went running as soon as we heard. What happened?"

"We don't know," Thisbe said. She saw how upset Fifer was and pointed to the cots with covered bodies. "Who . . . ?"

"We didn't see," Thatcher said. "I'm sorry. Henry said not to disturb the bodies—he'd be back soon."

Fifer sank against the cave wall, feeling faint. She hadn't seen Dev since he'd fallen. Had he even been found? Her head pounded, and she wanted to crumple up and fall apart. Why hadn't she insisted he stay on the ground? She felt her hope sinking.

But she couldn't give in to feelings right now. She was the head mage, and she needed to pull it together and lead her people through this. Whether Dev was under one of those blankets or not, people would be grieving and heartbroken tonight. Those two cots held people who meant something to others, no matter who they were. She passed her hand over her face and took a few deep breaths. Then, with a gasp, she looked sharply at Thisbe. "Where's Aaron? Have you seen him since he fell?"

Now Thisbe's face drained. Had they lost Dev and Aaron? And possibly Seth, too? "I'm going to be sick," Thisbe whispered, and ran out to the bushes nearby. But she didn't throw up. She just kept feeling awful.

Fifer came to her side. "We have to be strong," she said to her sister. She tugged at her shoulder. "Stand up, Thisbe!"

"You stand up!" cried Thisbe. She could hardly cope. This couldn't be happening, but it was. "Where's Rohan? Did he fall too?"

"I saw Rohan," Thatcher said, limping to the cave opening. "He's fine—he's helping carry injured people." Thatcher came out farther, looking haggard. "Listen, everything is chaotic right now. You can't think the worst about everyone. And the people of the seven islands need you to lead them through this part, too. You can do it, Fifer. You too, Thisbe. Get them through this."

Fifer nodded. She was relieved to hear that Rohan was all right. She needed to pull herself up with that information and go find out who else was alive. "Come on, Thiz. Let's go find Rohan." She glanced at Thatcher. "Thank you."

Thatcher gave her a sympathetic nod. Then he tapped his

chest, reminding Fifer that she was the head mage of Artimé.
And that he was with her.

It gave her the strength she needed.

Back by the water, Rohan and Sean were carrying Seth at a
swift walk toward the cave.

"Is he okay?" Thisbe asked, her voice wrecked.

"He's breathing," said Sean, and then his face crumpled.
"Somehow Henry got him breathing again."

"Thank the gods," Fifer said. The twins got out of the way,
then continued to the shore, scanning the faces anxiously and
keeping a mental tab on who was here and who wasn't. Henry
took charge, assessing the injuries and administering medication.
Sending the more serious patients to the cave hospital ward. A
few of the mages who'd been patched up and cleared to go swam
out to help the squirrelicorns retrieve the remaining people
who'd fallen into the lake, and Florence emerged unscathed on
her own. Luckily, the lake had immediately extinguished the
burning clothes of many of those who had fallen, saving them
from extensive burns. But for those who'd been knocked out
before hitting the water, their situation was a different story.

Simber limped ashore with two soggy but conscious mages on his back. He knelt to lay them down near Henry and turned to go back in the water, seemingly resigned that his life today was about as bad as it had ever been. Spike Furious, everyone's favorite whale, stayed in deeper water, helping to collect other swimmers.

Fifer ran up to Henry. "Have you seen Dev?"

Henry looked up, frazzled. "No. I mean, I don't think so. I hardly know what he looks like."

"How about Aaron?"

"Fifer, I've got a lot happening here. . . ." Henry's eyes shone with unshed tears.

Fifer cringed. "Sorry. How can I help?"

"Check on that row of people sitting up over there. If they're feeling good, you can call a dragon to take them up to the square. And if you see Lani, tell her I need her to come find me. Claire Morning too. And Sky and Crow. Tell them to meet me in the cave."

Mystified and frightened, Fifer nodded. She went to do what Henry had asked, wondering why he wanted to see those specific people. Was it because they were reported missing too? Or injured? Or because . . . he needed to give them bad news?

Lani—did that mean that one of the bodies under the blanket was Samheed? Fifer's stomach churned. Being head mage was hard. And this might be the hardest time she'd ever been through.

Just as Fifer started looking for the people Henry had listed, the formerly mind-controlled dragons, who were still mightily confused about where they were and the identity of the strange dragons surrounding them, began fighting in the air above them, causing quite a stir. All six dragons from the land of the seven islands rushed to break it up, and Drock tried again to explain what was happening. He told them where they were and that they were free to go back to their lands if they wished, and encouraged them to do so immediately.

Happy that Drock was taking care of that problem, Fifer turned to see Thisbe trailing her.

"I've located Ms. Morning," Thisbe said, out of breath. "And Lani. I sent them to Henry."

"Have you seen Samheed anywhere?" Fifer asked. "Or Dev or Aaron?"

"Not yet," Thisbe said. She felt anguished for her sister.

Where was Dev? And Aaron? And who was under those blankets? "Wait!" she said, pointing. "There he is!"

"Dev?" asked Fifer, whirling around.

"No—it's Samheed. Thank goodness."

"Oh my . . ." Fifer was overwhelmed. That meant Samheed wasn't one of the deceased people, which was great. But then who . . . ?

"Samheed, you might want to go to the cave to find Lani," Thisbe told him.

"Sky!" Fifer shouted as she came up the shore with Simber. She ran to get the woman's attention and found Crow at the edge of the water waiting for his sister. "Crow, Sky, you need to go to Henry in the cave immediately if you're all right. Do you need help?"

"Why?" asked Crow. "Did something happen? I think we can make it."

"I don't know," said Fifer, tears welling up. "He asked for you." She followed as they limped to the cave.

Samheed and Lani, Sky and Crow, and Claire Morning gathered around the beds with Henry, who spoke to them quietly.

LISA McMANN

Fifer and Thisbe remained at the entrance, pulses pounding. Trying to be ready for anything.

Fifer looked at Thisbe. "Where is Dev?" she whispered. And then her voice broke. "He can't swim."

Thisbe didn't know what to say.

As the girls stepped away to give Henry privacy to speak to the people gathered there, Aaron came running up. He had bandages around his arms and burns on his cheeks. "Are you two okay?"

"Aaron!" Thisbe exclaimed, and now her tears threatened. The girls jumped at their brother, and the three held each other tightly, shedding tears of relief. And then, from behind, someone cleared his throat.

Fifer turned sharply and saw a sorry, but welcome, sight. "Dev," she whispered. She opened up her arms, and he slid into them.

The Worst Part

You're all right?" Fifer asked Dev, pulling away.

"I am, thanks to Simber," he said.

"Not everyone is so lucky," Fifer murmured as Henry came out of the cave. His expression was so broken that no one had ever seen him like this before. He was clearly taking his duties hard.

"I've never seen him so upset," Aaron murmured.

Rohan slipped away from Seth's bedside and went out of the cave to find Thisbe, knowing something was coming and wanting to be there for her.

"Friends and family," said Henry with tears streaming

LISA McMANN

down his face, "I'm so sorry. This battle was never going to be without consequences. We've lost some dear friends and family, including Lani's and my father, Gunnar Haluki. And we've also lost Sky and Crow's mother, Copper, who fought with all she had and rallied her entire island to join in this venture. And Seth . . ."

Fifer and Thisbe gasped.

Henry heard them and lifted a tired hand. "Seth is alive. He's hanging on, and Carina and Sean are monitoring him. Everyone, I'm so sorry. The Revinir did everything she could to take as many people down with her as she could. And while I'm glad to see you all standing here alive before me, I am . . . devastated."

Thatcher held and comforted Henry as the young man cried, and Lani and Samheed came out of the cave and embraced them both. Their father had been a governor under the High Priest Justine's rule, and he'd been the one to defy her and sneak into Artimé using a wolf charm so no one would detect it was him. He'd pushed his daughter Lani into being declared Unwanted a year early because he knew she would flourish in Artimé. And he'd been co-ruling Quill for many years with Claire Morning.

Claire stood in numb silence as Samheed went to console her and give her a hug. Her clothing was burned and torn, and she had several lesions on her skin as well. Their dragon had been hit hard. Just inside the cave, Sky and Crow hung on to each other, staring at their brave mother's still body. Numb with grief, they barely noticed as Copper's assistant Phoenix led leagues of Warblerans and the leaders of Artimé to gather around in support of both families. The people of Warbler were in tears over the loss of their leader. And the people of Artimé's tears blended with theirs.

Copper had taken over after the Revinir—called Queen Eagala back then—had disappeared into the volcano aboard the enchanted pirate ship. She had nursed the island back to health over the years with her kindness and support and steady, firm hand in leadership, encouraging the oppressed people to experience and enjoy their new freedom. And now she'd died fighting to retain that freedom, for the Revinir surely would have gone back to Warbler once she'd conquered everyone and everything here.

"I'm so sorry about these devastating losses," Rohan said to Thisbe and Fifer. He and the other black-eyed people had gotten to know both leaders during their time in Artimé.

"I'm sorry too," said Dev, even though he'd only heard of them and had never formally met them except to fight alongside them today. He could tell they'd been so well loved. As Henry went back to check on Seth, the people dispersed.

Feeling stunned about how everything had gone down, Thisbe, Fifer, Rohan, and Dev fixed up their wounds, then checked on Aaron, who'd taken the brunt of the dragon fire and was feeling some serious pain now that the shock had worn off. They found him a bed in the cave so he could be close to the medicine he needed. With his pain heightening, he began to take a turn for the worse.

Once they'd done all they could to help Henry in the triage center and comfort the mourners, and the overhead dragon battle had settled down, the four found Maiven and Drock conversing at the edge of the water. They joined them.

"How is everyone?" Maiven asked them anxiously.

"Trying to absorb the news," Thisbe said. "Our friend Seth is in very bad shape. And Aaron is badly burned."

LISA McMANN

Fifer pressed her lips together. She was worried sick about Seth but knew he was in the best possible hands, and she needed to keep her focus. "How are things in the square?"

"I'm about to go help Florence with the soldiers who are inside the catacombs," Maiven said. "Some of them were under the Revinir's mind control and others, from the farther-out villages, were only serving her because they were forced to. We aren't sure if the mind-controlled ones are still affected or if, like the dragons, the death of the Revinir freed them from it. We hope for the latter."

"If necessary, we can make more ancestor broth," said Thisbe, though the thought pained her.

"Let's head up then, shall we?" Fifer asked.

Drock flew them up from the crater lake to the square, where Florence met them. Fox, completely restored, was standing with Kitten and Matilda.

"How is everyone up here?" Fifer asked anxiously. "It's so good to see you all. Matilda, what a fine job you did. Thank you. And you too, Kitten."

Fox thumped his tail expectantly.

LISA McMANN

"And we'd have never made it through without Fox," Thisbe said generously. "Dev said you were very important in the dungeon mission." She turned back to Florence. "Everyone else is okay, I hope?"

"Just a few minor injuries that are already being addressed," said Florence. "But I see you had some casualties down there." She paused, a pained expression on her face. "Who are they?"

Fifer broke the news about Copper and Gunnar, and told her about Seth and Aaron.

Florence closed her eyes and bowed her head. After a minute, she opened them again, and a teardrop fell. "I don't know what to say," she said, her voice hitching. "Lani, Henry, Sky . . . Claire . . . They've all been through so much already."

"This has to be the last time," Fifer vowed. "No more battles. It's time for both worlds to recover and live in peace and harmony together."

"We are well on our way toward that now," said Maiven. "Together we will work to repair everything that has broken over the past forty years. Fifer, shall we make a pact between our two worlds to strive toward peace and harmony?"

LISA McMANN

"We most certainly shall, Grandmother," said Fifer with a solemn smile. The two shook hands in the square.

"Once everything has settled," said Maiven, "we'll have a summit meeting to discuss our common goals and plan how to reach them."

"In the meantime," said Fifer, pointing to the elevator, "we have some people to take care of."

Another Funeral

The next morning, Aaron woke up from a deep, troubled sleep in the cave to find Samheed at his side, looking worried.

"What's going on?" he said weakly. "Are Fifer and Thisbe okay?" He tried to sit up.

"They're fine," said Samheed.

"And Seth?"

"He's improving."

Aaron's face relaxed, then darkened. "What are you doing here?" he asked. The two hadn't spoken much since their most recent spat when they were trapped in the library under the reign of Frieda Stubbs, and they'd never resolved their differences.

"I'm sitting with you," Samheed said, looking up to study the cave ceiling. "Obviously."

Aaron tried to relax, but it was difficult with all the snark enveloping him. "Where's Lani? Or . . . anybody?" *Anybody but you*, he wanted to say.

Samheed's eyes glistened. "Gunnar . . . died. In the battle. So did Copper."

"I heard the news yesterday before I passed out here," Aaron said. "I'm sorry." He imagined the way Lani and Henry and Sky must be feeling, and his heart broke for them. Especially Sky, losing her mother so soon after Alex. It made his own problems feel small. After a moment, he looked at Samheed. "How are they?"

"They're handling it. We're having a funeral in a few hours. They're going to bury them alongside Alex."

Something about that sentence made reality slap Aaron hard in the face, and he choked up. "Three brave leaders together," he said when he could get the words out. "I like that Alex's grave won't be alone."

Samheed sniffed, and tears leaked from his eyes. The two men cried together.

"I want to go to the funeral," Aaron said after a while. "Will you . . . help me?"

Samheed pressed his lips together, determined not to break down again. Then he nodded. "Yeah. Of course." The two held each other's gaze for a moment. Then Samheed whispered, "I'm sorry about everything."

Aaron nodded, the lump in his throat growing thicker. "Me too," he said.

As Aaron had expressed, it seemed fitting that such great rulers be buried together. It marked the sacrifices of people from another land who gave everything to support their neighbors in need during the rule of the Revinir. Samheed, Aaron, and Simber, still battered, hitched a ride up to Dragonsmarche with Pan. Then Samheed helped Aaron onto Simber's back and the three went slowly, limping down the path to the gravesite. The chaos was over, and all was quiet and peaceful as they held the funeral.

Within the calm gathering came other curious things, like Maiven and Ashguard reuniting. The two leaders from the land of the dragons hadn't seen each other in forty years, and each had presumed the other dead. Neither knew they'd shared the same dungeon for the past many years.

With that reunion came one more. Asha approached the notoriously grumpy man with caution as the funeral dispersed. "You're my grandfather," she said. "I'm Asha. I remember you."

"Ah, Asha," he said. "Dev told me you were here. I remember you, too. And I could have picked you out of the crowd. You look so much like your mother." Tears sprang to his eyes. He held out his hand and they shook solemnly, and he wasn't grumpy at all for a while.

Dev watched them, thrilled to see the reunification, but a little bit sad that after all of this time, he still had nobody. It was more than clear that this girl was indeed the rightful heir to the palace and would probably live there with Ashguard. In his library.

Which left Dev not only without kin, but without a home.

All the emotions of the battle and the deaths, and now this, came welling up, and he excused himself to find some privacy among the trees. His rush to find cover caught Asha's

LISA McMANN

eye, and she frowned. "What's wrong with Dev?" she asked.

"Perhaps he's sad," said Ashguard. "We're at a funeral, after all."

"Maybe," Asha said, but it seemed strange that he would go off by himself when he was like many of the black-eyed youth who didn't really know the people who'd died. "He said he found a painting of my mother among your things."

Ashguard nearly smiled. "He used to deliver food to the prisoners. He worked for the king since the time I was imprisoned—he was just a young boy when he first started with the food cart, barely able to see over the top shelf."

"Almost as bad as carting dragon bones through the catacombs," Asha said. She thought about what Dev's life must have been like and was glad she'd had her mother until she was seven years old. "Do you know of any news of Ari?"

"No, nothing at all of your brother," said Ashguard. "I fear the worst."

Asha dropped her gaze. "I was afraid of that. I just . . . Every time the Revinir roared, I kept having the same memory of him as a newborn being taken away. Though it wasn't an actual memory. It was a vision."

"It couldn't have been a memory since you were but a year old at the time," Ashguard agreed. "You couldn't possibly remember such a thing."

"The visions were peculiar. And now that the Revinir is dead, I likely won't have them again. I believed that because I was visualizing that particular scene, it had to mean something. Like maybe . . . he was alive. And I was supposed to find him."

Ashguard listened intently as Asha explained the vision and how Thisbe and Rohan had figured things out with their own visions. He frowned as he listened. When she finished, he said, "Does Dev have any kin?"

"Not that I know of."

"Perhaps that's why he's sad." Ashguard grew thoughtful for a moment, then narrowed his eyes and tapped his lips. "I wonder . . . Follow me. Let's go talk to the boy."

The two went into the forest in search of Dev, and they found him at the base of a tree with his face in his hands. When he heard them approach, he looked up and hastily wiped his eyes, then scrambled to his feet. "How may I be of service, Ashguard? Do you wish for help back to the road? Surely you must be weak after your imprisonment."

Ashguard studied the boy, then asked him and Asha to stand in a patch of sunlight that peeked through the tree cover.

They obliged. Asha stood a couple of inches taller than Dev, but it wasn't their height that caught Ashguard's eye. It was their faces. He looked from one to the other, noting the similarities. Their complexions, the lines of their jaws, the shapes of their noses.

"Son," said Ashguard carefully. "Do you have . . . family?"

Dev's eyes went wide, and he tried to stop the tears from starting again. He didn't trust himself to speak and shook his head. "I thought I did," he finally said, choking up. "But it turns out I was wrong."

Ashguard studied him. "How old are you?"

"I believe I'm nearly fourteen. But I'm not sure."

"Why aren't you sure?"

"Because I was stolen from my family when I was a baby and given to the king, to be raised as his daughter Shanti's whipping boy. She would be almost fifteen now if she'd lived, and I'm a bit younger than her." He looked up at the curmudgeon. "I found a painting in the palace," he said. "The girl in the painting looked so familiar. I couldn't understand why until I remembered Asha from the catacombs. It must be a picture of her mother. She's . . . she was beautiful." He blinked back the ache behind his eyes. He was processing. Giving up on his dream that he belonged somewhere. To someone.

"Dev," said Ashguard. "Is that your real name?"

"It's the name the king gave me."

Ashguard and Asha looked at one another, eyes widening. "And, Asha, if my memory hasn't failed me, you must be nearly fifteen, is that right?"

Asha smiled. "That *is* correct, Grandfather."

The old man almost smiled. He turned back to Dev. "I think there's another reason why you felt that the picture of my daughter seemed so familiar," he said. "I know the portrait you're talking about—it was in the small vestibule on the fifth floor, hidden away in the desk drawer, wasn't it?"

Dev nodded, feeling numb.

"That picture is familiar to you because my daughter looks like you," said Ashguard.

The silence among the three was intense as Dev figured out what Ashguard was saying to him. "Dev," said the ruler with a rare smile finally appearing, "I think you are my grandson."

"And you're my younger brother," said Asha, gazing at him.

Dev's heart beat wildly, as if it couldn't take this news. He had a hard time processing the words. All he could think of to say as he crumpled to the ground in tears was "Please . . . get Fifer."

The Beginning of the End of the End:
Saying Good-bye

The dragon-woman never resurfaced in the crater lake after Spike shook her loose. But despite not seeing proof of her death, everyone was certain that was the case this time because the dragons had immediately been freed from her control. Plus the ghost dragons had gone on to their next life, and Maiven and Drock were able to unite as dragon and black-eyed ruler, the way it should be.

At the next volcano submersion, Spike Furious left the crater lake with tremendous fanfare from the leaders of Artimé for her incredible feat in avenging Alex's death. Spike needed no glory, only the satisfaction that she had successfully taken down the monster who'd killed the Alex and had caused so much pain to the others in Artimé, whom she loved.

The success and recognition was enough to lift the whale's spirits quite high for the first time in a long while. She made her way quietly back to the seven islands to await further instructions, while Talon returned from his post monitoring the Island of Fire volcano to help with the mind-detoxification process of all the soldiers of the land of the dragons.

Over the next days, everyone worked to build unity and bring stability to the land, even as they grieved over the ones they had lost. Before long, Seth was awake and surrounded by visitors in the hospital cave. "I can't believe you almost died," Fifer said to him as she perched on the edge of his bed.

"It wasn't the first time," Seth reminded her. "We've been through some real scrapes together, haven't we?"

Fifer nodded. "I'm glad you're okay."

"Me too."

Prindi entered the cave and took a few tentative steps toward the cot. "Am I interrupting anything?" she asked.

Seth's pale face turned bright red, and Fifer couldn't help but notice. She glanced at Prindi, then back to Seth. "I was just leaving," Fifer said, squelching a grin. In the past, she might have felt a need to flee the situation, but not this time. She leaned toward him and gave his hand a squeeze. "I've got soldiers to feed broth to. I'll see you when you're back on your feet."

In the quiet rest times, Dev and Fifer found themselves looking for each other to talk about how everything had progressed. "I have a family," Dev would say, as if he couldn't believe it. "A sister. A grandfather."

"And the palace is yours," said Fifer. "Rotten roof and floors and all. Good luck." She laughed.

"We're going to restore it," he said. "Asha and I. And Ashguard, too, when he's got his strength back."

"I love that." Fifer smiled, imagining it, but something about that hit her hard and made her ribs ache. She blew out a breath. "I'll have to come visit sometime to see how it's going."

Dev was quiet, and the two looked at each other in the dim light. Dev felt something stir deep inside him—a longing he couldn't quite define. "That . . . would be nice," he said. "I mean . . ." He grew flustered. "I wish . . ."

Fifer gazed at him. When he didn't finish his sentence, she whispered, "And I wish."

He leaned toward her, and Fifer leaned toward him, and they pressed their lips together. When Fifer pulled away, she said, "I will miss you very much."

Dev closed his eyes and leaned back with a heavy sigh. "Everything is always so difficult."

"It seems especially so, with us," said Fifer.

With heavy hearts, they went back to work. And soon all of the people of the land of the dragons were restored to their old selves, and the people of the seven islands were stable enough to fly back to the seven islands and recover in their own homes.

Their dragon friends were ready and eager to go home to the Island of Dragons. Which meant Fifer's time in this land was coming to an end.

Fifer found Thisbe helping Henry and a few others pack up the hospital cave. "Are you coming home for a while?" Fifer asked. "Or staying here with Rohan and Grandmother?"

"I'm staying," said Thisbe. "I'm going to train with her. Learn how to rule this land, so that when she passes away—hopefully not for a long time—I will have built up the confidence of the people. And then I'll take over."

Fifer looked out over the lake. "And what about the rest of the black-eyed rulers?"

"They are free to take up housing at the castle or wherever they wish. Dev and Asha will be at Ashguard's palace, obviously—" Thisbe stopped short and looked at Fifer's face. "Why are you so sad? Is it because of Dev?"

Fifer felt an impulse to lie . . . but she wasn't going to do that with her sister ever again. "Yes," she said. "I can't believe it, but I think my little heart has melted for him."

"I think it's lovely," Thisbe said. "That you like him, I mean. Because he certainly has fallen for you, too. It's too bad you'll be so distant from each other."

"It'll be all right," said Fifer, though she struggled to feel it. "I need to be in Artimé, and he has his new family and the palace to rebuild. We'll see each other again. Sometime."

"You're definitely going to visit me," said Thisbe. "So you'll see him then." She thought about that for a moment. "It's so strange that we're going to be so far apart, permanently. I feel like I'm losing a piece of me."

"Me too," said Fifer. *Maybe even two pieces.*

LISA McMANN

It would be okay. Fifer would be very busy in the days to come, rebuilding Artimé after Frieda Stubbs had wrecked it. Fifer had ideas on how to improve the mansion so that it would be even better than when Alex was ruler. There was much to do. The job would keep Fifer's mind off things.

Samheed came by to help Aaron onto Ivis's back. Seth was transported there too, with his arm in a sling and a bandage covering some of the burns on his cheek. He looked a lot better than before. When Seth saw Thisbe and Fifer coming, he waved at them to join him. "Sorry I'm not sticking around to help, but I'm really looking forward to my bed," he said with a small laugh. Then he grimaced and held his stomach.

"Remember the first time we came here?" asked Thisbe.

They both nodded. The three had been through a lot over the years, not just since their first visit here, but since the time they were very young. And now it felt like they were heading in separate directions. Sure, Seth was going back to Artimé with Fifer, but he was also developing a bit of a tight bond with Prindi, who lived here and was planning to stay. So they'd be visiting each other too, maybe. It made Fifer feel better to know she wasn't alone.

As they helped more people board the dragons, Fifer spotted Clementi and Asha together, looking tearful. Asha was staying here—was Clementi going back to Artimé? It seemed so. Something about others feeling loss right now really resonated with Fifer. Maybe she and Seth and Clementi could visit together sometime. Only this time there would be no mission except to be with the people they'd grown to appreciate and love over the past little while—people who had made a lasting impression on their lives.

Maybe it wouldn't be so bad after all.

Fifer kept telling herself that until it was time for her dragon to depart.

Carina and Sean returned to the village outside Ashguard's palace to find Ol' Tater still standing under the canopy of trees where they'd left him. Carina had thought about just transporting him back to the Museum of Large directly. But she looked at his smiling face and remembered how happy he'd been to stomp around at the water's edge in Artimé. And it gave her an idea. She quickly penned a note to Maiven and sent it off.

Moments later came the response. "She said yes!" Carina exclaimed, then read from the note: "'There's nothing there he can harm, and Thisbe can control him if needed.'"

Sean smiled. "It's perfect. He'll be so happy stomping around."

Carina placed her hand on Ol' Tater's side. She closed her eyes and concentrated on the now abandoned crater lakeshore where the hospital cave had been. Then she whispered, "Transport."

In an instant, the mastodon statue was gone.

"Now let's go wake him up," said Sean. "And then we can go home. Our family all together again, at last."

The remaining Artiméans decided to make one more trip to the gravesite to offer their respects to the fallen leaders before going with Pan to Artimé. Fifer invited their friends from the land of the dragons to join them if they were able . . . and to say good-bye.

While young Daniel played with the unopened seek spells on his uncle Alex's grave, patting them like balls that always went back to their same space again, Fifer stood with Aaron and Kaylee and Simber and Florence, feeling absolutely messed up inside. Samheed, Lani, Claire, Sky, and Crow were already there. Fifer was sick about their losses—Gunnar and Copper were great warriors, and great parents. And it was still stunning to think they'd lost them both. They'd given everything they had to save the people of their world. But now Fifer's dear friends were hurting because of it.

Again she thought back to how this all began, with her and Thisbe and Seth making a rash decision to rescue the captive dragons. If they had left well enough alone . . . if they had let Alex send Hux back to fend for himself . . . would everything be different now? Would Alex and the rest still be alive?

There was no way to know for sure. The Revinir's power had been increasing. She would have become a dragon-woman whether Thisbe and Fifer had entered the picture or not. If they had sent Hux away, would they have even known about the Revinir's rise to power? Or that she was Queen Eagala in dragon form? Or that she'd intended to come after them all in the seven islands? Would she have struck at full power without warning and devastated their people?

No one knew which outcome would have produced greater

LISA McMANN

losses, but Fifer had to believe that being proactive and going after the Revinir had saved lives in the long run. Being unexpectedly attacked by a dragon army would have been disastrous. The way they'd gone about it had given Florence ample time to train their armies, despite the losses they'd experienced along the way.

The analysis helped Fifer feel a little better about the way they'd gone about things. They could have done better . . . but they also could have done much worse by ignoring the situation.

Thisbe, Rohan, and Maiven came down the forest path to join them, and that started Fifer's tears. Her dear sister . . . if only they could communicate through their minds from the great distance between Artimé and here. That would help with the separation. Perhaps with time, as their connection grew, their system would improve to be as good as Matilda and Charlie's. For now they had send spells. And the volcano network could get them to each other's world in fairly quick time when riding on Spike Furious or a dragon for the rest of the trip. It wouldn't be so bad.

Fifer embraced her sister and held her close—so close that

when Thisbe tried to pull away, she couldn't, which made Thisbe realize how Fifer was feeling in this moment. And that made Thisbe squeeze her sister harder. They understood without words what a momentous time this was for both of them.

"Where's Dev?" Thisbe asked quietly when they finally released.

"I thought he was coming, but maybe . . . he couldn't make it." Fifer's voice broke, betraying how sad she felt. "There's a lot to do at the palace."

Thisbe frowned. "If he doesn't show up because of that, I'll have some sharp words for him."

But Dev didn't come. Soon they left the graveside area and made their way to the road, where Pan waited to take the majority of them to Artimé, leaving Thisbe behind to work with Maiven. They reached the road, and the others helped Simber and Florence onto Pan's back before settling themselves. Fifer looked back as tears pricked her eyes, wondering why Dev hadn't come.

In the distance she could see someone approaching. Soon Fifer realized it was Dev on the back of a young dragon, flying quickly toward them.

Fifer studied him, then turned to Florence and Aaron. "Hold on a moment," she said. She slid down Pan's wing and walked toward Dev. Dev and the unfamiliar dragon came to a stop.

"Who's this?" Fifer asked coolly.

"I'm sorry I'm late, but you're not going to believe this," said Dev, looking harried. "This is Astrid. Reborn."

"What?" Fifer exclaimed. "The ghost dragon?"

"Yes—she found me. This is her next life, and she chose to spend it with me. And get this—she remembers absolutely everything I say."

"That's unbelievable!" Fifer said. "Astrid, how wonderful to see you! I never had the chance to thank you. Are Gorgrun and Quince and the rest of them returning to us as young dragons too?"

"I haven't seen them yet," said young Astrid, "but I don't doubt it."

Dev, still breathing heavily, got off Astrid's back and instructed her to stay close by. Then he turned back to Fifer. "She's giving me a run for it, I tell you. Very fast, and still learning how to smooth out the ride. I'm a bit shaken."

Fifer let a smile escape, but it felt bittersweet. "I thought I might not see you again before we left."

"It would have wrecked me," Dev said. "I would've had Astrid chase after you until we reached you. I'm sorry I wasn't here when I said I would be. It was quite a shock when Astrid showed up, and I lost track of time."

"I understand."

Dev studied Fifer's face and took an unsure step toward her. "Are you angry with me?"

"You could have sent a message," Fifer said.

"Ah. I keep forgetting I have these magical tools."

"I suppose I could have sent you one too," Fifer admitted.

"So . . ." Dev straightened his shirt collar and twisted his skirt back into place, then looked up, eyes pleading. "Don't go."

The words slammed into Fifer, and she took a step back to catch her breath. "I have to."

"I know."

"Maybe you should come with me," said Fifer, but then she cringed. She knew he needed this time to get to know his family. It wasn't fair to ask. But then again, it wasn't fair for him to ask her to stay here.

Dev smiled sadly. He knew they were both just trying to make it work, and there was no way to do it. Not right now, anyway. "I'm really going to miss you," he said, and his eyes filled. "Thank you for . . . teaching me . . . things." He couldn't manage to get the words out. Fifer, along with Thisbe and Drock and Astrid had taught him that he mattered. That he was worth something. And Fifer had taught him that he could give his heart away and she would protect it, not harm it.

"Me too," choked Fifer. The two went together in an embrace that told a story of all the trouble they'd gone through. From their first meeting in the village where Thisbe and Fifer had been abducted to their time trying to free the captive dragons, to the moment he'd appeared at their forest camp in tears after Shanti had been killed and he'd had nowhere else to turn. But the part that meant the most to both of them was the time they'd spent in the palace library, learning how to navigate being on the cusp of growing up and making life-altering decisions in order to save the world from a tyrant.

They held each other close, sniffling and whispering about how they'd see each other again eventually. And then they whispered more words—words that let the other person know they wouldn't forget them. And, in fact, that they'd be on their minds whenever the darkness of rebuilding ravaged worlds threatened to overtake them.

They drew apart, still clasping each other's forearms. Dev pushed aside a strand of Fifer's hair that had drowned in her tears, and she wiped one of his away with her thumb. Then they pressed together one last time in a kiss.

Fifer pulled away, not wanting to. But she knew her people back home needed her more than she needed to be with this boy. "Good-bye," she said.

Dev smiled. "I'll see you," he said, and his tears began anew.

"Okay," she whispered. Before she could change her mind, Fifer turned and ran blindly back to Pan. Florence helped her up, and they all kept quiet about what they'd just seen, which was the kindest thing they could have done for Fifer.

In moments, they were flying toward Artimé. Toward home. Fifer turned to look back as they went, finding Dev still standing in the road with his dragon, watching them go. He held his hand pressed to his chest, and raised the other when she turned.

With dry eyes now, Fifer raised her hand in response.

She couldn't imagine anything keeping them apart for long. And amazingly, in this world of uncertainty and endless battles, there was nothing that could. In a time when wars were ending and worlds were rebuilding, it felt like Fifer's life story was just beginning.

The End of the End of the End:
Behind the Last Door

Decades passed. Peace reigned in the land of the dragons and the seven islands.

Queen Maiven Taveer lived jubilantly for several more years, uniting the land of the dragons, and she worked with Thisbe to finish returning it to the glory it once was. They buried her alongside the other leaders, and the transition to Thisbe's rulership was bittersweet but seamless.

Fifer ruled Artimé and, over time, made some major structural changes to the mansion as they repaired it and restored it to its full potential. She created multiple exits from all of the remote rooms so no one would ever be trapped again. And she opened up all the residence hallways to everyone, removing the hallway labels so the people in Artimé could choose which apartment they felt most comfortable living in—including her. She'd felt uncomfortable moving into such a lavish head mage apartment so far away from her friends. So she stayed where she was and turned the head mage apartment into a museum honoring Alex, and released the magic protecting the secret hallway so that everyone could come and go as they pleased.

Ito and Sato passed away peacefully of natural causes. Not even Henry could quite define the power of the magical seaweed. They knew it had helped Aaron live again, and it had extended the lives of the scientists. But to everyone's relief, it didn't make anyone immortal after all. Henry decided to leave it alone forever, in the sea where it belonged.

Many years later, Claire Morning passed away too. After a long time, Carina Holiday and then Sean Ranger said their last good-byes to Seth, Ava, and Lukas and their families and friends.

Simber, Florence, Ms. Octavia, Kitten, Fox, and all the other statues stayed static as ever. Kitten wasn't sure how many lives she had left, but all she needed was the one she lived now. The rest of the people of Artimé grew old. And finally the day arrived when Aaron Stowe, who'd never fully regained his robust health after that last battle, was on his deathbed.

Kaylee and Daniel and the rest of Aaron and Kaylee's children and grandchildren gathered around. Fifer and Dev were there with their family. Thisbe and Rohan and all of their descendants arrived on Drock's back from Grimere. Samheed and Lani, Sky and Crow, Simber and Panther, Florence and Talon, Seth and Prindi, Asha and Clementi, and Henry and Thatcher all watched and waited for the imminent passing of this great, yet complicated person.

If Aaron had one wish, it was that the end of his days in this world would happen just like this. Surrounded by love instead of hatred. Kindness and goodness rather than jealousy and spite. It was just as he had imagined this moment to be, now that he knew without a doubt that he, too, was capable of moving on despite the magical seaweed.

Aaron had turned his life around. He'd made something good come out of the bad things he'd done. He'd learned the power of an apology, and the strength of trying to make up for the wrong things he'd done. He'd learned the pain of constant remorse, but he didn't regret that feeling, for it had healed him as well. And it had taught him how to treat people.

It had been a rocky road at first, with stumbles and setbacks everywhere. But through it all, there had never been a moment when no one believed in him. There had always been someone: his brother, Ishibashi, Kaylee . . . Samheed. He'd found them, or they'd found him, and they'd offered second chances when he hadn't deserved them. Dearest Ishibashi—what would Aaron have done without the man? How he missed him. And Alex, who'd never given up trying to make him see that he belonged in Artimé. Kaylee Jones, who knew about his past and loved him for the man he'd become, not the one he'd been. And his sisters, who ruled with power and with compassion.

When the time came for Aaron to take his last breath, he heard a voice calling to him. It seemed . . . familiar, yet distant. Warm and inviting. But Aaron wanted to be here, surrounded by his family. He was well familiar with the sorrow that came with death, and he wanted to delay that for his family as long as he could, though he knew it was inevitable.

"I can't come right now," Aaron tried to say. "I'm taking

my last breath with my family. This is the most important moment of my life."

But the voice persisted.

Aaron, no longer sensing an urge to breathe, felt a cool peacefulness envelop him. He felt his soul rise up and leave his still body behind on the bed. He moved like a shadow past his tearful loved ones, feeling a rush of gratefulness that so many had been able to come to pay their respects in his dying moments. It was all he could ask for, and he wanted to touch them, embrace them one last time before he left. Yet the voice continued to call, to spur him onward, and he followed it.

He felt himself moving out of the hospital ward, across the black-and-white marble floor to the glorious staircase. He traveled up effortlessly to the second floor, and over to the not-a-secret-to-anybody-anymore hallway. Finding his footing on the dark stained-wood floor, Aaron moved down the familiar wing, where the greatest of Artimé's leaders had spent some of their most life-changing moments. He went past the door to the head mage quarters, which was now a museum. Past the door that led to the remote rooms like the lounge and library. And the door to the Museum of Large on the right.

The familiar voice, which he still couldn't place, led him beyond them all.

He came to a stop at the final secret door. The one nobody had ever seen the other side of in all the years of living here. The one Mr. Today had never written a single word about to explain its existence. The door no one had ever been able to enter no matter how they tried to unlock it. Confused, Aaron looked around, but he was alone. He watched as his hand touched the doorknob. In a blink, the knob turned and the door creaked open, just a crack.

The voice in Aaron's ears grew louder. Calling to him from inside this room. Who was it? So familiar . . . yet unidentifiable. Aaron, feeling an overwhelming longing to go toward it, pushed the door open. He stepped inside.

The room was vast and dimly lit, full of comfortable chairs and tables topped with books and puzzles and games, like the best, coziest library. With a start, Aaron realized people filled the seats. Aaron stood there for a moment to let his eyes adjust to the darkness. Where was he?

He took another step inside, and the door behind him closed with a soft click and disappeared.

People in the nearest chairs turned at the sound. The one closest hesitated a moment, then got up.

Aaron wanted to gasp, but he found he no longer needed to take in air. The person approached, and Aaron felt like it might be impossible to stay standing. Something deep inside his chest, an aching wound that hadn't gone away in many years, sealed up. "Alex? My brother? Is it you?"

"Aaron," said Alex with a crooked smile growing on his lips. "You're here at last. I've been waiting so long."

In that instant, Aaron realized exactly what this room was for. And he understood why no one had been able to open its door.

"Alex," said Aaron, wanting to weep, but finding overwhelming joy pushing the tears back. "I thought . . . I believed I'd never see you again." He clutched at his chest where the hole had been since Alex's death and found it healed.

"It's me, brother. I'm so glad you're here."

The two embraced, and Aaron was surprised that Alex, despite his ethereal look, was as solid as ever to the touch. When Aaron released his hold on his dear twin, he saw more familiar faces. Sigfried Appleblossom worked in a corner with a look of bliss on his face as he wrote with pen and paper. Liam Healy sat at a table playing chess with Claire Morning, while Gunnar Haluki and another woman looked on.

"Is *everyone* here?" Aaron whispered. "I can't believe it."

"Most everyone. It's the best surprise," Alex agreed. He looked eagerly at his brother. "Do you have any news? It's been some time since we've had an update." He indicated Sean Ranger, who'd been the most recent one to arrive some years before.

"News . . . ," said Aaron, feeling a bit overwhelmed. "Of Sky, you mean?"

"Oh, yes—I hope she's continued to have a good life. And . . . others? Our sisters?"

"Everyone is as well as can be," said Aaron, "though I expect to see some of them coming through here soon. We're all getting a bit feeble." It was strange. Aaron didn't feel so feeble right now.

"We'll have all the time we need for stories later," Alex said. "There are some friends who would like to greet you."

Movement in the room caught Aaron's eye, and he saw three men coming toward him. "Ishibashi!" he cried. He embraced the man who had changed his life so drastically, and had died so shockingly, which had changed Aaron's life a second time. "I'm so sorry about what happened," he began, and he started to choke up, overwhelmed. But the man stopped him.

"It is but a distant memory, and you have apologized enough for the wrongs of the entire universe," Ishibashi told him. "Your feet are solid, and your slate is wiped clean. Today begins a new life. Everyone starts fresh." He smiled warmly as he gazed at Aaron. "It is my greatest joy to see you again. Ito and Sato and I look forward to hearing your stories of our friends."

Aaron nodded. He was shocked by all of this, yet it somehow seemed very natural all of a sudden, as if he'd been planning to come here forever.

He saw a splash of orange hair catch the light. "That's Meghan Ranger, isn't it," said Aaron. "I didn't know her well."

"It is," said Alex. "She's my dearest friend—I can't tell you what comfort it gave me to see her when I arrived. But come. I must take you somewhere." Alex took Aaron's arm, and together the two meandered through the vast library. Large carved pillars grew to the sky, and thousands of books papered the walls. "The lights are dim for the moment," Alex said. "That's to let us know someone is coming. We've been wondering who it would be. I'm really so glad it's you."

"I . . . I'm . . ." Aaron wasn't sure how he felt. Overjoyed to see these faces he thought he'd never see again. But sad to miss the ones he'd left behind.

"It's okay not to feel glad just yet," Alex told him. "There's a bit of adjusting to do. It's very hard to leave the others, but they do all right, don't they?"

"We have all managed to make it through the losses, though yours was *especially* difficult for me and Thisbe and Fifer. And . . . we've . . . we've fixed things in Artimé and the land of the dragons, Alex. We've made it better. All for you. Fifer has kept it so. I suppose you knew that by now."

Aaron glanced at Carina Holiday, who ran up to him and embraced him. He hugged her back, and she touched his cheek adoringly. Aaron squelched a grin. "I can't believe this place," he said. He and Carina and Sean had had a great life growing old together, and he'd missed them dearly.

"You'll get used to it," Carina said, stepping back. "I can't wait to hear about my children once you've had a chance to

LISA McMANN

settle in." She went back to where she'd been sitting, and Sean waved from afar. Aaron lifted his hand in response. They would chat later.

Alex smiled. "I'm so glad to hear that peace has continued under Fifer's rule. We'd heard as much once Sean arrived. Has it been years since then? It's hard to tell."

Aaron's mind was growing fuzzy about that too. "It seems like quite some time." He hesitated, then glanced at Alex. "May I . . . approach . . . the others?"

"By all means. They're only holding back to keep from overwhelming you."

Aaron nodded and went over to Claire. She saw him coming and stood up. "Aaron," she said warmly, and the two embraced.

"It is good to see you again," said Aaron. "I thought I might never . . ."

"I know how you feel," said Claire, her voice musical as ever, and the two laughed.

Aaron caught Liam Healy's gaze. "Hello again," he said. "Do you . . . remember me?"

"Of course, Aaron. It's nice to see you, too," said Liam.

"And . . ." He hesitated a moment, scanning the room. "Ah, she's coming now."

"Who?" Aaron turned to find Secretary Eva Fathom coming toward him. His face paled. He'd done her wrong countless times. "Oh no." Things had been going so well up until now.

"Chin up," Alex whispered. Aaron lifted his gaze to face her and tried not to cringe in shame.

"Hello, Aaron Stowe," Eva said evenly. "I see you've managed to find your way here." She eyed him for a moment and crossed her arms over her chest. "Whoever is in charge of that is awfully generous."

"Eva," Aaron said, trying to find words. He'd been the one to send Panther out to the lawn before she'd been tamed, and Eva, trying to protect Artimé's children, had been killed by the beast. "I'm . . . so sorry. Not a day has gone by that I haven't thought of you and the things you did to help push me toward the right path."

"Too bad none of those things worked while I was alive," Eva said with a cold smile, but then her expression thawed a little. "It seems your presence here isn't a mistake, so I look forward to hearing more. I trust we'll have plenty of time for that."

"I . . . hope . . . so," Aaron said weakly.

Eva took his hand and shook it firmly. "Let's start fresh, shall we?"

"Yes." Aaron felt a small bit of relief. "Thank you. That would be nice." He relaxed slightly as Eva left to join Liam and Claire, and now the lights rose a bit. Music drifted out of nowhere, and Aaron wasn't sure if it had been playing all this time or if it had just started. Behind them Mr. Appleblossom began reciting a soliloquy from whatever he'd been writing. Laughter crescendoed from several small groups. The feeling of the room began to lighten.

But Aaron's heart began to sink. He glanced at his brother. "All of these people are good," he said in a low voice. "They all fought for good things their whole lives. They aren't . . . like me."

"Remember what Ishibashi said," Alex reminded him. "Come along."

At the far end of the library was a small crowd of people surrounding a table, and the conversations were flying.

"What's going on?"

"Oh, it's just a little bit of fun and games," said Alex, guiding

LISA McMANN

Aaron that way. "But I think we'll need to break it up. There's one more person you'll want to say hello to right away."

The brothers approached the group, and the people at the table parted, revealing an old man with white hair that stood up and waved in the slightest breeze. He took a look at the newcomer, and the laughter faded from his face. The people around grew silent, and some slipped away. The old man stood up, and the others made room for him to approach.

Aaron felt a new wound open up inside him, like a black hole. "Alex," he whispered. "What should I . . . ?"

But Alex melted into the background as the man with white hair came toward Aaron and stood before him.

Aaron wanted to turn and run. Retrace his steps. Go straight back out to the secret hallway and slam the door shut. Perhaps there was some seaweed Henry could give him that would bring him back to life for a while longer. Anything to avoid this confrontation. He didn't expect it—he wasn't ready! He couldn't possibly become ready for this, ever, even if he'd had lots of time to prepare. Aaron stood, feeling weak, as the white-haired old man stopped before him. An image of the last time they'd stood face-to-face flashed through Aaron's

LISA McMANN

Dragon Fury » 458

mind—it had been the moment Aaron had killed the man.

The entire library grew silent, and a brave few came closer to watch.

"Hello, Mr. Today," said Aaron in a whisper. "It's . . . I'm . . ." He couldn't manage to complete a single thought.

Marcus Today studied Aaron, his gaze darting from the scars on Aaron's face to the white in his stubbly beard, to the limp in his step, and then back up to the fear in his eyes. The original head mage and creator of Artimé slowly lifted his hands to his chest, where the deadly heart attack spells that Aaron had thrown met their mark. He felt the damage they'd left as if the incident had only happened yesterday.

Aaron's eyes brimmed. The shame he felt, the feelings he'd carried through decades, never able to free himself from it, was too much to bear. Yet he held the man's gaze. He would face whatever he needed to face to make up for his actions. It was the life Aaron had been living since his days with Ishibashi.

After a long moment, Mr. Today removed his hands from his chest and slowly held them out to the newcomer. "Welcome, Aaron," the old mage said with a healing warmth to his voice.

LISA McMANN

The words flowed through Aaron and soothed him. He closed his eyes.

Mr. Today continued. "I've been waiting so long for you. And I'm glad you are finally here. Tell me, friend: How does it feel to be eliminated?"

Aaron opened his eyes and stared. "What . . . does that mean?"

The old man smiled warmly and beckoned to Alex. Then he stepped back and seemed to melt into the crowd.

Alex returned to Aaron's side. "It's what he used to say when the Unwanteds showed up at the death farm after the Purge. I think he means you're an official Unwanted now," said Alex. "I believe it's his way of saying he accepts you for who you are. Exactly as you are."

"I have no words to match the way I'm feeling right now," Aaron murmured.

Meghan appeared on his other side, and her sudden presence made Aaron feel as though they'd known each other well, even though they'd hardly interacted. "From the sounds of it—and believe me, I've heard a lot of stories—things might have gone a bit differently if you'd been declared Unwanted from day one, like you should have been."

LISA McMANN

Like you should have been. Aaron wasn't sure what to say. In the past, whenever he'd thought about that very thing, it was accompanied by loads of guilt and regret. But those feelings were finally beginning to slip away. Could Aaron truly belong here, with the asterisk behind his name permanently removed? Was he no longer an exception to the rule?

Alex and Meghan took the stunned newcomer by the arms and guided him to the far edge of the room. The light increased, and the walls of books began to grow transparent and fade away. Soon there was no room at all, and the increasing light led the way to a new, beautiful world, as wonderous as Artimé . . . perhaps even more so. Soon they were standing on a different lawn with water and trees and the outline of a city in the distance.

"What's happening?" asked Aaron. His mind whirled, though not in a panicky way. But he didn't want to forget where he'd just come from and the people he'd left there. Kaylee and his children and grandchildren, and Fifer and Dev, and Thisbe and Rohan, and his friends all hovering at his bedside. "What about . . . the others?"

"Try not to fret," said Meghan sympathetically. "They'll

be along in time. I had to wait ages to see my brother, but once he came, it seemed like no time had passed." She glanced at Aaron's face to see how he was handling things. "Are you feeling a new spring in your step? Shall we explore this place?"

"Is it new to you, too? Where did the library go?" Aaron asked as others from the library began to stream past them into the world. Like Meghan had suggested, the weight of his old body seemed to be peeling off, and movement became easy again, as in his youth.

"The library is always here when we need it to receive someone," said Meghan. "Like you, today."

"But," said Alex, "every time friends join us, they bring a new world with them for us to explore."

"So you don't always sit in the library?" asked Aaron. "Waiting for the next one?"

"Please," Alex scoffed, but his voice was teasing. "We come from Artimé, and we are warriors. We have worlds to conquer and all the time we need to conquer them."

The thought of a world to conquer surprisingly didn't bring up any negative feelings for Aaron. In fact, his body began to buzz with excitement. "Worlds?" he whispered, full of wonder.

"Different worlds," said Alex, his voice quivering in anticipation. "Every single time."

Aaron glanced wistfully behind him, then turned toward the light.

"Come on, you two," Meghan said with finality. She linked arms with the twins and pulled them toward the city. "Let's join the rest. It's time to see what tremendous adventure awaits."

Acknowledgments

So many people were involved in the Unwanteds and Unwanteds Quests series over the past dozen years, and now we are done. I'm in shock. But I am also deeply thankful for everyone who had a hand in making it.

Thank you to Michael Bourret, Liesa Abrams, Mara Anastas, Karin Paprocki, Owen Richardson, Elizabeth Mims, Brian Luster, Penina Lopez, Katherine Devendorf, Jessi Smith, Lauren Carr, and Lauren Forte. And to Sarah Woodruff, Caitlin Sweeny, Anna Jarzab, Michelle Leo, Nicole Russo, Beth Parker, Alissa Nigro, Mary Marotta, and Valerie Garfield. To Emily Polson, Anna Parsons, Gabrielle Audet, and Michaela Whatnall. Thanks also to Ellen Gutowsky, Sarah Lieberman, Steve West, and Fiona Hardingham.

Thank you to Matt McMann for brainstorming with me, reading every first draft and giving me feedback, and writing so much flap copy. And for talking about these books every chance you got. Thank you to Kilian McMann for all of the artwork you created for my presentations and for giveaways. Thanks to Kennedy McMann for the reams of extra content you created. Thank you to Joanne Levy for keeping me organized and answering so many questions.

I'm so grateful for all the educators who have invited these books into their classrooms and libraries, chose them for reading lists, and book-talked them endlessly. Special thanks to Tricia Kiepert and MaryJo Staal for your unwavering support. Thank you to the reviewers who recommended these series, the librarians who kept them on the shelves, the booksellers who hand-sold them, and the parents who bought them. Special thanks to the kids who saved their money and spent it on books—me and authors everywhere see ourselves in you. And a big thank you to Elias Deuss, who created and maintains the very awesome Unwanteds app.

Thanks especially to you, my Unwanted readers. You are passionate and enthusiastic and creative and talented. You teach me about what it's like to be a kid these days. You share your art and your stories and your hopes and fears. And you kept me going with your encouragement through fourteen books. I hope you won't forget these great times we've had—I know I never will. And I hope you'll pick up these books again someday and start the adventure all over from the beginning.

I am with you. And I know you are with me too.

ABOUT THE AUTHOR

Lisa McMann lives in Sacramento, California. She is married to fellow writer and musician Matt McMann, and they have two adult children. Her son is an artist named Kilian McMann, and her daughter is an actor, Kennedy McMann. Lisa is the *New York Times* bestselling author of over two dozen books for young adults and children. So far she has written in genres including paranormal, realistic, dystopian, and fantasy. Some of her most well-known books are the Unwanteds series for middle-grade readers and the Wake trilogy for young adults. Check out Lisa's website at LisaMcMann.com, learn more about the Unwanteds series at UnwantedsSeries.com, and be sure to say hi on Instagram or Twitter (@Lisa_McMann), or Facebook (Facebook.com/McMannFan).

Don't miss this series from
LISA McMANN

"Gripping, action-packed, and filled with humor and heart.
Kids will go wild!"

—Katherine Applegate, #1 *New York Times* bestselling author
of the Newbery Medal winner *The One and Only Ivan*

HARPER
An Imprint of HarperCollinsPublishers

www.harpercollinschildrens.com